Also by J. Penner

Adenashire
A Fellowship of Bakers & Magic

A FELLOWSHIP OF LIBRARIANS & DRAGONS

J. PENNER

Copyright © 2024, 2025 by J. Penner
Cover and internal design © 2025 by Sourcebooks
Cover design by Erin Fitzsimmons/Sourcebooks
Cover art © Katie Daisy
Map art by Travis Hasenour
Internal art © Clara Fang
Internal images © Sonya_illustration/Getty Images, Leyla Ozcan/Getty Images, Mimomy/Getty Images, Olga Shipilova/Getty Images, Kseniya Ozornina/Getty Images, Tatyana Sidorova/Getty Images, Ekaterina Kudriavtseva/Getty Images, Daria Ustiugova/Getty Images, Garsya/Getty Images

Sourcebooks, Poisoned Pen Press, and the colophon are registered trademarks of Sourcebooks.

All rights reserved. No part of this book may be reproduced in any form or by any electronic or mechanical means including information storage and retrieval systems—except in the case of brief quotations embodied in critical articles or reviews—without permission in writing from its publisher, Sourcebooks.

No part of this book may be used or reproduced in any manner for the purpose of training artificial intelligence technologies or systems.

The characters and events portrayed in this book are fictitious or are used fictitiously. Any similarity to real persons, living or dead, is purely coincidental and not intended by the author.

All brand names and product names used in this book are trademarks, registered trademarks, or trade names of their respective holders. Sourcebooks is not associated with any product or vendor in this book.

Published by Poisoned Pen Press, an imprint of Sourcebooks
P.O. Box 4410, Naperville, Illinois 60567-4410
(630) 961-3900
sourcebooks.com

Originally self-published in 2024 by J. Penner.

Cataloging-in-Publication Data is on file with the Library of Congress.

The authorized representative in the EEA is Dorling Kindersley Verlag GmbH. Arnulfstr. 124, 80636 Munich, Germany

Manufactured in the UK by Clays and distributed by
Dorling Kindersley Limited, London
001-352699-Jun/25
CPI 10 9 8 7 6 5 4 3 2 1

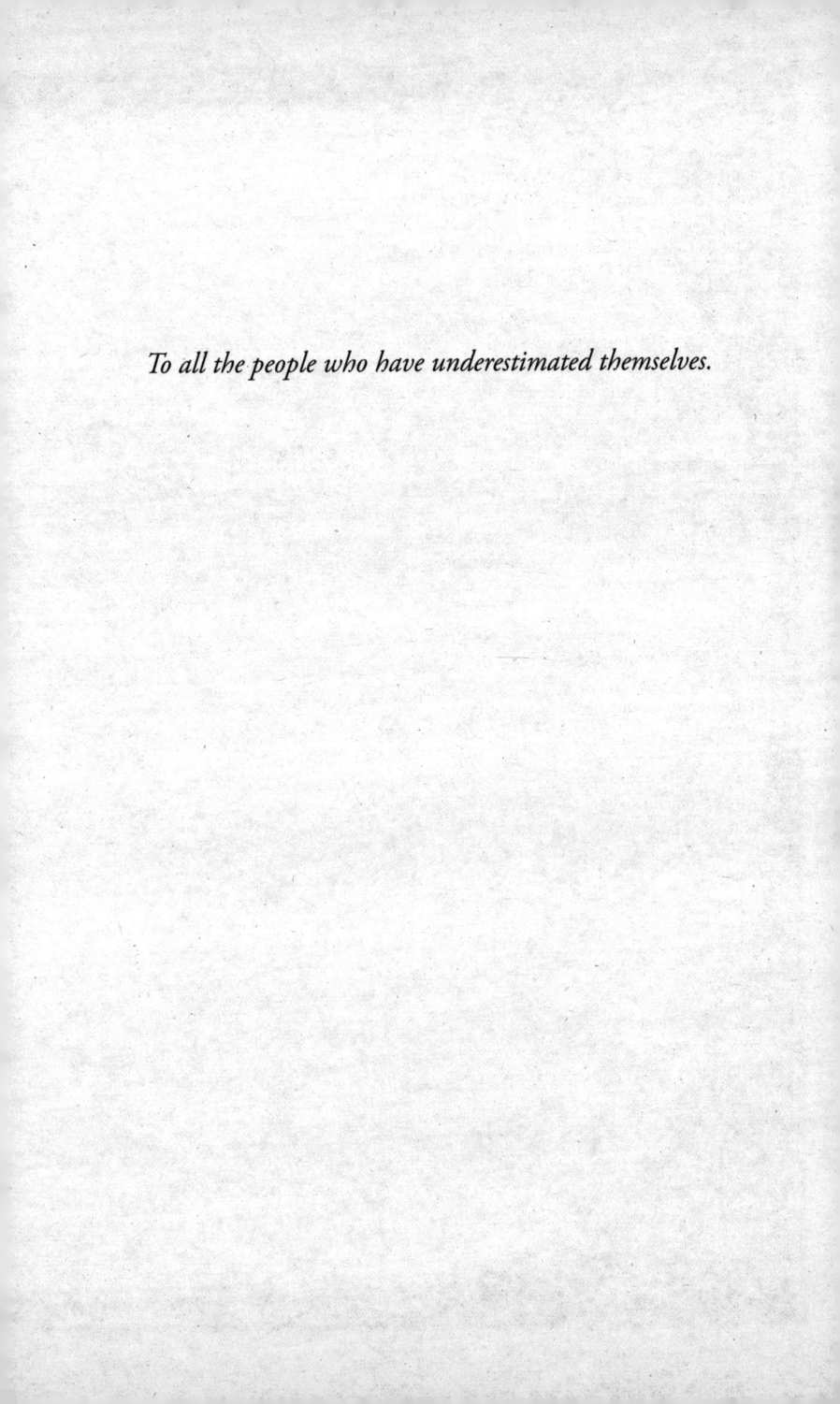

To all the people who have underestimated themselves.

DUNDES HEIGHTS
THE SEA OF THE SOMERDOWS
ADENASHIRE
Mount Blackdon
Stouling Forest
COLMORE MOUNTAINS
LANGHEIM

THE NORTHERN LANDS

RIDGELANDS

THE PRESMAR GULF

THE SOUTHEAST SHORES

DRYWARD

THE SOUTHERN DESERT

N

THE LOWER OCEAN

1

In the back office of a bookshop nestled in the heart of Adenashire, Doli Butterbuckle's dwarven umber cheeks flushed hot.

With her free hand, she grabbed a handful of scrawlish It's About Tome customer receipts from a pile on the desk beside her and fanned her scorching face. But she couldn't drag her eyes from the ivory parchment, where a dwarf warrior carried on a forbidden—and *steamy*—love affair with her handsome sworn enemy. Doli clutched the rough paper as though to keep the text from jumping off the page.

"Oh, stars." She sighed and settled deeper into the chair, devouring the next words while still fanning her face.

She'd once again lost herself in a torrid romance novel when she was supposed to be staffing the store.

The cozy room with its large mahogany desk and overstuffed furniture was where she generally ended up when sorting through new books. But when one caught her eye, she often found herself enveloped in the tattered, yet still luxurious blue velvet chair with her feet nowhere near touching the floor. The chair was easily big enough for an orc and could have sat multiple dwarves.

The office air lingered with the must of leather and old books and the smoky aroma of burned-out beeswax candles bought at the local market. Soft light streamed in from a small window just behind the chair, and the atmosphere allowed Doli the escape she needed.

That included escape from considering the letter in her pocket she'd received a few weeks prior. The one from her mother back in Dundes Heights—a place and family the dwarf had been glad to get some distance from when she moved to Adenashire over half a year before.

Envisioning herself as a warrior in a passionate love affair was a pretty good job perk since her only warrioring, or love affairs for that matter, consisted of making sure her friends were happy and taken care of. Ever since she'd met Arleta Starstone, Jez, Taenya Carralei, and Theo Brylar (short for Theodmon) at the Langheim Baking Battle, she'd fed them a steady diet of her magical tea. Although Jez preferred rum. Lots of rum.

Her new life in Adenashire was not exactly a battlefield. Or a romance. And making rum was not a magical talent she possessed.

With another sigh, Doli leaned her face close to the pages.

The hero stepped from the warrioress's bedchamber, leaned against the doorway, and said in a husky tone—

"That story is one of my favorites." Verdreth's booming orc voice came from the door.

He gave a deep chuckle as a startled Doli screamed, threw the book, and released about half of her receipt fan high into the air. "I…I was about to put out the new stock."

But the green-skinned orc, standing there impeccably dressed and holding a tiny teacup in his large, meaty hand, smirked as his eyes followed the papers fluttering to the wood-planked floor.

"I figured as much," he said in a gentle, yet amused tone. "Make sure you don't miss the copy of *My Heart's Battle* lying there under my desk." Verdreth tipped his head slightly and leaned down as if attempting to get a view of the stray tome.

Doli knew Verdreth was not at all angry at her. The orc rarely became angry at anything and was often found lost in a book himself. In fact, he and his orc partner, Ervash, who both lived next door to Arleta and Theo, had become father figures to her over the last months.

But that didn't make having your boss-slash-surrogate dad finding you in the middle of reading a romance story—and realizing that he knew what level of *romance* that book held—any less embarrassing.

Doli's mouth gaped as her brain worked to find more words. But just as a coherent sentence struggled to make its way past her throat—

Ding. The bell on the shop's front door chimed against the glass like a finchlette's tune.

Doli leaped from the chair and landed her boots with a thud on the wooden floor. "Customers!" she said, gesturing a little too vigorously toward the door.

Verdreth grinned, showing off his tusks, and adjusted the tiny pair of spectacles at the end of his nose. "Yes. Tend to that first."

The dwarf quickly smoothed her pink, floral skirt with a lovely ruffle along the hem and ran her hands over her dark, loose curls.

"You look good," the orc noted and took a sip of his tea.

Doli's eyes glistened, and a grin curled at the corners of her plump lips. She already knew the pink hue of her dress perfectly complemented her dark skin tone. It wasn't magic, but she had a proper gift for fashion. And with that, she bounded down the hall and out toward the shop, still a little flushed from the book's words.

The flushing didn't cease when Doli entered the sales floor and laid eyes on a hulking figure who stood staring intently at one of the bookshelves. She practically skidded to a halt and stood gaping at the gargoyle with light blue skin and delicately curled horns on top of his head, wings tucked tightly against his back as if trying to avoid disturbing items on the shelves and display tables. The particular shelf he was examining sat right beside the staircase leading up to the second floor, where Doli and Jez's rented rooms were found.

Gargoyles were uncommon in this part of the Northern Lands, as they kept to themselves in the cities northeast along the Ridgeland Mountains. They were an interesting bunch whose skin became like armor if they needed to protect themselves, and sometimes when experiencing powerful emotions.

He wore a linen shirt with zigzag stitching and loose gray cotton pants with the hems tucked into his boots. The shirt's neckline was cut in such a way that Doli caught a glimpse of his muscular chest. But her gaze was caught by the long, thin blue tail with an arrow-like point resting lightly on the floor and sliding from side to side like a snake who'd been out in the sun too long.

"Oh, stars." The words slipped from Doli's mouth before she could stop them, and the gargoyle turned her way, nearly knocking a stack of books from the end of the shelf.

His hand flew out, catching the tumbling books, and his emerald eyes moved at once to Doli. He casually looked her up and down, which was not a great length, her being a dwarf. "I apologize for my clumsiness."

At his obvious regret, Doli immediately moved toward him. "Oh, no. It's fine. There's no harm."

He shook his head. "These shops are often too small for me, so I tend to avoid them, but from the outside this one seemed a bit roomier."

Doli grinned while her heart pounded against her rib cage. Although she'd never seen a gargoyle in person, she had read about plenty in her books. Plenty. The memory brought a twinge of excitement to her chest, but she quickly clamped the feeling down. "That's because an orc owns this shop. He makes sure there's enough space for those of the larger…variety."

This choice of words seemed to amuse the gargoyle since

his lips curled into a crooked grin. Which Doli didn't mind the sight of one bit.

"So you're not the owner?" he asked.

Doli looked down at herself and chuckled. "Last time I looked, I wasn't an orc. No. I just work here."

Gently the gargoyle placed the fallen books back on the shelf as if they were precious treasures. "Working with the written word is never simply a job. It's a calling."

Gargoyles were the self-proclaimed historians of the Northern Lands. They were highly educated and knew about every truth and lie in history concerning every part of the realm. This second part made them either loved or hated among the people groups, depending on how much each would admit to their pasts. Too many of those in charge liked to manipulate their history books to make their decisions look better than they were, rather than learning from their mistakes. The Head Librarian of the gargoyle people was considered to hold a high, sacred position and rarely made any public appearances to avoid corruption.

But even for the general gargoyle population, books, even nonhistorical ones, were revered.

Doli stepped closer to him, warmth traveling over her entire body. "Well, I'm Doli…Doli Butterbuckle. What exactly are you looking for today?" She put on her smile and the standard air of sunshine everyone loved.

Before he had a chance to answer, the bell chimed again as Jez, tailed by Arleta, flung open the door, and Doli nearly jumped.

"It came!" Arleta squealed, pointing at the hefty, ornate wooden box in Jez's clawlike hands.

Arleta was fully human, with long, chestnut hair pulled back in a low bun. She'd likely been working in her bakery, A Little Dash of Magic Bake Shop, since she had telltale flour speckled on her blouse and olive-toned face. Jez, a fennex, stood tall with a long, bushy, fox-like tail and two furry ears atop her head of white hair. Her normally sand-colored cheeks were flushed peach under a scattering of freckles. The fennex's usual scowl was replaced by an awkward grin as she clutched the box like a child anticipating the Yule holiday.

The dwarf's eyes flitted between her two dear friends and her gargoyle customer, who'd turned back to the books but was occasionally looking over his shoulder at the commotion.

"Open it," Jez demanded, a rare excitement in her tone as she held the box toward Doli.

But the dwarf didn't take it. Instead, she bit at the inside of her cheek for a moment before she asked, "Why didn't they deliver it to me?"

The fennex rolled her eyes. "Because I told the guy *I'd* deliver it to you."

Pinching her lips, Doli peered around Jez, whose full tail partially blocked her view of Arleta. "And you had to stop and get everybody?"

Arleta shrugged and wiped her hands on the sides of her apron. "Not everyone. Theo and Tae aren't here."

Theo was a woodland elf and Arleta's unlikely Fated. Taenya was her business partner, and also an elf.

"What's going on?" Verdreth rounded the hall into the main shop, teacup still in hand.

Suddenly the place was incredibly crowded to Doli. Too many people. Too many books. Even the gargoyle was looking at her, which hadn't been a bad thing only a few moments before but now was making her stomach flop like a fish.

She had known the box was coming weeks ago when she'd received the letter from her mother—some kind of inheritance from an uncle she'd barely known. But Dundes Heights was a place she'd hoped to stay away from and not even think about, at least for a while longer. The box, covered in intricate dwarven carvings of powerful magic wielders involving gemstones and the earth, reminded her that she was different from them. Tea magic was the best she could do…and she had that eye for fashion. Not very dwarflike, a fact her family had often reminded her of. Sometimes intentionally. Sometimes simply by existing.

Jez hefted the box and scowled. There was her normal demeanor. "We both knew if you received it in private, you might tuck it away in your room and not tell us about it."

Doli wanted to scowl right back at the fennex but didn't dare. Not with everyone looking. So she kept her sugary-sweet expression plastered on her lips. "Now why would I do that?"

Nose wrinkled, Jez held out the box while her claws gripped the sides. "Open it."

Groaning, Doli held out her hands. Not quite sure what to expect when it came to the weight of the box, she braced herself. "Fine."

Jez passed it to Doli and the weight plunged into the dwarf's arms, making her stumble backward.

"Ohhhhhh!" she exclaimed, but she caught her breath as she was abruptly stopped midair by something. Doli eyed her savior…a blue tail.

The gargoyle steadied her while Jez grabbed the box from Doli's hands.

"Are you okay?" Arleta asked Doli, her hazel eyes as big as fine china saucers. Then she rounded on Jez. "What were you thinking?" she scolded the fennex.

Jez growled, the sound rumbling in her throat.

Nervous, Doli ran her hand over the right side of her curls and looked at the gargoyle. "I'm fine. I…I didn't catch your name," she said, his tail still wrapped around her waist.

He loosened it and the tail floated to the ground, but before he could answer, Jez stepped up.

"Yes. Who are you?"

The gargoyle edged back, wavering his attention between Doli and Jez. "Sarson."

"And have you lived in Adenashire long? I haven't seen you before." Jez ran her narrowed gaze up and down Sarson's tall, muscular frame.

Doli opened her mouth to save him from Jez's grilling, but Verdreth was faster.

"Is there anything in particular you were browsing for, sir?" the orc asked, sweeping his arm toward the shop.

Sarson bobbed his head, likely glad to be released from Jez's interrogation, and followed Verdreth into the historical section of the bookstore.

Doli raised up on her toes and called after the gargoyle. "Thank you!"

He turned his head back toward her and bowed it slightly before continuing his low conversation with her boss.

The fennex hissed. But most likely not loud enough for Sarson to hear.

"Seriously, what's wrong with you?" Arleta asked her.

"I don't like him." Jez kept her voice low. "Anyone with a wingspan like that is trouble."

The dwarf glanced at Sarson and wondered to herself how extensive his wingspan might be before she turned back to the fennex. "You don't like anybody when you first meet them." Doli shook her head with an air of exhaustion.

Arleta leaned against the wall next to a table of new books. "She's right. You hated Doli and me when we all met at the Baking Battle. Now you can't live without us." The human raised one brow.

"Ugh," the fennex said, box still in hand. "You people have no idea what you're talking about. I'm taking this upstairs to your room, Doli. But you *are* opening it tonight."

"Oh. Sure thing," she said in honeyed tones. But all she could really think about was how Sarson's tail had wrapped around her waist.

2

Doli perched on a rickety white step stool with peeling paint, her elbows deep in spice cookie dough in the shared kitchen between Doli and Jez's rooms above the bookstore. The ornate box waited on her perfectly made bed behind the closed door of her room.

Out of sight. Out of mind. Sort of.

The living space was cozy, not too big, not too small, and the cedar paneled walls gave the place a welcoming amber glow. The furniture was sparse, only two rocking chairs by a simple fireplace with a wood beam mantel. Beside it was a stack of wood Theo had brought up to them the week prior. A small table with stools was pushed against the left-hand wall for dining. A clock with large, scrolled numbers hung on the wall. All in all, it was much sparer than any place Doli had ever lived. Her home in Dundes Heights had shown the signs of her family's obvious wealth: expensive carved furniture, plush fabrics, and gilt in every direction. But she didn't miss it. She kept her new, simple home stocked with vases of freshly cut wildflowers and had brought a few favorite knickknacks to strew around the place.

The place looked pretty, and homey.

On the counter was a small jar of plum jam she had recently canned along with a dozen others, saved for cookie making whenever she needed to take a break from the world and the people in it. That included her friends, though she loved them dearly. But there were days it was hard to keep her face on, to maintain such a chipper attitude all the time.

Her plum-jam-filled spice cookies always made life better. The recipe had been her grandmother's—the only dwarf in her family who had really seemed to understand her. Grammy's long gray locks were forever pulled back into tight braids and coiled atop her head like the crown she deserved. The style complemented her umber skin coloring, a near match to Doli's. The woman always had a kind expression and word for her granddaughter, and Doli had loved every moment with her. Despite her brawny, mining-built arms and typical dwarven leanings toward rare gems, Grammy was a tender soul who never said no to eating or crafting a delicious pastry to support her granddaughter's passion. She had taught Doli everything she knew about baking and readily accepted a cup of magical tea when they finished baking cookies or a cake.

Thinking about her grandmother made Doli's hand

tingle with magic, yearning to make a cup of tea. Lavender with two lumps of sugar…Grammy's favorite.

Unfortunately, Grazigrett Butterbuckle had passed away when Doli was only a girl. Those few years spent with her had been nowhere near long enough for Doli. When she thought of her grandmother, emotions never failed to well up inside her. And this day was no different.

"Why can't you be here for me to talk to?" she whispered.

Doli removed the fragrant cinnamon-and-brown-sugar-scented dough from the bowl and placed it on the well-floured counter. She blew out a quick breath to calm her nerves and held back the tears that threatened the corners of her brown eyes. Grabbing the rolling pin, she pressed out the dough into a perfect, thin layer.

From there she cut it into rounds, placed a small dollop of purplish jam into the center, and squished the soft edges between her fingers to seal each cookie. Then, as Grammy had taught her, she flipped it seam-side down to make the shape of an apple seed and placed it on a tray.

Once all the cookies were filled and on the baking sheet, the dwarf climbed down from the step stool and reached to open the small oven door. The kitchen was nothing like the extravagant one she had used when she'd competed in the Langheim Baking Battle months before, yet she was grateful to have a kitchen at all in her upstairs apartment. Not everyone had the indoor variety in Adenashire, but the orcs had made sure one was installed before she and Jez moved in.

When the cookies were baked and cooled, she'd lovingly

glaze each with a mixture of sugar, syrup, and water and leave it to dry before enjoying with a cup of tea.

The oven was halfway open when the apartment door clicked and swung wide, squeaking on its hinge, revealing Jez, who must have finished her shift closing the bookstore.

"Okay," she growled, her tail flicking side to side as the door drifted shut. "Let's do this." Unlike Doli, Jez mostly wore simple clothing, and that day was no different. The fennex wore a plain white shirt with tight-fitting olive green pants held up by a worn brown leather belt.

Doli pushed the cookies into the oven and closed the door. She held herself there for a beat and squared her shoulders, pressing down the uncertainty twisting in her stomach. Once she was ready, she turned on her boot heel, plastered on a sunny demeanor, and conjured her sweetest voice. "Oh good, you can help me assemble the other batches on the sheets for baking."

The fennex pursed her lips and narrowed her eyes at Doli. "You're making cookies?" Her pointed ears twitched on the top of her head.

"Yep, just got the first batch in." Doli held her flour-covered hands into the air as if to prove her words. A small flour cloud floated in the air for a second before descending to the ground. Even Jez would have to agree that opening a dusty wooden box while preparing cookie dough was a bad idea.

"Now?" The fennex sauntered to one of the rocking chairs and slouched down into the seat, which creaked and scraped lightly against the flooring.

Doli shrugged as if clueless, knowing full well what Jez was getting at. "Why not? I thought I might take a batch over to that nice gargoyle in the morning since one of the books he wanted won't be in until tomorrow. You know… home delivery. And Adenashirian hospitality."

Mentioning the gargoyle would distract Jez. Even though Doli hadn't much cared for the fennex's comments about him earlier in the day, getting her worked up about a different topic was better than talking about the box sitting on top of her floral-print pink blanket.

"That gargoyle?" Jez groaned. "Shit. What was his name? Sartop?"

Doli rolled her eyes as she wiped her hands on a soft tea towel. While snapping at Jez might have been satisfying in the moment, she spoke sweetly. "Sarson…and language."

"Stay away from him, Doli." Jez sat up and leaned her hands out on her knees. "Gargoyles never venture out of the Ridgeland Mountain area, and if they do, there's a *reason* for it."

The dwarf crossed her arms over her ample chest and raised a brow. "Such as the reason both of us left our homes? We needed a new change of scenery?"

She shook her head. "That's different. Our families are annoying."

"Okay. Tell me how you *know* it's different for him."

"I mean, he could be shunned or something," Jez said with frustration in her tone. "They really don't leave their cities. Not even to travel."

Doli returned to her workstation and stepped up on the

stool to continue her cookie making. "And how do you know so much about gargoyles?"

Jez grabbed a poker from beside the fireplace and jabbed at the barely flickering logs. "Listen. I just don't want you to get hurt."

Doli laughed, and the sound came out a sweet song, but inside she wanted to let Jez have it. "Well, I appreciate your concern. But I'm simply being neighborly, not asking him for his hand."

The fennex released an exhausted sigh as she stood, replaced the poker, grabbed a couple of new logs, and threw them onto the minuscule fire with a thud and puff of ash. Walking back to the kitchen, she washed her hands in the porcelain basin and slipped in next to Doli, who already had three cookies prepared on the new tray. The fennex eyed the process for a moment, then picked up a dough round, loaded it with jam, and made the apple seed shape with precision before placing it on the sheet.

The two had the next batch done in no time, just as the air filled with a spicy baked aroma that made Doli's stomach growl in anticipation.

And just as someone knocked at the door.

Doli furrowed her brow at her friend. "Who's that?"

Jez bit her lips, displaying one of her fangs in the process. "It might be Arleta...come to watch you open the box."

"Arleta?" Doli asked and swiped the cookie sheet from the counter.

"And Theo."

"Theo too?" Doli jumped to the floor with her metal

tray in hand, nearly dropping it before placing it next to the oven.

"And Taenya." Jez leaned against the counter.

With a huff, Doli removed the finished cookies from the oven and replaced them with a new batch. "And while you were at it, I suppose you invited Verdreth and Ervash over too?"

The fennex twisted her lips. "Possibly. Listen, I don't get why you're so upset about this. We do practically everything with all of them."

Carefully Doli placed the hot tray on the counter to cool but didn't turn to Jez right away. Instead, she gnawed at the inside of her cheek, trying to formulate words that would make sense. She knew her behavior wasn't logical. The box only represented her past, and it didn't change the person she was that day. But somehow she thought it might bring everything crashing down. What if she accidentally revealed to her friends that her personality wasn't always a ray of sunshine? That she had bad days too…and a past she'd rather forget.

Doli turned on her heel and allowed a familiar curl at the corners of her lips. "I don't know. Perhaps I'm afraid a ghost will emerge from the box." It was a silly excuse. Even so, it might be enough to throw Jez off the scent.

Jez wrinkled her nose for a moment, then waved her hand in the air as if swiping away the concern. "I don't know what you're talking about, dwarf."

But Doli was already on the way to open the door, which did, in fact, reveal Arleta and Theo on the other side.

"Hello." Arleta tugged at the end of the long, brown braid hanging over her shoulder. She wore a pretty peasant's dress with puffed sleeves, free of flour.

The human leaned down to give Doli a quick hug, which of course Doli returned. The contact did make her feel a tiny bit better.

Theo came in behind Arleta. He was tall, as was everyone compared to a dwarf, but a head over Arleta, with golden blond hair. He had pointed ears, pale skin, and a seemingly forever friendly expression, particularly around his Fated.

After Doli and Arleta finished hugging, he slipped his hand around Arleta's waist and escorted her into the kitchen. The two of them were rarely far apart for long if they could help it.

"The others are right behind us," he said. "They're all pretty excited to see what's inside your inheritance box."

"She thinks it might be a ghost," Jez blurted out. A lock of her white hair trailed across the sand-colored skin on her forehead.

Theo's eyebrows shot up, interest piqued. "A ghost?"

Doli waved off the remark. "I don't know what Jez is talking about."

The fennex narrowed her brows at Doli, but the dwarf ignored it.

"Well, we're all excited, ghost or no ghost." Arleta clasped her hands and turned her attention to the cookies on the counter. "Ooh. Are those the jam spice cookies you told me about?"

Doli nodded and left the door ajar for Taenya, Verdreth, and Ervash when they arrived.

"I'd love the recipe if you're willing to share it," Arleta said. "I think they'd make a great special offering at the bakery when Yule rolls around."

Doli had to agree. All the warm spices made for a delicious winter cookie to share with family and friends. And keeping Grammy's tradition alive meant the process should never be kept a secret. "Sure thing. We can do a lesson."

As the rest of the group came filing through the door, Jez remained silent, nose twitching, as if she were mulling something over.

Taenya was first, followed by the two middle-aged orcs, who had to duck slightly to enter. But by the anticipatory looks on their faces, they didn't mind at all.

The woodland elf woman was dressed in a pair of brown slacks and a fitted cotton shirt outlining her slim frame. She strolled into the kitchen, took a spot next to Jez, and mimicked her, lounging against the counter. Taenya tucked her bobbed auburn hair behind her pointed ears, leaned in, and whispered something to Jez that Doli couldn't hear.

The fennex waved her off and crossed her arms over her chest.

"I haven't seen you in a day or two," Ervash said to Doli, running his hand along the slightly curled right tusk jutting from the corner of his mouth. The orc had his black hair piled up on top of his head and tied off with a leather cord. He wore a loose-fitting shirt with the collar cut low, displaying his impressive chest muscles. Though he looked like he could be a captain of the guard, he spent his days as an artisan working with paints, canvas, and wood.

"Well," Doli said, voice chipper, "I'm happy to have you."

Verdreth stood eyeing the cookies hungrily as if the orc hadn't eaten in days.

"Those aren't ready, Dad," Arleta said with a mild rebuke in her tone. "And I have a large bag of bakery leftovers for you and Ervash back at the house anyway."

Verdreth met her with a sheepish, fangy grin and adjusted the spectacles on his nose. "Thanks."

Arleta had lost her parents in a carriage accident when she was a teen. Since Verdreth and Ervash were both her neighbors, as well as gentlefolk, they stepped in as surrogate parents for her. Arleta had only recently started calling them both "Dad," and they seemed to relish it.

Although she would rather have snuck out the door when no one was looking, Doli squared her shoulders and stepped into the middle of the room. "I'm ready for the big reveal, if someone would retrieve the box from my room."

"I'll get it," Jez said immediately and left Taenya's side to make her way into Doli's room.

Her bed with its floral coverlet could be seen through the open door, along with a collection of delicate teacups and saucers perfectly arranged on a set of shelves next to her nightstand. A soft whiff of vanilla wafted into the living area from the perfume she not only sprayed on herself daily but also around the room to keep everything fresh.

Jez hefted the box from the bed and carried it to Doli while everyone looked on. "Where do you want it?" she asked.

Doli bit her top lip and gestured at the floor. "Here, I guess."

The fennex placed it on the ground with a small thud.

Doli looked around at her friends. "Here goes." Before she could change her mind, she quickly unlatched the golden buckles and flung open the lid, half expecting to see a letter inside, but there wasn't one. Not that she could see anyway.

In near synchronization the friends stepped closer to the wooden box and peered inside. It was filled with wadded-up paper. Doli reached in and started pulling paper out until she felt something hard wrapped in one of the sheets. Beside it was a plain metal box the size of a small sack of flour, plus a leather pouch. The dwarf picked up the pouch and loosened the cord.

From inside she drew out a small mining hammer. Her insides twinged. She had no idea what she would use it for, except possibly pounding a steak. She would most definitely not be using it for mining, as her uncle had apparently hoped.

She set it aside, then pulled out the paper-wrapped object.

"What do you think it is?" Arleta asked.

Doli set it on the table and began unwrapping. The hard object was curved and might have been pottery. "I'm not quite sure."

As the paper twisted off, she tossed it to the floor, unveiling the ugliest vase she'd ever seen.

The bright orange handmade vase had a painted dwarf on the front...which from a different artist would have been fine. But this one had needed a few more lessons before painting this portrait of a long-dead ancestor of Doli's, whose irregular proportions looked as if a child had painted them.

Doli stared at it.

"Ugh," Jez said, which was what everyone else was thinking by the astonished looks on their faces.

Ervash tipped his head and gazed at it. "Maybe if you—"

But Doli only burst into laughter. "No, it's terrible. But for some reason, no one in my family will say so! And now it's all mine."

"Do we have to keep it?" Jez grimaced.

Doli walked over to her other vases and plucked out several flowers, then brought them to her newly inherited piece and plopped them inside.

"That doesn't help," Taenya admitted.

Doli stepped back and studied the vase. "Nope. It doesn't. It's still hideous." But she let it be and peered into the bottom of the box. She found one more pouch sitting beside the metal box.

She pulled the leather strings and emptied the contents into her hand. Out came a gold necklace with a pink stone pendant.

Her eyebrows raised with interest. "Oh…this is much nicer."

The others agreed while Jez picked up the vase and shoved it into a corner on the counter.

Doli immediately fastened the necklace and admired it. "Maybe my uncle's taste wasn't so bad after all." With the necklace on, the dwarf wasn't sure why she'd dreaded opening the box so much. "Only one more thing."

She reached for the metal box and lifted it. A small latch secured the top and she pinched it to open, but it stayed tight, despite appearing as if it needed no key.

"Might need magic," Jez said from the side.

Doli eyed her. "Think tea magic will do?"

The fennex shrugged. "I dunno. But worth a shot."

To Doli's side, Arleta walked to the oven and took out the next batch of cookies and placed it on the counter next to the first.

Doli placed her hand over the lock, and in the same way she always envisioned tea in a cup, she instead thought of the lock popping open. Her hand tingled with warm, sparkling magic, and the lock gave a little snap. The dwarf gave a light chuckle. "It worked."

"What's inside?" Ervash asked impatiently, possibly because of the uneaten cookies calling his name.

Doli pried open the lid and found the inside lined with magenta velvet. Lying on its side was a pristine, bright pink egg. The lustrous shell gleamed in the firelight, and everyone's eyes widened.

"Oh, stars in heaven," the dwarf gasped, recognizing it immediately as a dragon's egg. It was so bright and pretty that Doli couldn't help but graze the top curve with her finger.

And a crack formed along the left side.

It had begun to hatch.

3

A haze of smoke hung around the candlelit bookstore table where Jez and Doli sat poring over books on dragons. Before them sat the cracked pink egg as if it too waited for answers.

They'd been reading for so long that everyone else had gone home for the night, but not before Arleta, with Doli's instructions, had gone up to the apartment to finish rolling and baking the spice cookies. At one point during the evening, the orcs had also brought in a load of sandwiches and eaten most of them themselves, being the largest and generally hungriest of the bunch.

Doli had only been able to stomach a few bites, despite the tender chicken and delicious creamy sauce Verdreth had spread on two slices of freshly baked rosemary sourdough bread. So most of her meal still sat on the table before her.

In reading multiple books, Doli had already learned that most dragons resided in the Mount Blackdon area of the Northern Lands, as well as how difficult raising dragons could be. Most young dragons were not good with their flame abilities, so accidents happened. Things burned down. Plus, they needed a very specific diet and care. The dwarf had no idea if she'd be able to get some of the supplies she'd need once the dragon hatched.

She eyed the egg. The crack had already grown at least an inch since the last time she'd looked. So it *was* going to hatch.

How would Doli be able to work at the bookstore if she had a baby dragon flying around all over the place, possibly burning up books? Or the entire bookstore?

Stars, she didn't even want to think about the mess she was in.

Most dragons had strong elemental magic. They could all produce fire, of course, but some also included earth, wind, or water, or a combination of several depending on their heritage. Because of this, they were extremely sought after, especially by people with not-so-altruistic intentions. Word that a dragon had been hatched in Adenashire would not *remain* in Adenashire. Not for long, at least.

Doli had been relishing her new, quiet life where the expectations of her were totally different from what they had been in Dundes Heights. Only in the last weeks had everything begun to unravel. And that night? Even more so.

"Maybe we can find another dragon and give it back before it finishes hatching, and no one will even know it was here," Doli said.

Jez shook her head, pulled an open book closer, and read aloud. "'Once dragons begin to hatch, they form a bond with the last living being that touched their eggs prior to beginning the process.'"

"Bond?" Panic welled up inside Doli's chest. "And what kind of process?"

"Says here that the hatched dragon will refuse to leave their guardian's side until the time is right," Jez said.

Doli scoffed. "What does that mean? And why in the stars would my uncle have willed a dragon's egg to *me*?" She ran her hand over her loosened ebony curls in frustration.

Jez's ears twitched on top of her head. "And I don't think finding a dragon would help even if one was around." She flipped to the next page of a book entitled *Dragons and Their Lore*. "There seem to be multiple dragon clans, and they don't all get along. Who knows what they might do with a rival clan's egg?"

"Could there be a friendlier clan who could help me figure out what the 'right time' is?" Doli dropped her head down into her arms on the table. "Better than we can at least." Her voice was muffled by her encircling arms.

"Yeah, I don't think that's an option. When was the last time you heard of a friendly dragon clan?" Jez's tone was flat and matter-of-fact.

Doli never had. Even in her flight-of-fancy books. They'd

probably eat her. She grazed her fingers over the pink jewel on her necklace.

"Plus there's this whole passage about the bond. Apparently the dragon's life is also tied to the person it bonds with. They can die without them."

"Die?" The dwarf screeched and shot straight up in her chair. The intensity of her movement set the candles flickering. "I don't want a dragon that I might accidentally kill if it eats the wrong cookie off my counter. Let alone by accidentally breaking some magical bond that I know nothing about." Her face contorted as her brows sank toward her eyes.

Not looking up, Jez said, "It doesn't say you might kill it *that* easily. It says nothing about cookies, but I need to do a little more reading."

Doli huffed.

Nose twitching, Jez leaned back in the wooden chair, calmly placing a paper bookmark on the page where she'd left off at and staring at Doli with brows raised.

"What?" Doli threw her hands into the air.

Jez deadpanned. "What? You know what."

"No, I don't," she insisted with a hint of indignation. "You'd probably be upset if a dragon was unexpectedly forced on you too."

"I would. But that's not all that's going on here." The fennex sucked her teeth and then leaned her elbows onto the table.

The dwarf glared at her friend and then eyed the egg, whose pink color she would have adored in any other circumstance. "Yes…it's *my* dragon. Not yours. I'm well aware."

Jez sighed and glanced at the egg. "I mean, whatever is going on with you did not start with this egg."

"I don't know what you're talking about." But Doli knew very well what the fennex was getting at. The dwarf wrung her hands under the table like a dish cloth.

"Since we're friends and I do my best to respect your privacy, I hold back on my scent magic. But Doli, your emotions are flipping out all over the place these days. I don't need magic to tell me something is going on with you." She tapped the end of her nose with her clawed finger. "I can practically smell them when you're coming down the street with my good ol'-fashioned fennex sniffer. Let alone being in the same room. It's torture."

Heat rose in Doli's chest. Part of her had hoped she'd been hiding her feelings well. She'd had so many years of practice. She was always the perfect host, the perfect friend, the one with a smile for those she knew and random passersby. Everyone thought so. But these last few weeks, she'd been feeling as if she were coming undone. Doli steeled herself and forced up the corners of her lips. "I'm fine."

"That's reassuring." The fennex returned her attention to the egg, still in its velvet-lined box. "Then I guess you're fine with this dragon egg situation all of a sudden too?"

Without warning, Doli's eyes filled with liquid. Her body became like a pile of goo from a spell gone wrong, and she slumped in her chair, tears pouring down her cheeks.

The fennex groaned. "Oh, damn it. Don't start crying. I have no idea how to deal with something like that! I take it all back! Forget I mentioned anything. You're probably fine and we'll figure this whole thing out together." When Doli didn't stop, Jez whipped her head around the bookshop's empty sales floor. "Where's Arleta when I need her… or Verdreth?" She cursed some more under her breath.

Doli sat there staring at the egg, defeat flooding through her veins and emptying out into her stomach. The few bites of chicken sandwich she'd eaten threatened to come back up at any second.

The fennex jumped to her feet and rifled through the deep pockets of her linen pants. Quickly she pulled out a handkerchief and proclaimed, "I'm not sure this is clean." But she held it out to Doli anyway.

In her distress the dwarf took it, but she only tucked it away on her lap to be polite. "What am I going to do?" Tears gushed down her cheeks like a waterfall, but thank the stars, the food in her stomach stayed in place.

Jez paced behind her chair but had no solutions to offer.

And Doli didn't feel at all ready to confess the warring conflict inside her which had been bubbling up the last few weeks, though if she were honest with herself, it had been going on for nearly her entire life. Putting on an air of happiness and helping others had been her only way of dealing with her problems for as long as she could remember.

But caring for a dragon? This problem was bigger than she'd ever expected. Caring for herself and her grown friends was already enough to tax her ability to hold herself together. Was this some kind of test her family had dreamed up for her? But why would they do such a thing? She couldn't answer that question, other than the fact that they had always tried to push her into becoming a person she didn't want to be.

They couldn't seem to accept that sunshine and tea might be the person Doli was. And what was so bad about that?

Doli gazed around the room, hoping to find a book that had just the right answer in it. Her eyes landed on the historical section of It's About Tome. The sight held her attention as her mind worked.

"What if we asked the gargoyle?" Doli asked suddenly.

Jez whipped around, eyes blazing. "The gargoyle? Why in the stars would you bring him up right now? I told you, they're not trustworthy."

"You really know nothing of the sort," Doli argued, a squinch glad to be talking about something other than the dragon egg. "Have you ever met one before this morning?" She slipped off the chair with a thump as her boots hit the floor, and she planted one hand on her hip.

"Have you?" the fennex retorted, her lips curling at the corners enough to reveal her fangs.

Doli clicked her tongue in defiance. "I've read about them."

"In *which* books?" Jez tipped her head slightly to the romance section.

Cheeks heating, Doli didn't answer.

The fennex crossed her long arms over her chest and tapped her booted foot on the floor. "Those aren't accurate, you know. They set up extremely unrealistic expectations for life."

"And how much do you actually know about romance books, Jez?" The dwarf glared at her.

"I know…things."

"Of course you know *things*. But I'm talking about romance books. Not *things*."

Jez growled low in her throat. "I know that they are not the way relationships turn out. *Everything* is unrealistic."

The dwarf shrugged but wondered what relationship had hurt Jez that she'd be so sensitive about this issue. "What about Arleta and Theo? They seemed to have worked out in a pretty romantic way. The whole meet-cute when he delivered her Baking Battle invitation, struggles at just the right point like everything was going to fall apart, then the happily ev—"

"Meet-*what*? Ugh, never mind. They're different," Jez snapped, waving her hand in the air as if she'd smelled something stinky. "And we're not talking about Arleta and Theo. We need to get back to the dragon egg topic."

Doli blew out a long sigh, wiped the remaining tears from her cheeks, and straightened. "I *am* on topic. You're the one who got lost. Everyone knows gargoyles are historians and have contact with all the people groups, which would include dragons." She eyed the books on the table. "He could have contacts and information we don't know about. He might even be able to get in touch with them."

Jez opened her mouth as if to say something but quickly shut it. She took her eyes from Doli and began pacing again with balled-up fists.

One of the candles on the table flickered and went out.

"Possibly it's a sign we need to sleep on it," Jez said, relief in her tone.

"I'm fine with that." Doli's eyes were heavy despite the buzzing in her chest over the day's events. In the dim light she carefully gathered the egg, tucked it under her arm, and headed toward the staircase.

"Don't drop it," Jez called from behind.

"Ugh," Doli groaned. "Goodnight, Jez."

4

The sounds of Jez tinkering in the kitchen came through Doli's closed door. She pulled herself up in bed after lying there for a good fifteen minutes after waking. Even with the stack of fluffy white pillows, her head pounded as if she'd drunk way too much ale the night before. In fact, the only thing she'd drunk before sleep was the chamomile tea she'd conjured into a blue floral porcelain teacup, which still sat half full next to a burned-down candle on the nightstand.

The dwarf swung her legs over the edge of the bed, and her bare feet were at least eight inches from the floor. The bed that had come with the furnished rental was not sized for a dwarf, but she'd gotten used to the slight inconvenience. Not much in Adenashire was dwarf-sized.

Morning light streamed through the paned window like a hazy fog. From her spot on the bed, she could see that the iridescent dragon egg in its box had formed a second winding crack.

"Oh, my," Doli said under her breath, her nerves taking hold again. When she'd first awakened, she had immediately hoped the entire egg incident had been a dream. But it wasn't, and the dragon egg was well on its way to hatching. But when? How much time did she have? She wished she'd looked for that information in the books.

She made a mental note to do just that later in the day.

The dwarf slid to the floor with a thunk and walked over to grab her robe from a metal hook on the wall beside her door. She flung the yellow velvet garment over her cozy bedclothes and tied the fabric belt around her waist to secure it. She also adjusted the silk cap she wore to bed each night to protect her curls. Afterward she turned to the egg.

"Why would Uncle Thorras give you to me?" The question came out with a sigh. Moving to Adenashire was supposed to solve all her problems, not bring the problems of Dundes Heights—and new ones—to her.

But the egg didn't answer, of course, and she had no idea why she was talking to it. So Doli picked up the box, already feeling like taking it with her wherever she went was the right thing to do, and headed out into the living area, which smelled of scrambled eggs.

Sure enough, Jez's tall fennex frame stood in the kitchen, poking into the cast-iron pan with a wooden spoon. A plate of dripping butter and the broken shells sat on the countertop next to her.

Doli breathed deeply in and out to settle herself, not wanting to alert Jez to any problems through the scent of her stress. She raised her head high and put on a cheerful air.

"Want some?" Jez asked without turning, her long, fluffy tail flicking side to side.

Doli gazed down at the larger egg in her hands and her stomach flipped. "Seems a bit morbid, doesn't it?"

Jez glanced at Doli but kept working at the stovetop. "You think dragons don't eat eggs?" She turned her attention back to the pan, lifted it with her free hand to portion the eggs onto two plates, then brought them to their dining table.

On the table were forks, a stack of generously buttered toast with the golden liquid dripping down the side of the crust, and two teacups from the cupboard, along with two fabric napkins.

The dwarf looked down at the eggs again and decided that, yes, dragons probably did eat eggs. So her eating them would offend no one in the room. But then she looked back to the kitchen where the cooking mess still waited on the counter. She scowled without thinking.

"It will all get cold if I take the time to clean up first before we eat," Jez said, picking up her cup and holding it out toward Doli. "Could you make us some tea?"

She didn't mention the semi-sour mood that Doli couldn't seem to control.

At the request Doli's spirits lifted slightly, as did the headache still lightly beating over her left eyebrow. She walked to

Jez and set the dragon egg box down between the two simple white plates full of steaming scrambled eggs.

"The regular?" Doli asked the fennex as she put her hand over the cup, a couple of inches from the lip. She was always glad to make tea.

"Sure," Jez said and sat. "Except no sugar today."

Doli nodded and envisioned the simple black tea with a tablespoon of cream in her mind. Seconds later, magic quivered in her hand and continued up her arm until steam from the tea dampened her palm. She pulled her hand back. A few sparkles remained in the air and then vanished.

"Thanks." Jez plucked the cup from the table and took a sip.

Doli climbed into her chair and made her own cup. That day it was a black tea infused with currant, two tablespoons of cream, and two lumps of sugar. She chose a thick piece of buttery toast from the top of the stack and placed it next to the eggs on her plate.

She was about to ask Jez if she'd had any more thoughts about the dragon egg when the fennex pulled a letter out of her pocket and plopped it on the table in front of Doli.

"I forgot this came with the delivery yesterday."

Doli furrowed her brow. "What is it?"

Before she answered, Jez stuffed her mouth with a large bite of eggs. "How em I surpoz t' mo?"

The dwarf scowled but quickly nudged up the corners of her mouth. "What if it's a letter from my uncle…telling me more about the…" Her eyes flicked to the egg again and her stomach tensed. "Uh, contents of the box?"

The letter was addressed to her by her mother, Gingrilin Butterbuckle.

Jez shrugged and kept eating. "M'be."

Ripping open the seal by running her finger underneath it, Doli kept the smile on her face. But doing so strained against her plump cheeks, and the entire expression felt wrong. She locked it in place anyway as she pulled the parchment from the envelope, hoping that her mother was passing along more instructions from her uncle, something that explained the inheritance and somehow made the situation easier.

But instead when she unfolded the paper, it was her mother's looping handwriting.

Dearest Dolgrila,

She gulped, then tensed, at the sight of her full name. Her parents were the only people who still called her by it.

I hope you are doing well and settling into the simplicity of Adenashire. We all know how you couldn't wait to make your way in the world away from your father and me.

To another reader the sentiment might not sound *too* bad. But Doli knew the words were laced with the guilt she was supposed to feel for leaving, accompanied by her mother's grating tone of voice in her head. She'd heard it hundreds of times, especially before she left home for good after competing in the Langheim Baking Battle the previous year. Her parents had not wanted her to travel alone to the elven realm in the first place, but she was well past the age of needing parental permission for anything, and they couldn't stop her. She'd used her own gold for the trip, as well as the move to Adenashire. Her mother and father could never understand why Doli thought a life away from Dundes Heights could be better than staying. They were happy there, wealthy. So why wasn't Doli? If they would have simply taken the time to listen to her, she might have stayed.

"Is it a letter from your uncle?" Jez broke into Doli's thoughts. "About the box?"

Doli flitted her attention from the paper to the fennex. "My mother."

"Her again?" Jez scooped a dollop of eggs onto her toast and took a bite.

"It's amazing how one can't quite get their family to leave them alone." Doli's tone came out biting, and she immediately regretted letting her words leave the privacy of her mind. Her chest burned with heat underneath her nightdress and robe. "I didn't mean that."

Jez eyed her briefly as she continued chewing. "Yes, you did."

Doli fanned herself with the letter. "I didn't," she insisted with an overly sweet drawl to her voice.

The fennex finished chewing, swallowed, and let her gaze fall on her friend. "I love you, dwarf. But you're lying."

The heat pricking at Doli's chest moved up her neck and

settled on her cheeks, causing her to fan the letter faster. "It's so hot in here." Her eyes moved to the fireplace.

"It's not," Jez said flatly. "And with you distributing the scent of your emotions by blowing them all over the place, you're making your untruth even worse."

Doli huffed and returned to reading the letter. She needed to get it over with, then she could move on with her day.

Everyone was so disappointed you were unable to make it to your Uncle Thorras's Life Commemoration ceremony, so your father and I have decided to travel the incredibly long distance to Adenashire and will be there in—

"Shit, shit, shit." The curses she never used flowed out of her as she threw the letter onto the table and jumped from her seat. "Tomorrow? There's no way this can be happening!" She wrapped her arms around her stomach and squeezed.

Jez leaned back in her seat as if to get as far back from Doli as she could. "What's tomorrow?"

The fennex's question jolted the dwarf back to reality and reminded her that she had an audience. She immediately straightened, her chest heaving for breath. "My parents. They're coming. Tomorrow."

Thoughts jumbled in Doli's brain…how her parents would compare her to her sisters, Brudela and Whurigret, and how their use of gem-finding magic had enhanced the family business. Plus, both were married and already had children.

"Well..." Jez glanced around the room and then back at Doli, raising one brow. "For more reasons than one they can't stay here."

A look of horror crept over Doli's features. "Oh, stars, I hadn't even thought of *that*." She placed her hand to her chest as if to keep her heart from flying out.

Jez stood and sighed. She quietly walked over to Doli, bent, and placed her clawed hands on the dwarf's shoulders.

Doli immediately calmed while her friend led her back to the table.

"You have to tell me what's going on, Doli," Jez insisted. "If only so that I'll be ready for this visit."

Doli pulled herself up into the seat, breathing hard. "I'm sorry. I'm a mess!"

"I know you are." The fennex patted Doli on the shoulder and sat back in her seat. "If it's you and not me cursing up a storm, something is really up."

Doli had scolded Jez so many times for her use of crass language. Now *she* was using it too. "You heard that? I think it's all your fault."

Jez dropped her head into her hands and chuckled. "Yeah. This is about *me*."

Ignoring her, Doli glanced down at the no longer steaming eggs on her plate, scooped a fluffy portion with a fork, and stuffed it into her mouth.

Jez's eyes widened. "Oh, damn. You really aren't going to talk about this? Letting your problems fester is only going to make everything worse."

Doli wanted to shoot back that Jez wasn't the best at

talking about her emotions either. Ever since they had met, the fennex had kept her own problems to herself. But the dwarf's mind had cleared enough to realize that the words would not be helpful. The letter rested against the dragon egg box, open to her mother's handwriting stating they'd be arriving the next day.

That was what was important—getting past her parents' visit. And figuring out what to do about that damn egg.

Doli pressed down the fear bubbling inside her and looked back up at Jez. "I don't have a shift today at the bookstore, so I'm going to run some errands. I'll see if there's a room I can rent at the Tricky Goat and stop at the market, and then I *am* going to drop off a batch of my spice cookies to Sarson to welcome him to Adenashire."

Jez opened her mouth to speak, but Doli cut her off.

"We can deal with the other stuff later." She ate a bite of toast while Jez sat there with her arms crossed.

Maybe. Maybe not, she amended mentally. But she kept that thought to herself.

5

Reluctantly leaving the egg at home and carrying a basket laden with Sarson's book and her fragrant, jam-filled spice cookies, Doli headed into the Tricky Goat Inn and Pub to rent a room for her parents.

It was the only lodging in Adenashire, so there was no risk of them finding something else before speaking with her. She also didn't want them to complain about having to spend their own silver on a room, rather than staying with her and Jez for free. Mother would make it sound like no big deal but then keep bringing it up for the duration of their stay…and long after.

Again and again.

Several empty tables and chairs waited out front since the pub wasn't open before lunch and it was just prior. A group of crows cawed as they sat on the edge of the roof, most likely staking their claim for any dropped, discarded, or possibly still-wanted food that would be served on the porch.

She climbed the squeaky wooden stairs to the entrance. On the door was a large sign featuring a carved goat with two curly horns munching on a bunch of grass. One of its eyes was closed as if it were in mid-wink—the "tricky" part, she guessed. Doli pushed open the door and entered the darkish foyer. The windows facing the street were small and slightly clouded, so not much light fell on the walnut paneling. But her eyes adjusted quickly, and she wrinkled her nose slightly at the smell of old ale, meats, and assorted other dishes that were served in the dining area to the left of the check-in station.

The place was empty save for a large badger wearing a pair of striped woolen pants and a tidy cotton shirt, lounging in a puffy chair next to a fireplace. A cane with an ornate silver handle lay against the side of the chair. He wore a set of spectacles at the end of his pointy snout and held a copy of *The Daily Lands*. It was a small, local publication with news concerning Adenashire and the surrounding towns that Doli rarely paid attention to. When he flipped the paper around, Doli spotted the headline in large, bold lettering: "Massive Unicorn Stampede. Residents Urged to Use Caution."

Doli's eyes widened at the words, but she turned and continued to the check-in, where no one stood to help her. Behind it, secured on the wall, were twenty small wooden cubbies with room numbers at the bottom of each. She took in a settling breath and reached up to ring the service bell, which sat next to a blue ceramic vase with two wilted red roses. The bell was louder than Doli had expected, and her insides jumped at the sharp sound. She turned back to the badger and laughed nervously. "Sorry."

The badger lowered his newspaper and gave a silent chuckle. "No problem. Surprised me too when I got here." He looked her up and down briefly with his dark brown eyes. "You travel light."

Doli tipped her head in confusion for a moment until she looked down at her basket with its top covered by a pink cotton dish cloth. "Oh, no." She held up the container chin-high. "This is a delivery for a bookstore customer. I'm here to book a stay for my parents."

His eyes twinkled as he leaned his elbow on his knee. "Don't want them staying with you?"

"Um…"

The badger waved his clawed paw in the air. "You don't need to answer that. I'm being nosy." He held up the paper. "You see this? About the unicorns?"

As he flashed the paper, she caught sight of another headline: "Head Librarian Abruptly—" But that was all she saw before he put it down again.

"No, I hadn't." Doli was glad not to be talking about her relationship with her parents. "What was the story about, besides the obvious?"

"Well, apparently there were a couple hundred steeds involved. Looks like there was some kind of territorial dispute, but the investigation is ongoing." He pinched his lips shut right as Doli heard footsteps approaching behind her.

"Can I help you?" The woman's voice was breathy and sounded exhausted.

When Doli turned back to the station, there stood a middle-aged human woman in a plain cream dress with a black apron cinched around her waist with a matching fabric tie. She worked at pulling her wavy brown locks into a low ponytail, but several strands insisted on escaping. Eventually she rolled her eyes, seemingly giving up on getting it all secured. Doli recognized the woman as the innkeeper, Maven.

"I need to rent a room starting tomorrow," Doli said, putting on her sweetest smile. "The best one you have. But no hurry." It was obvious that Maven was having a hard morning already…and Doli could identify with that problem. Best not to make it worse.

The woman blew out a quick breath and flipped open the thick, leather-bound scheduling book on the counter.

"Did you say today or tomorrow?" Maven asked.

"Oh. Tomorrow." Doli could barely see over the top, but inside the book was a scrawl detailing guests' names, rooms, and fees.

The innkeeper scanned down the page and plunked her finger down in the middle. "Good, because we're completely booked today, but our suite will be available and ready tomorrow before dinner," she said. She lowered her voice and muttered, "If all the staff shows up for their shift."

The letter from her mother hadn't specified the time of arrival, but before dinner should work.

"Oh, thank you so much." Doli raised up on her toes to get a bit closer to the woman. "Are you okay, though?"

"Sorry." Maven waved a hand dismissively. "Rough morning."

Doli's brows furrowed in concern, and for the moment she forgot some of her own troubles, including the pink dragon egg she'd left in her apartment. "What's going on?" Asking helped her to feel more like her regular self, and she truly was curious.

Maven leaned her forearm onto the counter. "If you really want to know…"

Doli nodded. "Of course."

The woman paused for a moment before speaking. "This place really used to run itself. But that hasn't been the case in the last several months." Maven shook her head. "Perhaps it's only that I'm getting older."

"Thinking about selling?" The badger's voice came from behind Doli. He'd obviously been eavesdropping.

Maven's lips turned down in thought, and then she laughed. "I don't know. I hadn't thought of it. But after this morning? The buyer would get a good price." But when she glanced back at Doli, her mood had clearly been lightened by sharing her woes.

Both patrons gave small chuckles, and Doli was glad to have asked.

"Now," Maven said with a tiny glint in her eye, "let's get that room booked."

With the room booked and goodbyes bid to Maven and the badger, Doli headed down a secluded street just outside town. Trees danced overhead as the wind rustled through them. Unfortunately, her problems still hung in the air, and she knew she couldn't spend long at Sarson's house because she needed to get back to the egg. Whether it was all in her head or some kind of real connection, she already had a type of maternal bond forming with the egg, to protect it, at least until it could be returned to its rightful family. She had no idea what her uncle had in mind when he'd given the egg to her or if it was a simple mistake, but what had been done was done.

She checked the address on the bookstore receipt, and she was on the right path. Sarson's home should be not far away. A minute or two down the road she spotted the cottage.

It was white with a tall thatched roof. Fruit trees were loaded with ripe apples and pears. The place was lovely and simple, not at all what she would have expected of a gargoyle. From what she knew about them—not that she'd ever been to their territories in the Northern Lands—they were a fairly extravagant people. But after meeting Theo, a woodland elf, who chose to live simply instead of in a castle, it was possible that not all rumors of taste were true. She herself was a dwarf who preferred fashion and baking over mining any day of the week.

Doli picked up her pace and followed the path to the door painted a sunny yellow. This made her bubble as she rapped on the wood.

But there was no answer.

Frustrated, she pinched her plump lips and tried again, this time more loudly. "Hello," Doli called. "I have a delivery from It's About Tome."

Seconds later, heavy footsteps sounded inside. She had enough time to step back before the door opened a crack and a light-blue clawed hand appeared.

The tall gargoyle peered out as if he might want to close the door quickly in case someone was there he didn't want standing on his porch. "Oh. Hello," Sarson said in a gentle, yet surprised tone when he looked down and saw Doli.

Flutterbees whirled around in her stomach at the sight of him. As he opened the door wider, she could see that his white shirt was loose and open in the front, revealing the curve of his powerful chest muscles. The sight took the air right out of Doli's lungs. And then there were the large wings tucked tightly behind his back.

Quickly he brought his hand to the wayward fabric. "I'm sorry. I wasn't expecting anyone. I haven't really gotten out much since I moved to Adenashire." He worked on pulling the tie closed at the top of the neck.

A nervous laugh left Doli's mouth, and she held up her basket too high. "I brought you the book you reserved. It came in this morning on a delivery. And a housewarming gift." The words tumbled out on top of each other too quickly. But she managed to reach inside the basket and pull out the book, *History of Gargoyles*. She laughed again, not meaning to. "I'd think you'd already have this book. History is kind of what gargoyles do, right?"

A half smile curled at his lips. "You'd think that, wouldn't you?" He held up the book. "Thank you for bringing this. I had expected to pick it up myself later this week."

An awkward silence settled between them for a moment before Doli remembered the spice cookies. "Oh, and I made some cookies last night. I wasn't sure if anyone had welcomed you to the village, so I thought I might." She held out the basket to Sarson, and he gently took it.

"Thank you, Doli," he said softly.

Her breath immediately picked up. "You remembered my name." She had meant to keep the thought in her mind, but it came out anyway.

Sarson smiled, revealing his fangs, and he ran his free hand over one horn. "I always remember kind people."

Doli would have classified her behavior the afternoon before as clumsier than kind, but Sarson could think whatever he liked. "Thank you…Sarson." His name made those flutterbees take another loop in her stomach. But not knowing what else to do, she almost excused herself until she saw something behind him.

"You have quite the library in there," Doli said. And it really was. The shelves must have taken up the entire back half of the house. Row upon row of books could be seen, and that was just from the porch. She wondered how many more there must be inside.

"Um." Sarson glanced back into the house. "It's still completely unorganized." He paused for a second. "But would you like to see it?"

In Doli's mind it didn't appear to be unorganized at all… and she did indeed want to see it. "Yes, please."

As if he hadn't thought she might accept his invitation, Sarson stood in the doorway, not moving.

Doli stepped toward him and held out her hand in expectation. "Well?"

"Oh." He snapped to like a band. "Please, come inside."

The house was warm as she entered, not only in temperature but also the furnishings. The leather chairs and chunky wood table leaned masculine, but not to a point. Sarson also had several vases full of greenery and a few late-blooming wildflowers scattered around the place. The scent in the air was heavy with coffee and herbs with a hint of honey.

"You have coffee?" she asked. The beans were not exactly common in Adenashire or even Dundes Heights.

Sarson closed the door while he lifted the pink dish cloth covering the cookies. "I do. On my journey here I happened upon a farm. The beans were for sale, so I had to have a few bags." He chuckled. "The samples were so incredibly delicious I couldn't believe they weren't somehow magic. Would you like a cup?" After the question, he pulled out a cookie and took a bite.

"Would I? Of course." Doli salivated at the thought of the slightly bitter coffee on her tongue. It had been years since she'd had any.

His eyes danced and his tail swayed behind him on the floor as he chewed the cookie. "These are delicious. I think I'll grab myself a cup to enjoy too."

Doli clasped her hands behind her back and twisted gently at her waist. "I'm glad you like them." She had the urge to blabber all about her grammy to Sarson, but they'd only just met and she didn't want to assume he'd be interested in the stories.

The gargoyle bowed his head slightly and raised his hand to indicate the library. "My kitchen is outside, so feel free to look around in there. I won't be long." He started to turn but stopped. "I imagine you'll want sugar and cream?"

Doli bit her lip. "You imagine correctly. Although I do like it black as well."

"Me too." With that he excused himself, set the basket down on a counter, and walked out a door on the back side of the house.

Heat pulsed at Doli's cheeks as she waited to blow out the breath she'd been holding. After a moment, she ambled toward the massive collection of books. At one end of the case was a sturdy ladder with wheels on a track along the top. Sarson was so tall that he probably didn't need it to reach anything, even at the top. Her first urge was to climb up on the rungs and swing across to the other side, but she did no such thing and kept her feet on the floor.

In front of the shelves was a cozy seating area with two brocade fabric chairs and a small table between them. Perfect for sitting and reading with someone you care about. The thought of herself and Sarson sitting quietly in each, reading a book and sharing a snack plate of meat, cheese, and fresh breads ran through her mind, but she quickly cast it aside.

"You're being so silly, Doli. This isn't fiction," she scolded herself under her breath and rushed directly to the nearest bookcase, not looking for anything in particular. There were a lot of books related to the history of the Northern

Lands—elves, humans, dwarves, fauns, and everyone she could even think of plus several more. And as she ran her fingers along the spines, grazing the raised lettering, she couldn't help but wonder if they were official gargoyle-told histories…and what they had on dwarves. Her mind wandered and somehow came back to the real reason she was here, apart from delivering the book. To ask about dragons.

She quickly performed a deeper scan over the tomes to figure out how they were organized, by title, author, or topic. It seemed by topic, so she searched for D. Doli quickly spotted the word *dragon* on the spines of a book on the very top shelf when the back door clicked open.

Sarson entered with two cups of steaming coffee, and the rich scent hit Doli's nostrils at once.

"That smells amazing," she said, anticipating her first sip.

He brought the cups over and set them on the table near the bookcases, then returned to the basket for a handful of cookies, which he quickly plated from a stack of dishware on the counter. The gargoyle set the plate down with the mugs and joined Doli.

She eyed the book on the top ledge but decided not to ask about it yet. Instead she plucked the coffee from the table and sipped the creamy brew. It was honestly as delicious as she remembered, maybe more so. The brew warming her middle, she asked, "So what brought you to Adenashire?"

Sarson sat in the chair opposite her and took a cookie from the plate. "Retirement."

"Retirement?" The answer surprised the dwarf since Sarson appeared to be in his prime. "Why?"

He took a bite of his second cookie and furrowed his brows before he answered. "I can't really say more."

"Oh." Doli took another sip of her coffee, and she couldn't help but remember Jez's suspicion that gargoyles could be trouble or untrustworthy. She twisted at the pink gem on her necklace.

He raised his cup to his lips, and his eyes told her that he'd sensed her discomfort at his answer. "Adenashire was a sleepy place where I could be a hermit. I've wanted something quieter for a long time. Yesterday was one of my first real ventures into town. Until then I'd had everything delivered out here." He looked at Doli with a soft gaze. "You're my first visitor."

She grinned, almost forgetting about Jez's nonsense, and leaned to the edge of the chair. "I'm glad to be so." Her attention moved back to the books…and to the need to get back home. "Um. I saw you had a few books about dragons."

"Several," he confirmed with a tip of the head.

"Do you happen to have any about dragon types and maybe…eggs?"

Sarson raised his right brow. "I do, in fact." He stood and gestured to the shelves. "Would you like to see them?"

Doli downed her coffee and managed, "If you wouldn't mind, I'd actually like to borrow them."

"Oh. Not at all." He chuckled and reached for the books. "I do know where you live." Sarson grabbed two books from the top shelf as if he'd already known exactly where they were and what information was inside. Without even looking at them he handed the books to Doli. "These are just what you need."

Doli took them and looked down at the top offering, *Dragon Life, Egg to Adult*. "Thank you for this and the coffee. I'd really love to stay longer, but I have something to take care of this afternoon." The need to get back to the egg pulled suddenly on her heart like a string.

Sarson smiled. "Then I'll see you out."

Hefting the books into her arms, Doli made her way to the door. "It really was a nice chat."

The gargoyle opened the door to allow her out and gave her another soft gaze. "It really was, Doli Butterbuckle."

The flutterbees were back.

He had also remembered her *last* name.

6

The next morning, as she dusted the bookshelves in the store, Doli hummed a happy little tune she'd heard a bard singing on the street corner next to the market. Mostly she kept her work to the lower shelves within her arm's reach, since she would need a ladder for the rest unless Verdreth got to them first.

Her mind was alight with the memory of visiting Sarson the day before. He'd remembered her first and last name. So this meant one of two things. He either had an excellent memory…or she had made an impression on him when they first met in the bookstore.

No need to remember that she'd nearly fallen over during that meeting. Just that he'd caught her with his tail.

Doli liked to believe that it was mostly for the second

reason. And she was so caught up in the glorious thought that her other troubles seemed to melt away. She drifted into a daydream of picnicking with Sarson in a meadow outside of town. "What are you so chipper about today?" a feminine voice asked from behind the dwarf.

"Oh, stars!" The voice startled Doli from her daydream, and the feather duster she'd been holding was tossed high into the air. It landed on the floor with a thunk, and a small puff of dust scattered through the space. The dwarf's hand flew instinctively to her chest, where she'd fashioned a sling out of leftover fabric from a purple and white checked dress she'd sewn last month. That morning, she'd liked how the pattern complemented her forest green dress. Tucked inside the sling, the dragon egg was safe and warm. And unharmed.

But during the night, a third crack had formed and was making its way merrily down the side of the pink egg.

She spun on her boot heel to Taenya, who stood only a few steps from the entrance. The elf held a basket, and light streamed through her chin length auburn hair like a halo. She almost always dressed simply, not too differently from Jez. Although Jez wore more leather.

Today was no exception. The elf wore a plain pair of slouchy tan pants with roomy pockets below the hip and a gauzy white cotton shirt tucked in at the waist. A belt cinched everything in.

"I'm sorry, I didn't mean to startle you," Taenya said, grinning. Her green eyes twinkled in a way they had not dared to when she and Doli had first met at the Langheim Baking Battle. Taenya had won against Arleta in the final round and was a celebrated baker in the elven realm. But she had hated the life she led in Langheim, with her brother's constant expectations to be something she wasn't. The burden had made her into an angry person. After the Battle, she took her winnings, came to Adenashire, bought a bakery for Arleta—because she felt that Arleta should have won—and then the two of them became business partners.

Doli understood a thing or two about feeling forced to be someone you're not.

"Oh." Doli returned the friendly expression and plucked the duster from the ground, then held it high like a prize. "I'm simply distracted."

Taenya took a step toward the dwarf. "Well, it can't be about your family coming later today with a zippy tune like that."

Doli rolled her eyes. "Jez told you about my parents' visit?" She flopped down in one of the comfy chairs in the middle of the display floor.

"She told me," Taenya confirmed and placed her hand on the basket handle. She eyed the staircase leading up to Jez and Doli's apartment. "Speaking of Jez. Is she upstairs?"

Doli gently ran her hand over the egg through the sling's fabric. "Jez needed a break from peopling and went fishing at first light." She glanced at the large freestanding clock against the bookstore wall. "She's supposed to be back soon. She's covering the rest of my shift so I can make all the preparations for my parents' arrival this evening."

A look of disappointment washed over Taenya's features for two shakes, and the instant need to make her feel better bubbled in Doli's chest.

"You can always come back…or I can give her whatever you have there." Doli's eyes dropped to the cloth-covered basket.

Taenya shrugged. "It's only a blood orange tart I'd been experimenting with at the bakery this morning. I wanted to get her opinion on it."

The thought crossed Doli's mind that Jez had made a blood orange cake in one round of the Baking Battle. So she must have liked the flavor. Taenya must have noticed this preference as well.

Or it could have been a coincidence.

"Well, you could leave it up in the kitchen…or come back later." Doli's voice trilled as she fanned herself with her free hand and the air blew at the curls across her forehead.

Taenya pursed her lips as if in thought. "I think I'll leave it upstairs."

Doli pushed up the corners of her lips and gestured toward the stairs. "Be my guest." But she was also still thinking about the tart.

The elf nodded and turned to head up, but Doli caught her by saying, "Can I try it too? After Jez, of course?"

"Oh. Yes." Taenya twisted back to the dwarf. "I'd love that. I feel it may need something, and I'd love your notes as well."

Doli watched as Taenya vanished up the stairs, then stood back up to continue dusting. Moments later, the shop door burst open, and its bell rang multiple times. This time, she didn't startle until she actually turned around and found her parents standing directly inside the doorway.

Gingrilin and Uldrick Butterbuckle. In all their glory.

And glory it was. The same sunlight that had lit Taenya's hair reflected off the glittering jewelry both of Doli's parents wore. Gingrilin's coiled dark hair was threaded with gold twine and topped off with a large golden comb with a ruby inset. Doli's father had a long, dark braided beard and wore two golden ear cuffs and a set of begemmed rings on each finger. Their creamy, dark umber skin mirrored Doli's.

They were stunning and regal, as always.

Doli was not opposed to this kind of thing. She loved jewelry as much as the next dwarf, but she hadn't worn most of the pieces she'd brought to Adenashire because, in all honesty, they seemed out of place in the rustic town.

But neither of the two dwarves had apparently considered that fact, or cared, because they had worn their best outfits of luxurious satin, silk, and velvet and were loaded with two large leather bags, each likely stuffed with clothing just as fine. They would do nothing but stand out the entire trip.

Good thing it would probably only be for a night or two.

"Dolgrila!" her mother announced and flung open her arms, dropping her bags on the floor with a plunk.

"Be careful, dearest," Uldrick said, but Gingrilin seemed to pay him no mind.

"Mother?" Doli's eyes darted to her father, and he gave a little shrug. "You're so early. I hadn't expected you until later in the day."

Gingrilin continued toward her daughter and hugged Doli, squeezing her around the waist.

Doli leaned back slightly to avoid the dragon egg being damaged. Her mother didn't even seem to notice.

"Oh, Dolgrila." Her mother's voice was dripping with drama. "You don't even want to hear about the intense journey we've had. There were unicorns…so many disgruntled unicorns."

Doli knew that meant she was going to hear all about it. Probably five times. Or more.

At least she'd probably find out more than was in the newspaper story.

Her mother continued to squeeze Doli to the point where she had picked her up off the floor several inches.

Nearly breathless and worried about damaging the dragon egg that her mother appeared not to have noticed, Doli managed, "Can you put me down, Mother?"

The dwarf dropped her daughter and stepped back. "Oh yes, dear. Now let me take a look at you!" She folded her arms over her ample chest and brought her right hand up to her already pursed lips. "What do you think, Uldy?"

Doli gulped and brought her hand to the sling but immediately regretted it because she didn't want to talk about what was inside.

But of course, her mother reached for the fabric, knitting a sweater with her brows. "You're looking a bit *simplistic* these days. What's inside this, um, pocket?"

Doli edged back, momentarily doubting herself, but she reoriented quickly, knowing perfectly well that her dress was in fashion. It simply wasn't as over-the-top as the clothes and jewelry they wore. "This is, um, something I'm looking after for a bit."

"What is it?" Uldrick asked, his voice peppered with curiosity.

But Doli was not ready to go into all the dragonish details at that moment. She didn't even want to think about it *herself*. "You must be exhausted." Doli made a beeline for the dropped bags, but when she grabbed the handle and pulled, the luggage pulled right back. It stuck to the floor as if it were filled with stones. "Goodness. What did you bring?"

"Pshaw." Gingrilin waved her hand dismissively. "Just a few bits and baubles." She gazed around the bookshop, apparently forgetting about Doli's appearance or what was in the sling. "Now where should we put them for the week?"

"Week?" The question slipped out before Doli could slap her hand over her mouth.

"Well, yes!" Doli's mother said. " We wanted to be here long enough to look around the town, make sure you've settled in…open your inheritance box."

Doli froze and gulped. Was she supposed to wait to open it?

"Gini," Uldrick said, "we can get to all that soon." He turned his attention to Doli. "Will you please show us to our rooms?"

Although all she really wanted to do was hyperventilate, Doli steeled herself against the whirlwind that was her parents. She put on her most sugary voice and said, "Your *room* at the local inn will be ready for you after dinner."

Her father raised a brow. "I thought we'd stay with you. No need for the expense."

Doli's brain whirled at the thought of her parents staying with her and Jez up in the apartment. They'd be into everything, criticizing the furniture, the tiny kitchen. Asking too many questions.

Jez would surely end up putting her colorful words—and claws—to good use.

No one wanted that.

"Oh, no." Doli waved both of her hands in the air and kept her tone light. "I've arranged the whole thing. I even paid for the room."

Not for a week, of course. *That* would have to be remedied as soon as possible.

Her mother opened her mouth to speak, but Doli was faster. "I've been earning my own silver here at the bookstore. Please allow me to share it."

Gingrilin clamped her lips shut. Dwarves, at least the ones Doli had met, wanted to be seen as excellent hosts. This was unspoken. So if a dwarf offered to pay for someone else's way, it should be accepted. It was good manners. *Even* if strings were attached. That problem would have to be figured out later.

Doli knew this and found it annoying sometimes. But at the moment, the tradition had worked in her favor.

"But not until dinner, you say?" Uldrick struggled with his bags, still not setting them down.

Before Doli could answer, footsteps came down the staircase, and she looked up to see Taenya.

"Oh," the elf said. "You must be Doli's parents."

The couple turned their attention to Taenya. Relief washed over Doli to have the attention off herself for a moment.

"Why, yes, we are!" Gingrilin plastered on a huge grin. "Are you from Langheim?"

Taenya continued down the stairs. "I am. Doli and I met at the Baking Battle last year."

"Oh, how wonderful," Doli's father said with too much enthusiasm.

Doli knew neither of her parents found the Baking Battle all that important, but it *was* important that they were liked. Her stomach flopped, knowing it was a trait she'd inherited from them, although the manifestation was slightly different.

"Did you do well in the competition?" Gingrilin asked, and tacked on, "Our Doli didn't win, you know."

Doli scowled.

The elf tipped her head in interest as her feet touched the floor. "Oh, Doli did very well. She made a lovely batch of strawberry cheesecake scones that almost brought her to the finals."

Warmth from the fact that Taenya remembered her strawberry cheesecake scones filled Doli's chest. Plus, the elf didn't even mention the truth that she'd been the one to take the grand prize.

"Oh," Gingrilin said and glanced at her daughter. "That's lovely."

"Well." Taenya bowed her head slightly. "I must go now. Have to get back to work at the bakery. I hope you have a pleasant stay in Adenashire."

"Thank you, dear," Gingrilin said.

Doli's father nodded, and the elf made her way out the bookshop door with the bell ringing behind her.

Uldrick, still holding his bags, leaned close to his wife. "I don't think that elf did very well in the Battle."

Doli rolled her eyes again and let out a short, calming breath. "How about we put your bags upstairs? I'll lock up the shop, and we can go check the status of your room at the inn." Doli remembered Maven's tired demeanor the day before and doubted the room would somehow magically be ready. But it was worth checking, and it could waste some time.

She stretched her lips into a wide grin and took a step forward.

But that was the exact moment the egg in her sling jiggled.

And popped open.

A little high-pitched trill came from inside the pocket.

7

Uldrick's face contorted with confusion mixed with great interest. "What was that?" He finally dropped his bags onto the floor, and they plopped over on their sides.

Doli's breath picked up, and her heart pounded against her chest as the sling wobbled wildly.

"Um…" was all Doli could get out.

The dragon trilled again as it squirmed and pushed from its egg. Pieces of iridescent shell escaped the sling and tumbled to the floor while a tiny, clawed hand crept over the fabric. Panicked, Doli quickly shoved it back inside.

"Yes." Gingrilin took two steps toward Doli. "What do you have in there?"

"Nothing," Doli lied futilely, since there was already a

tuft of pink hair and tiny set of pointy horns peeking out of the sling pocket in full view of her parents. "Nothing." She twisted away from them as she shoved the baby dragon back in one more time. "Get back in there," she whispered, trying to keep her tone light.

"Is that…a dragon?" Uldrick asked as he and his wife edged in for a view.

"A dragon?" Doli managed, her voice cracking. "Why would I have a dragon?"

Faster than any dwarf weighed down by a cache of gold and jewels should have been able to move, Gingrilin whipped around and stepped in front of her daughter. Her eyes trained on the wiggly fabric, now with two clawed hands jutting from the opening. "*Yes.* Why *would* you have a dragon?"

Doli's wide nostrils flared as far as they could go, and her cheeks and neck heated as though flame had burst to life inside her. She clutched for the emerging dragon, who had managed to fling its tiny wings out wide. But it was too fast and leaped free. Doli's hands were empty. The youngster was airborne, dashing and diving around the bookstore.

"Oh, stars!" Horror widened Doli's eyes as she nearly bowled her mother over in an attempt to catch the baby. The only thing she was thankful for at the moment was that Sarson's dragon book had promised that dragons do not produce fire until they are at least a year old. So at least they would not be burning down the bookstore.

Not yet anyway.

But they were squealing, knocking books from the shelves

as they flew around the room and already making a general menace of themselves.

"Get back here!" Doli demanded to no avail.

"Doli!" Gingrilin shouted as she reached up to grab the little one but missed. "What in the stars is going on? Why do you have a dragon?"

Uldrick quickly opened and rummaged through one of his bags as his wife and daughter raced around the room, trying and failing to grab the tiny pink troublemaker. Gingrilin nearly took out a small table displaying a newly arrived book titled *Elf Culture*, but Doli steadied it before everything hit the floor.

Finally, Doli's father pulled out a family heirloom knitted blanket from the bag and held it high as the dragon looped the room. The dwarf jumped higher than one might expect for a person of his age and stature, and he wrapped the blanket around the dragon as it squeaked in protest. Like a professional baby bundler, Uldrick quickly smoothed back the dragon's wings, avoiding its snapping, yet thankfully still toothless jaws, and swaddled the rascal into a nice little cozy bundle.

Uldrick held it out to his daughter. "I think this is yours."

Doli quickly snatched it from him and held the dragon close to her chest as it whined to be let free again. Their little snout pinched in displeasure, and they opened their mouth and hissed as if trying to push out fire that didn't come.

Doli gazed down at the little baby, and all the chaos of the bookshop faded away, as if it was only her and the dragon and their own little world. She was finally able to get a good look at them instead of the pink blur that had been zipping around the bookstore for the last few minutes.

Which had passed like an age.

The dragon settled back into the blanket and slowly blinked their sky-blue eyes several times at Doli. A snap of magic traveled from the bundle through Doli's hands, then arms. In that moment, the dwarf knew the dragon was female and the name she'd already chosen for herself—Evvy. The two stared intently at one other, and their bond was sealed.

At least for the time being, the dragon confirmed that Doli would be her guardian. And she was safe.

But it wasn't long before Doli broke from the spell and found her mother shaking her shoulder.

"Doli! Will you please tell us what's going on here?" Gingrilin demanded. "Why in heaven and land do you have a dragon?"

The dwarf brought her gaze from the now-cooing bundle in her arms to her semi-screechy mother. "Because Uncle Thorras willed her to me," she admitted. "I already opened the box because I didn't even know that the two of you were coming to Adenashire until it was too late. Jez didn't give me the letter until the next morning."

With a furrowed brow Uldrick asked, "Why would Thorras will you a dragon egg?"

Doli frowned, and she gestured helplessly. "I asked the same thing. Where in the Northern Lands did he get it?"

Evvy squawked in displeasure, and all three of the dwarves looked down.

"Well." Gingrilin threw her hands up. "This is terrible."

Although Doli had, only minutes before, thought the situation was terrible too, the bond she experienced with Evvy had somehow softened that feeling. "It's not *exactly* the end of the Northern Lands, Mother."

"But how are you going to take care of such a child?" Gingrilin asked. "You need to give it to us, and we can go back to Dundes Heights and figure out what to do." She gazed around for a second. "This village is no place to have a dragon. It's so…dusty." She pressed her lips together and grasped for the bundle.

Doli pulled away from her mother, rage bubbling in her chest. "First off, she's not an *it*. And her name is Evvy. And Adenashire is just fine."

Gingrilin scoffed. "You've never been responsible, dear."

Uldrick placed his hand on his wife's upper arm, but she pulled away.

"What are you talking about, Mother?" Doli growled. "I'm a grown woman, and I've made my own way with my life. Is it what you wanted? Did I go into the family business? No. But I'm doing splendidly."

The little dragon turned its head to Gingrilin and hissed.

Gingrilin wrinkled her nose. "I didn't mean that the way it sounded," she said under her breath.

"Of course you did!" Cheeks flaring with heat, Doli made her way to the door with the dragon still bundled and only her little head poking out of the blanket.

Out on the street Doli suddenly regretted leaving the bookstore as her stomach dropped into the earth. But she couldn't go back in there. Tears stung at the corners of her eyes. Her parents had never understood her, and that day was no different. She looked over her shoulder to see her bewildered parents through the window shrugging and throwing their hands into the air.

Doli huffed and gathered Evvy closer, making sure to pull the blanket up so the dragon stayed out of sight from nosy onlookers, which she knew were plentiful in Adenashire.

Down the road was the bustling street market. Scents of roasted meats and sweet popcorn prepared in large metal drums hit her nose immediately. And it seemed the smells traveled through the blanket to Evvy as well, since she had already poked her snout out from the fabric again, and her little nostrils moved in and out as she sniffed.

But Doli had no time for the market or even how cute little Evvy was. She needed help, and fast. Help with her parents, help with the baby dragon.

So she left the bookstore behind and ran. She ran two streets over and straight into A Little Dash of Magic Bake Shop. In the window was an array of frosted cakes, pastries, and pies. Every single one of them looked heavenly.

She was pretty sure that at least Taenya would be back and working, but Arleta might be there too. Doli burst through the door, and the first person she saw was Theo, sitting at one of the tables with a mug in front of him. Lying beside him on the ground was Faylin, a large gray and white forest lynx, whose primary role was as Theo's, and now Arleta's, house cat—although he claimed they were his humans.

"Hello, Doli," Theo managed to get out before she spun the other way.

She could see Taenya in the back kneading a large batch of dough, and Arleta was stocking fresh and crusty rosemary berry pastries, likely from running out during the morning rush. She wore a white apron with a red stain on the left that perfectly matched the color of the pastries.

"What in the Northern Lands is going on, Doli?" Arleta's hazel eyes grew large as she wavered her gaze between Doli and Theo, who had stood but still held a cup of steaming liquid.

Doli bent over slightly, one hand on the bundle and the other on her knee, trying to catch her breath. When the dwarf had finally filled her lungs with sufficient air, she righted herself and held the blanket out at arm's length.

"She…she hatched!" Doli managed as the dragon worked against her confines. "But my parents… They were right there. They saw the whole thing and told me I wasn't responsible and wanted to take Evvy back to Dundes Heights."

"Wait." Taenya came from the back holding a dish towel and wiping her hands. "Who's Evvy?"

And just as the elf asked, the little dragon twisted against her bundle and somehow slipped free. She flew straight for the pastries on the counter display, snatched one from the top of the stack in her toothless jaws, and flew up to the highest shelf in the bakery. She perched and began devouring the goodie while little crumbs fell to the floor.

"*That's* Evvy," Doli said. She dropped the blanket, turned to the front door, locked it, and quickly twisted the sign hanging on it from OPEN to CLOSED.

Evvy still sat purring as she clutched the pastry in her back claw and munched away.

"Well," Theo said, humor in his tone. "She has good taste."

"Do dragons even eat sweets?" Doli asked, trying to remember everything she'd read in the last two days. It was all mostly a blur.

Arleta leaned against the counter as she watched the baby. "Apparently they do."

Bang, bang, bang came from the door, and they all turned to see a gray-haired halfling woman peering through the glass.

"Sorry!" Taenya called. "We're closed for a bit. Check back in, uh—" She gazed around at the group, but Arleta gave a shrug and no one else answered. "In an hour."

The woman scowled but turned and left.

"She'll just go to the market and get something else," Faylin grumbled, his chin still resting on his paws, not even opening his eyes. He did flick his tufted ear in annoyance.

Likely that his nap had been disturbed.

The little dragon finished up her snack and began licking her back claw. Her tiny pink tongue flicked in and out of her mouth to groom her scaly body and wings.

"She sure is cute." Arleta sighed as if in love.

Evvy stopped grooming and closed her mouth but left her tongue lolling out as she surveyed the bakery.

"Aww," Taenya sighed. "A blep."

A what? Doli's brow furrowed. They were right, though… Evvy was adorable. But an obvious problem. How was she supposed to deal with her parents, or get anything done at all with this baby dragon around? Dwarf babies were nothing like this. They didn't get up and run around moments after being brought into this world.

A gentle hand grazed her shoulder, and she looked up to see Theo.

He gave her a sympathetic shrug and gestured to the table he'd been sitting at beside Faylin. "Would you like to have a seat? I think we can all figure something out."

Seconds later Verdreth appeared at the door huffing and puffing. Arleta quickly came out from behind the counter and let him in.

The orc looked up at the dragon, who was grooming once again, and then back at Doli. "Would you mind telling me why your parents are camped out in the middle of my bookstore?"

8

"Oh, my parents!" Doli knew she shouldn't have left them alone in the bookstore, but no logic had mattered when she'd needed to get away from them. Doli rushed toward the orc at the door, fully intending to go back there, collect them, and figure out what she was going to do next.

Verdreth, wearing a tidy blue shirt and gray vest with matching pants, shrugged and didn't move to unblock the entrance. "They didn't even notice me since they were selling a stack of books to a customer who seemed incredibly interested in unicorns."

Doli pinched at the bridge of her nose and groaned. "I'm so sorry. I totally forgot to even lock up."

Adenashire was a safe place with very little crime to speak

of, so even if her parents weren't in there hocking books, it was highly unlikely any would have been stolen.

Chuckling, Verdreth said, "They were selling so many I was thinking of hiring them full-time." His eyes twinkled.

Doli stared at him flatly. "You wouldn't dare." She knew he was joking, yet even the thought of it made the hairs on her arms stand on end.

"No. No, I wouldn't." The orc pushed his round spectacles up on his nose. "Bad idea."

Theo cleared his throat behind her. "If you're leaving, I think you might have forgotten something."

When Doli turned back to him, he was pointing up at the baby dragon perched on the edge of the shelf, surveying the chaos below that she was partly responsible for.

"Where is my mind these days?" Doli said, balling her hands into fists and quickly releasing them.

"Why don't you let us help you?" Arleta asked, sympathy thick in her voice as she came out from behind the counter. "The morning rush is over. There's no need for all of us to stay here for at least a couple of hours." She glanced over at Taenya, who nodded in agreement.

Doli gulped and breathed hard.

"I already have Ervash on the way to the bookstore," Verdreth said. "If you need time off for the rest of your shift, we can cover it."

Doli let out a huge sigh of relief and simply sat down on the floor where she had stood. Reflexively she unlatched the teacup on her belt, put her hand over the cup, and conjured a steaming cup of tea. She drank it like a shot and immediately made another before her nerves truly started to settle.

Theo sat down next to her. "I realize you have a lot going on with your parents' arrival and the dragon. But besides that, are you feeling okay?"

Doli's heart jumped at the question, and any relief she'd felt from the tea disappeared into buzzing zips of lightning in her stomach. Jez had mentioned the same thing, but Jez could smell her emotional state *and* lived with her. If everyone else was noticing her recent state of mind, then she really had been doing a poor job of holding it together.

She gulped down the rest of her tea, returned the cup to the holster, and said in her finest sunshiny tone of voice, "I'm fine. You're right. There's just a lot going on, but I feel better now."

She didn't. It was a bald-faced lie. In fact, her insides compressed like they might twist her into a loop if that were possible. Before the elf could respond, four small pink feet with tiny claws on each toe landed on her shoulder.

Evvy nuzzled Doli's cheek and gave a high-pitched whine.

"Aww," all four of the others cooed in unison as if Evvy had them under a spell.

Maybe she did. At least a little one.

Doli had noticed in the dragon books that some types had magic to influence others, but she hadn't studied those parts enough to really understand the ability. It could also simply be that the dragon was incredibly cute with her enormous eyes, toothless gums, iridescent scales, silky wings, and stumpy tail.

Doli reached for the fabric sling and pulled it open. The little dragon took the dwarf's cue and crawled from her shoulder into the warmth of the sling. She nuzzled in, shut her eyes, and immediately began snoring quietly.

The dragon's warmth, which was great, settled into Doli's chest and made her body relax. She looked up at Verdreth. "Do I need to get my parents out of the bookstore? They can't check into the inn until dinner. Plus, I need to head over there to make sure Maven has openings for a week."

"They're here for a week?" Theo chimed in. He had his own trouble with his mother, so he was likely sympathetic to Doli's feelings about hosting her parents for such a long time.

Doli turned to him and raised her brows. "Yup."

"Stars," Theo breathed like the word was a curse.

"I do think Ervash and I can handle them for a bit." Verdreth glanced over at Arleta. "You think I could get a dozen pastries to go? You know…to keep the Butterbuckles fed?"

She chuckled lightly and gave him a sweet expression. "Sure, Dad. On the house. I'll even throw in a few extra just for you."

The orc's cheeks turned a darker shade of green as a blush.

He and Ervash loved being Arleta's surrogate fathers. Each of them still acted a little giddy in their own way when she called them Dad, even though she'd been saying it regularly for months.

The orc approached the counter to collect his treasures. Crossing his arms over his broad chest, Verdreth leaned in to study the vast selection of almond bear claws, strawberry mint tarts, cardamom lemon bars, salted chocolate chip cookies, blueberry pastry braids, and several other varieties Doli had yet to identify. Arleta plucked them one at a time for the order.

"Make sure to get a couple of the blueberry ones."

"Of course," Arleta said as she continued to load the bag, and Taenya walked over to help.

Everyone knew berry-flavored anything were the orcs' favorites. They would eat and enjoy any type of goodie made with the fruits.

When Arleta was finished, Verdreth took the bag, leaned over the counter to give Arleta a quick peck on the cheek, then looked down at Doli. "We'll keep them busy all afternoon. Don't you worry." Then he left.

"If you want, I can go see Maven," Theo said as the door swung shut. "I stayed at the Tricky Goat for over a month last year before Arleta and I were"—he gazed up at her from the floor, love dancing at the corners of his mouth—"official."

The human rolled her eyes slightly, but her lips curved into a shy smile. "It took me a while to come around."

Before Arleta had competed in the Baking Battle and met Theo, Doli, Jez, and Taenya, she hadn't quite found herself. She and Theo were fated to be together, but before she could accept that fact, she had to love herself first.

"Okay, okay." Doli waved her hand in the air and stood. Normally she loved a good romance story, even one told on too many occasions. But this was not the time. "Don't you two get all lovey-dovey right now when there are things to be done!"

Taenya chuckled from behind the counter as she wiped it down with a cloth. "You sound like Jez."

The dwarf whipped her attention to the elf. "I do not!" Her tone was outraged.

"Yeah. You do," Theo and Arleta said in unison.

Jez *was* grumpy most of the time, while Doli, at least in theory, was the opposite. While Jez was one of her best friends and everyone knew and accepted the fennex's temperament, Doli did not want to be seen as an irritable person.

Quickly she checked Evvy, who was still sound asleep in the sling, straightened her skirt and hair, and snatched her father's blanket from the floor. "We simply have jobs to do and no time to waste." She put on her gentlest tone of voice. "Theo can head over to the Tricky Goat and get my parents' lodging taken care of. I'm going to go home and find out what I need to feed Evvy."

"Do you want me to tag along?" Arleta asked while reaching underneath her bun as if to untie her apron.

"No," Doli said. "Not right now. I think I can do this on my own, and it will give me a few minutes to myself." She tipped her head. "That is, if I can sneak past my parents and up the stairs."

With Theo heading to Maven's, Doli made her way back to the bookstore but entered through the back door by the way of the alley. Once inside, she passed the empty office and crept down the hall on tiptoe.

From her vantage point she could see both of her parents deep in conversation with a customer, a human man about thirty years old and ginger-haired. Gingrilin held his hand, and despite the tension in his arms, there seemed to be no escape.

"You wouldn't believe the journey we had." Doli's mother held up a book with a unicorn on the cover. "We were surrounded, I tell you…surrounded!"

Doli's father came around a freestanding bookshelf with a pile of books nearly as tall as he was.

Verdreth staffed the checkout desk, and Ervash sat slumped in one of the chairs with his elbow resting on the arm, his hand supporting his chin. For such a midmorning hour, he already looked completely exhausted with his messy bun poking out in all directions.

Doli had been there many times when dealing with her parents. But at that moment, she only needed to reach her room without them seeing her. Not rescue her friends.

First, Doli dashed behind a display while her father still unloaded the stack of books in front of the customer. The man raised his brows in what appeared to be utter bewilderment.

"I really only came in here for—" the man managed before he was cut off.

Gingrilin took a book from her husband and shoved it into the man's hands. "Did I tell you about—"

Doli didn't want to hear any more of her mother's words,

so she darted behind the nearest bookshelf, then a chair, and somehow made it to the bottom of the staircase. She made it about halfway up before the dragon squealed.

"Oh, those are *very* interesting," Verdreth boomed.

Doli didn't look but assumed he'd seen her and covered. She placed her hand over the now squirming dragon and raced up the rest of the staircase as quickly as possible. At the top she glanced down at her parents, who were still completely occupied. Verdreth waved as though to shoo Doli to her room.

She jogged to the door while struggling to keep the dragon in place and her father's blanket tucked under her arm. She turned the handle and rushed inside just as the rapscallion wiggled out of the sling and escaped.

"Evvy!" Doli called, exasperated. She dropped the blanket on the floor.

The dragon paid her no mind and flew over to the fireplace, perched on the mantel, and sat there hissing and fluttering her wings.

"What's going on?" Jez came out of her room while she finished pulling on a fresh shirt. "Oh." Her eyes trained on the hissing baby dragon.

"*That's* what's going on." Doli placed her hands on her hips and leaned her back against the door. "I really need to figure out what to feed her."

Jez pursed her lips for a second, walked to the kitchen, and retrieved a large, already prepared fish fillet from a plate on the counter. "How about this?"

Evvy stopped hissing and stretched her neck out while

her tail flicked from side to side in a happy dance. She launched from her spot on the mantel, flew across the room, and grabbed the white fillet in her toothless jaws. Within seconds, she'd sat on the counter, ripped the piece of fish into long strips, and gulped the first chunk down without even chewing or swallowing.

"I'm guessing she likes meat and fish." Jez leaned her hip against the kitchen counter while her fluffy fox tail flicked back and forth.

Doli pinched at the bridge of her nose. "She also likes pastries." She eyed the loaf-shaped package that must have contained the blood orange tart that Taenya had left for Jez.

"Smart girl," Jez chuckled and offered Evvy a second fillet.

"You sure you're okay with her eating all your fish?" Doli grabbed a dragon book from the floor and sat at the dining table in an exhausted plop.

"Meh." The fennex swiped at the air with her clawed hand. "I didn't really go fishing for the fish. That was just a bonus."

"How *are* you feeling lately?" Doli asked, looking up from the book cover. "I'm sorry I haven't asked."

"Tired and like I needed a break from you all," Jez said with a half smirk.

It was a joke but based in reality. Doli knew that Jez had been kind of a loner before meeting her, Arleta, and Taenya. The fennex had told her more than once that she'd decided that her life was better with her friends in it, but they could also be exhausting.

Doli smiled back. "Well. I'm glad you got to go…and I do like having you around."

"I like being around. Sometimes." She tossed Evvy another small piece of fish, and the dragon caught it with her back claws. "Now that's enough for you."

Evvy tipped her head and batted her eyes while Jez wrapped the remaining fillets in paper and tucked them into the cold box.

Doli flipped open the book and turned to the chapter on baby dragon diet. Jez was right—meat, fish, some greens and vegetables. Nothing about fruit pastries.

"I think I need to head down to the market and get a few things for her," Doli said, closing the book.

The dragon had curled up in a tight little ball, tail wrapped around her body, and fallen asleep right on the kitchen counter. The fennex stared at Evvy, her gaze as soft as Doli had ever seen it.

"Why don't you do that?" Jez whispered. "I can watch Evvy."

"Oh." Doli stood and removed her fabric sling. "Are you quite sure?"

"Pshaw." The fennex didn't take her eyes off the baby. "How much trouble could she be?"

9

Doli made it down the stairs and out the back of the shop without her parents spotting her, mostly thanks to Verdreth, who had made tea and sat blocking their view of the staircase as he dutifully listened to her mother's story.

The redheaded customer had apparently escaped, but Doli wondered how much in books it cost him to do so.

Gingrilin stood swooning and sighing as she acted out the scene while Uldrick played the role of the unicorn stampede, with a piece of parchment rolled into a cone and attached to his forehead. By the look and sound of it, one would have thought they'd nearly lost their lives in the harrowing voyage to Adenashire.

A bona fide hero's journey.

Doli rolled her eyes and adjusted the strap of her cloth shopping bag on her shoulder as she slipped into the alley. Overhead the sky was clear. There was a slight breeze, and finchlettes sang a sweet tune in a nearby oak tree. It would have been a perfect day for picnicking.

She filled her lungs with the crisp air and followed her nose straight to the market. The aroma of smoked meats drew her in since that was exactly what she planned to buy for the dragon. Doli had noticed how many pieces of Jez's fish Evvy had eaten, plus the pastry from the bakery. Despite her body size, which was barely bigger than a three-week-old kitten, the little dragon had a voracious appetite and could apparently stuff a massive amount of food in what should have been a small stomach.

So smoked, dried meats should be a good choice. They could keep much longer and would take up less space in her and Jez's kitchen.

Doli did her best to calculate how much might be needed, but she had no idea how fast Evvy might grow…and how large. The thought made the dwarf's stomach plummet as she imagined a dragon bigger than the orcs stomping and attempting to fly around the apartment. There was no way Adenashire would accommodate a dragon long term. She quickly brushed the thought away.

"One problem at a time, Doli. You can do this," she muttered as she approached the market.

Mr. Figlet, the quokkan market owner, stood near the entrance and tipped his hat at her. He wore a smart outfit of a fitted sage green shirt and pressed wool trousers, complete with shiny new black leather boots.

"Welcome," the marsupial said, stuffing his hands into his deep pockets.

Quokkan were entirely adorable with their big button eyes and furry round faces. But Doli knew better about Mr. Figlet. Before Arleta had come in second place at the Langheim Baking Battle and had rented stalls at the market to sell her baked goods, he'd never treated her with much respect. Full humans didn't have a drop of magic in their veins, and some people, like Mr. Figlet, tended to hold it against them.

Since then, their relationship had improved…slightly.

Doli gave him a quick nod and headed straight to the smoked meats seller. But first she passed multiple tempting booths, including one selling colorful, sparkling hard candies in all the colors of the rainbow.

A tall centaur worked busily at his smoker, and puffs of fragrant smoke billowed into the air as he tended to the various cuts inside the drum. Doli's stomach grumbled, making her realize that in all the chaos she hadn't yet eaten that morning. She'd only had those two cups of tea at the bakery.

Displayed on the table in neat piles were multiple types of smoked and dried meats and fish in varying shades of brown from light to dark. Each was labeled with the variety as well as the seasoning. Her stomach grumbled again at the sight.

"Would you like a sample?" asked the centaur with light sepia skin and fur on his back half, his tail swishing behind his body. The half man, half horse was surprisingly adept at working in such a small space. But from what Doli knew, he was a near-permanent fixture at the outdoor market, so he'd had years of practice.

"Um, yes." Doli wanted to ask which he thought a dragon might like best but then thought better of it. The longer they could keep Evvy's existence secret, the better. Doli smiled at him. "Which is your favorite?"

The centaur's brown eyes lit up, and he pointed immediately to the sweet and smoky beef. "It's a simple flavor, nothing fancy and not too sweet. It's been my favorite since I was a colt."

"Then I'll try that one." Doli reached out as he plucked a small piece from the back of the display and dropped it into her palm. She popped it in her mouth and was instantly surprised at how tender the meat was. The sweet, savory flavors flooded her taste buds, and although part of the appeal could have been her hunger, she was pretty sure that the meat would have been delicious any time. The dwarf finished chewing before she said, "I'll definitely take two bunches of that, along with the same amount of the spicy lamb, annnd…" She surveyed the options. "And trout sticks."

"The lady knows what she wants!" The centaur chuckled and placed all of Doli's selections in a bag.

He handed her another sample, this time of the spicy lamb. The flavor added a little heat, but not so much that she'd need water. The second sample was as tender as the first, and Doli nearly groaned with pleasure. "How is this so good?" she asked.

The centaur grinned. "A little bit of magic and a lot of family tradition."

"Well, hats off to that." For a second, Doli was more like herself again. She loved talking to people and helping them feel good about themselves. It really was the person she wanted to be—*and* be able to have a bad day here and there.

The seller finished her order, folded down the top of the bag, and handed it to Doli. "That will stay fresh for months if need be."

The bag was heavy in her hand. Doli had no idea how long it would last Evvy, but hopefully at least until the next market day. Definitely not months if she kept eating like she had that morning. She handed over a good amount of silver and knew she'd have to pick up some extra shifts at the bookstore if she was to keep Evvy fed.

"Thank you so much," she said. She turned to head home and immediately collided with someone's hip.

The bag of smoked meats flew up into the air, and the surprise once again took Doli's feet right out from underneath her. But before she could land unceremoniously on her rump, something snaked under her arms and pulled her back upright. She looked down at a blue tail with a pointed end peeking out from under her arm.

"I'm incredibly sorry," Doli managed as she looked up at Sarson, who was grinning.

"We meet again," he said, keeping his tail in place as if to confirm her balance before taking it back.

Doli bit her lip, and for seemingly the hundredth time, heat flamed her cheeks at the sight of the gargoyle. Not to mention that it was the second time he'd saved her from making a complete embarrassment of herself.

That day he was dressed in a cloak with a hood pulled over his head. A bag slung over his shoulder had bunches of carrots and radishes sticking out of the top.

"Um, yes" was all Doli could manage as she dug her boots into the dirt to ensure better footing.

He stared at her for a second, then reached into his cloak pocket. "I was hoping I might see you, since I brought you something." Sarson pulled out a giant book that looked at least seven hundred pages thick and held it out to Doli.

His large, clawed hand partially blocked the lettering on the cover, but Doli could easily make out the title, *Dragon Types and Their Prophecy*.

"You seemed so interested in dragons yesterday that I made sure to find this book," Sarson said. "It's one of my favorites, but you were in such a hurry I didn't have time to locate it before you left."

Doli took the thick book from him, and the weight sagged in her grasp, making her nearly fall forward that time.

"Oh, stars," Sarson said and immediately placed his hand under the book. "It is a little large."

A nervous laugh escaped Doli's lips. "It is for me, at least."

They stood there for a moment in awkward silence while a group of chattering women passed. One of them did a double take at Sarson and then turned back to her group in a hurry, as if she had some sort of commentary to share.

Sarson wrinkled his nose. "I'll be done here at the market soon, and then I'd be glad to take this back to the bookstore for you?" It was a question as he pulled the book gently from Doli's grasp.

There were all sorts of thoughts Doli could barely untangle in her brain. "I still need a few things," she managed to say. "But I can grab them on the way out. I'll come with you." She had no idea how she'd go unnoticed at the bookstore with a gargoyle in tow, but she didn't need to deal with that immediately.

Soon…but not immediately.

They walked past the candy seller, and Doli made a mental note to stop there the next time she wasn't having a dragon emergency. At the vegetable stand she loaded up with cauliflower, carrots, and brussels sprouts since she thought the dragon might have fun plucking the sprouts from the stalk one by one.

"What do you plan to make with the sprouts?" Sarson asked just as Doli finished handing the seller his copper.

"Oh." Her mind completely blanked, and she knew she should have come up with a story before she'd left, but she also hadn't planned on meeting Sarson here. "My roommate, Jez, loves them roasted." The words tumbled from her mouth…and were completely untrue.

Jez hated brussels sprouts and claimed they should be banned from the Northern Lands due to their horrible, bitter taste.

The large stalk hung out the top of Doli's shopping bag and she tried to shove it down further, but it was no use.

"Shall we go?" Doli kept her tone perky as she glanced up at Sarson. In the few moments they'd been at the vegetable stand, she'd noticed several more eyes on them from their fellow shoppers...and there was no way she was the one attracting the attention.

So far, Sarson had only been a perfectly nice person.

"I think that's wise." Sarson pulled his hood further over his head, but there was no hiding his gigantic frame and the wings sticking out the back of the cloak, even if they were tight against his back. It was so rare to see a gargoyle outside their realm that people seemed compelled to stare.

She couldn't help but recall Jez's words about not trusting him. Was that why so many people were staring?

Luckily the bookshop wasn't far. But on the way, Doli decided it would be best for her to go inside by herself so that Sarson didn't have to meet her parents. And then she wouldn't have to worry about Jez spotting him and making comments.

"Thank you so much," she said as they reached the entrance, and she held out her hand.

"Oh." A look of disappointment turned down Sarson's expression. "It's still very heavy."

"I'll manage, and I do appreciate you loaning me the book," she said, trying to peek surreptitiously through the window to see if her parents were still there. "I'll get it back to you as soon as I can."

Sarson handed over the book, and this time the dwarf took it with both hands and supported the weight with her legs. But she still let out a grunt.

"Are you sure you've got it?" Sarson asked, concern wrinkling between his brows. "I can bring it inside for you."

The word *no* had just formed on Doli's lips when a wild-eyed Ervash flung open the front door, chewing something. "What took you so long?" He swallowed whatever had been in his mouth and stared right at Doli. "We need you inside right now!" His gaze flicked to Sarson. "Good day, sir. We seem to have…an emergency."

Doli's stomach sank into the cobblestone street. *What did my parents do now?*

The orc frantically waved her inside while Sarson reached to lift the book from Doli's struggling grasp. The dwarf gulped and followed Ervash.

Sarson came in behind, and the door had barely shut before—

Crash.

The noise had come from upstairs. And it didn't sound good.

"No, no, no! What in the stars are you doing?" Jez's muffled voice yelled from the second floor. "Stop…stop…stooooop!"

Doli was certain this had nothing to do with her parents.

10

Ervash, whose dark hair had completely fallen out of his top bun and was in disarray all over his shoulders, locked the door and ushered them farther into the bookstore. His breaths came quickly, and Doli noticed he had a small net attached to a handle in his hand.

Bang, crash. The sounds came from upstairs.

"That's for Evvy, isn't it?" Doli's attention wavered between the orc, Sarson, and the staircase. Her stomach was flopping like a fish over what she was about to walk into.

The orc eyed Sarson, looking uncertain about answering in front of a stranger. "Uhhh…"

"Who's Ev—" Sarson got halfway out.

Crash. The horrible noise was followed by heavy footsteps. *Boom, boom, boom.* From the weight, probably Verdreth's.

Doli didn't wait another second. Without answering Sarson, she hiked up her skirt and bounded up the stairs with her groceries still in tow. The dwarf didn't look back, but two pairs of leaden boots clunked behind her.

After reaching the top of the stairs, she beelined to the door, flung it open and dropped her grocery sack on the floor. The apartment was in shambles. The blood orange tart was broken in half, and pieces of it were scattered all over the floor. The two chairs before the fireplace were knocked to their sides. Books were splayed open and scattered from one end of the room to the other.

The fennex and the orc were running wildly about the room in a vain attempt to capture the tiny dragon, who evaded them joyfully.

Ervash stepped in behind Doli. "Here!" He threw the net to Verdreth.

The orc caught the handle easily, then swiped at Evvy and missed as the baby dragon zipped to the other side of the room. Doli was sure she saw Evvy stick out her tongue at Ervash.

"Damn it," Verdreth swore under his breath. He'd nearly lost his spectacles in the effort but just managed to catch them before they flew off his face.

Stunned by the disorder, the dwarf halted as if her feet were frozen in place. "Evvy," Doli managed a plea.

The little dragon turned in midair at the sound of her name. She let out a high-pitched squeal, and her eyes lit up at the sight of the dwarf. But that didn't stop the chase. As if it were some kind of game.

"Is *that* Evvy?" Sarson finally made his way into the room and shut the door behind him. Quickly he lowered his hood and reached into his pocket.

The little dragon did another loop around the room, then finally dove from the ceiling and landed on Doli's right shoulder. She rubbed her scaly face across Doli's cheek while purring as if nothing untoward had happened.

"Where in the stars have you been?" Jez shouted, baring her sharp fangs while her fox tail flicked in annoyance—as if she hadn't been the one to volunteer her dragon-sitting services.

Evvy whipped her head around to the fennex, hissed once, then immediately returned to snuggling the dwarf.

Doli placed her hand gently on Evvy's raised spine between her tucked wings to keep her in place. "Um. Was I gone that long?"

"Yes!" Both Jez and Verdreth shouted in unison.

Doli knew she hadn't. It had been just long enough to buy what she needed for Evvy at the market. But she gazed around at the mess, plus the sweat pouring down her friends' faces, and guilt pulled at her stomach anyway.

"I have no idea what I'm supposed to do." Doli's feet remained steady, but tears burst from her eyes. "I suppose my parents are still downstairs too. With some cornered customers they won't allow to escape before they buy five books on unicorns." The words flooded out like a gush.

Ervash blew out a quick breath. "No, Theo fetched them right before chaos took hold." He pinched his lips, then muttered, "And that guy only bought one unicorn book. I told him he could return it tomorrow."

"Thank the stars," Doli said. She looked around again at the mess, imagining how much harder this might be with her parents looking on.

Judging her choices.

Jez stood, leaning against the wall between her room and the kitchen with her arms crossed, her breathing agitated.

"I'm sorry, Jez," Doli said. Her chest buzzed with nervousness as she petted Evvy's back and tail. "I should have sent you to the market."

The fennex gave a huff, but something in her expression revealed a twinge of her own guilt. "It wasn't your fault."

"This dragon is going to be more difficult than we thought," Ervash said as he ran his hand through his tangled hair.

Which of us thought it was going to be easy? Doli kept that to herself since she was pretty sure no one wanted to hear it. They needed solutions.

Evvy purred and continued rubbing her face on Doli's.

Sarson opened the book he'd had in his pocket and pointed at the top of a page. "She's a Fervour dragon."

Evvy perked up, stretched out her neck, and let out a little trill.

"A what?" Jez furrowed her brows at the gargoyle.

"A Fervour," he said again and turned the book around to show a drawing of a small pink dragon that looked almost exactly like Evvy. "She's from the Dawn order. But even among their people, Fervours are extremely rare. So rare that a Fervour egg might only successfully hatch once in five hundred years." After a moment he flipped the book back around and gazed down at the page. "Fervours have the gift of fire, as well as the ability to influence the emotional state of others. As younglings they have a particular talent to influence those around them to care for them, despite the fact that they are notoriously high energy. They also have the magical ability to control objects."

Doli decided it was no wonder that everyone who had met Evvy had instantly felt a connection with her, including herself.

The dwarf was about to suggest cleaning up when warmth radiated from the little dragon onto her shoulder, then a tingling traveled down her arm and out to her entire body. A pink aura enveloped Doli and Evvy as the others watched.

"What's going on?" Verdreth asked, probably directed at Sarson since he was the one with the information, but Doli couldn't tell with the pink glow blocking her view. Evvy caught Doli's gaze and their minds immediately connected, though not in words.

But seconds later, Doli's emotions had settled completely, and the glow dissipated.

The little dragon looked around the room, then closed her golden eyes, and both chairs suddenly flipped upright. The orange tart mess swept itself into a pile. The books on the floor levitated, then returned to neat stacks on the dining room table. One by one, everything that had been broken or out of place returned to how it had been before the chaos.

Sorry. This time, the simple word came from the dragon into Doli's mind as Evvy batted her eyes at the dwarf.

There was no way for Doli to stay mad at her.

"She's sorry," Doli relayed to the group, not taking her eyes off Evvy.

Jez let out a sigh of relief.

"Intriguing," Sarson said, then held up the book again. "Oh yes. And they only hatch when they have been paired with the right dragon—or person, in this case—to begin their lives with. Their eggs can lay dormant for up to a thousand years. So Fervours can be hidden for centuries, with their souls waiting on the other side, until they find the person who is meant to initiate the hatching process. But once hatched, they will remain connected to their initial caregivers for the rest of their lives, even in their adult state."

Everyone in the room looked at Doli.

"So Evvy truly chose me?" The dwarf was stunned, not quite sure what to think about this new revelation. "It wasn't a mistake?"

Evvy curled back her little reptile lips and trilled again. The sound vibrated the scales on her throat and the surrounding air.

Doli blew out a huge breath, feeling a bit better about the situation even though her mother's words that Doli wasn't responsible still wormed their way through her brain. She knew she *was* responsible, but it was hard to completely throw off how her family saw her. She looked up at Sarson. "I'd really love to borrow that book so I can read more about Evvy."

He revealed his white fangs, and his eyes crinkled. "Yes, of course. That's why I brought it to you."

After everything that had just happened, Doli had nearly

forgotten about her chance meeting with Sarson at the market. She giggled sweetly.

The gargoyle closed the book and placed it on the kitchen counter. Then he looked around at the others, his expression slightly shy as if he'd forgotten they were even there. "It was nice to meet you all again."

Jez glared silently, as if dark thoughts were churning in her mind.

"Yes," Verdreth said in a much jollier and welcoming tone than he'd voiced minutes before. "And remember you're welcome in my bookstore anytime. I'll be getting a large history shipment next week. Lots of gems."

"I'll be sure to drop by," Sarson said and bowed his head slightly.

After that the four of them stared at each other for a moment while Evvy snoozed on Doli's shoulder, apparently exhausted from all the trouble she'd caused.

But no one seemed to be angry at her anymore.

"I'll be off then," Sarson said. "I can let myself out downstairs." He gave Doli a wink. "And don't forget, I'm around if you want to go over anything. I do know quite a bit about dragons even without the books." He started to go, then turned back to Doli. "I'd recommend keeping Evvy out of sight if you can. Dragons… They can attract attention. Sometimes the wrong attention."

Doli nodded.

"We're headed down too." Ervash gazed around at the clean room. "Need to open the store back up. And I'm famished."

"Oh yes." Verdreth pushed his spectacles up on his nose and retrieved the net from the floor. "We still have some pastries from Arleta left, I believe."

Ervash's expression turned to guilt. "About those…"

"I knew you smelled like blueberries when you came back with the net!" His partner gave an annoyed growl and shook his head.

"Thank you," Doli said to Sarson, ignoring the orcs. "I appreciate the offer." Part of her wanted to take him up on it right that moment. Going back to his little cottage with the enormous library and having a cup of tea together sounded lovely. But she knew it wasn't the right time.

That, and Jez cleared her throat and broke the moment.

"Okay. Well, you know where to find us," Ervash said, waving. The three of them left Jez and Doli alone with Evvy.

The room suddenly got quiet.

"You don't think it's strange…" Jez finally spoke but suddenly broke off and slunk to her room.

"What?" Doli eased Evvy off her shoulder and cradled the little dragon in her arms. The baby looked utterly peaceful with her eyes closed and snoring lightly. Evvy stirred and rolled over onto her back, revealing her lighter pink belly.

The fennex came out with a fluffy pillow in her hands. "I have an extra one, so you can make a little bed out of this for Evvy." She placed it on the chair next to the fireplace and patted a little depression in the middle.

Doli didn't really want to put the dragon down, but she did have things to do, including putting the groceries away and digging into the book so she could learn more about

Evvy. Then she needed to deal with her parents. "What's strange?" The question slipped out of her mouth as she walked over to place Evvy on the down pillow.

The little dragon curled up like a kitten and wrapped her tail around the front of her pink body.

Jez and Doli stood in front of the chair and stared at Evvy for what seemed like a very long time. Just the act of staring made Doli's brain feel fizzy and drunk.

Finally Jez spoke as if she'd remembered what she was going to say. "Don't you think it's strange that Sarson and Evvy showed up around the same time?"

Doli snapped out of her cute baby dragon spell and looked up at Jez, whose right ear was flicking.

"What are you talking about?" Doli demanded.

"Plus, all this talk about attracting the wrong attention," Jez half growled.

Doli's jaw tightened. "He's probably right."

The fennex shrugged. "Or maybe he wants Evvy's magic all to himself. I told you nothing good happens with all that wingspan to spare."

"Ugh," Doli groaned at her friend as she watched Evvy yawning on her pillow. "You're impossible."

11

"See! I told you there was something off with Sarson." Jez sat at the dining room table and jabbed her clawed finger down on the book page she'd been reading. "'Dark magic can be used to imitate and force the bond between a newly hatched Fervour dragon and its guardian.'" She held up the book. "See, right here on the page!"

Doli had barely fallen asleep in the chair before the crackling fireplace, and at Jez's demand for attention her eyes snapped back open. She held Evvy in her arms while stroking the little dragon's spine all the way to the tip of her tail. The baby purred in contentment.

"What are you saying, Jez?" Doli demanded. "That what Evvy and I have isn't real? *And* it was a mistake?"

The fennex looked up from the book, shook her head, and backtracked. "That's not what I'm saying at all."

"Please elaborate then." After a full day of caring for the dragon, she was too tired to really be mad at Jez, even though the fennex likely deserved it. Plus, she needed to keep her head because she had to leave soon to have dinner with her parents. Theo had somehow taken care of everything with Maven and got Doli's parents checked in early. Doli had an inkling that Theo may have cleaned the room himself, and she owed him a giant thanks. Despite all that, a twinge of annoyance that Jez was still determined to argue that Sarson was a problem pricked at her chest. There were so many more important things to learn about *dragons*.

Doli took in a calming breath, picked Evvy up with both hands, and held the dragon up to her face. The two of them stared at each other, and the dragon, with her little front legs draped over Doli's thumbs, gave the dwarf a slow blink.

"What if Sarson used some kind of magic to ensorcel you?" Jez squinted and continued reading intently.

Oh, stars.

"Ensorcel?" Doli rolled her eyes, puffed out her cheeks, and then made pouty lips at the little dragon. But she could still see Jez out of the corner of her eye. "He doesn't exactly seem like the ensorcelling type." Although Doli wasn't actually sure what a person who ensorcelled acted like.

"Gargoyles can have strong magical abilities," Jez insisted. "Has he mentioned this? Not that he'd reveal it, most likely." She muttered the last part under her breath and scowled.

Doli didn't answer. And there was nothing to tell. Sarson

had not mentioned any unusual magical abilities, not even the fact that, like all of his race, his skin could harden to a stonelike texture for protection. Instead, she kept occupying Evvy…as well as distracting herself.

Evvy gave a little whine of amusement at Doli's silly expression and landed her front foot, claws retracted of course, on Doli's chin.

"*Dark* magic." The words came out in a low, ominous tone, and Jez's eyes grew as large as saucers as she raised the heavy splayed-open book off the table.

Doli repositioned Evvy in her arms and fully turned toward Jez. "Are you trying to tell me you think Sarson is an evil gargoyle wizard who somehow orchestrated this entire thing with my uncle's inheritance? That somehow he *arranged* for Evvy to bond with me? And he did so by offering me coffee and letting me borrow books? This is the most likely scenario you can come up with?"

Jez finally looked up and raised her brow. "When did he move here again?"

Doli groaned. "Not too long ago. Possibly a couple of weeks?"

"Wasn't that around the time you received the letter from your mother that the package was coming?" She looked down at the book and then quickly back at Doli. "And then he shows up at the bookstore right before Evvy hatches." The fennex held up her finger as if she'd just had a revelation. "And you 'ran into' him at the market and he ended up back here."

Doli scoffed as she rocked the dragon. "You're being ridiculous."

"Am I?" Jez narrowed her gaze to imply that Doli was the ridiculous one.

Doli wrinkled her broad nose. "Yes. Yes, you are. Stop spinning conspiracy stories about someone who's a perfectly nice person!"

A log on the fire tumbled off the burning stack, and flames licked up the back of the fireplace.

The fennex stared at it for a moment, then said, "And wait… He offered you coffee? When? What if it was a potion?"

Doli stood without answering Jez's absurd question, deposited Evvy on her pillow, and walked over to Jez. "Maybe it's time you tell me what your problem with gargoyles is."

Jez sat back in her seat and leaned as far away from Doli as she could. Her nose twitched. "I don't have a problem with gargoyles in *general*."

The dwarf planted one hand on her hip. "Yes, you do. From the moment he walked into the bookstore, you had nothing but negative things to say about him. Sarson hasn't done anything to you, me…any of us. So I must assume you don't like gargoyles."

Jez waved her hand between herself and Doli as if she were trying to clear the air. "You said it yourself—I'm always negative about anyone new. Suspicious."

Doli narrowed her eyes and leaned in closer to her friend. She whispered, "Yes, but this is different."

The fennex huffed. "Why? Because you like him?"

Doli scoffed and threw her hands in the air. Frustration

at her friend pulled her chest tight, but she stopped herself before she could yell at her. There *could* be a perfectly rational reason why Jez was behaving irrationally. Instead, she replied in a calm tone, "Please don't turn this back on me. What is your problem with gargoyles?"

"I don't have a prob—" Jez started to say but Doli held up her hand to cut her off.

"What is your problem with *Sarson,* then?"

The fennex slowly closed her lips and spread them in a thin line. Doli waited patiently, hands firmly on her hips.

"*Nobody* likes gargoyles" was the weak answer Jez finally came up with.

And then the deflection clicked for Doli. "What history have the gargoyle librarians recorded about the fennex that has somehow offended you?"

Heavy footsteps sounded in the stairway.

"That must be Taenya," Jez said as if she were somehow excused from answering Doli's interrogation.

Doli backed up. Jez took the opportunity to close the book, stand, and slip away from the dwarf.

"We're not done here, though," Doli said, turning her attention back on a sleeping Evvy. "I'm going to bring this up later."

The little dragon was kicking her feet and vibrating her wings as if she dreamed about flying. Doli walked over and stroked her head to calm the agitation brewing inside her own stomach.

A knock came from the door.

"Door's open," Jez said as she flicked Doli a look.

The handle turned and Taenya poked her head inside. "All safe?" she asked, the amusement in her voice tempered with hesitation. The elf came through with a bag in her arms, and Evvy shot awake and sniffed the air.

Taenya was dressed in what Doli noticed was a new blouse, or at least one she hadn't worn before. It was different from the elf's normally simple style with a small frill at the end of each sleeve. The cotton shirt was a pale green, accentuating her eyes and complementing her auburn hair, which was partially pulled back in two combs on the sides of her head. The look was closer to the dwarf's style, and she liked it very much but decided to keep that to herself for the moment.

"It's safe," Doli said. "Evvy and I had a little talk about destroying things. But your tart got ruined."

Taenya's face fell.

"What tart?" Jez perked up for a second.

"Taenya brought over a blood orange tart for you to try earlier...but it was one of the things Evvy destroyed," Doli muttered.

"Oh," Jez said and quickly glanced at Taenya. "That's too bad."

"Maybe next time," Taenya said, shrugging.

The dragon took flight toward her and fluttered around the top of the bag, dipping her face inside.

"Yes," Taenya said and closed the door. "I brought us some food."

Evvy let out a trill and clasped her hands together. She quickly turned and zipped to the kitchen, where she landed on the counter, fluttering her wings excitedly.

The elf hefted the bag and walked over to where Evvy waited. Jez was back at the table with her nose in the book.

"I stopped at the Tricky Goat and had them make me a few entrées." She brought out several wooden boxes with lids that pulled back to reveal the meals inside.

Maven had been testing an eat-at-home menu for several months. For an extra fee you could take a box home and then return it empty to get your deposit back. Jez had used the service several times and had her favorites.

While Taenya unpacked, Doli folded the blanket she needed to return to her father.

"I got a lamb stew." Taenya held up the box while Evvy licked her lips. The elf looked down at her. "That's for me."

Evvy gave a sad whine and blinked wide eyes at the elf.

"Don't worry," Taenya said, reaching into the bag. "I didn't forget you. Pork tenderloin with a honey glaze and a side of buttered mashed potatoes and greens."

The little dragon's lips curled back into a gummy grin, and she held out her hands toward the box.

Taenya opened the lid and savory steam wafted out. She placed it before the dragon, who immediately half crawled inside and dug in.

"I got you the shepherd's pie, Jez." Taenya retrieved the last box, walked over to the table and placed it in front of the fennex, along with a fork from the counter. "Extra peas on the side."

"Thanks." Jez didn't even look up.

But Doli tipped her head in interest. That meal was Jez's favorite, extra peas and all.

"Well. Wish me luck," Doli said. "And you too."

The dwarf walked to Evvy and stoked her back. The dragon was purring as she ate, ripping strips of the pork and gumming it with her jaws. She had a clump of buttery mashed potatoes on the side of her face, but Doli didn't mention it.

"We're going to be okay." Taenya sat across from Jez with her meal and dug into the thick stew. "I have some games for Evvy, and Jez mentioned earlier that you have more for Evvy to eat."

Doli let out a long breath. "I made a trip to the market today. Jez knows where everything is. Right, Jez?" She raised her voice at the end of the question.

The fennex finally put down the book and closed it. "Yes. Yes."

"Now please be good," Doli said to the munching dragon. "I won't be long, *and* we made an agreement."

The dragon bobbed her head and returned to munching her dinner.

"Are you sure you're going to be okay?" Doli turned back to the elf and fennex as they quietly ate their dinner.

"Just go," Jez said, her mouth full of peas.

Doli's mouth pinched, remembering that Jez thought her first time dragon-sitting would be easy too. Apparently the fennex's memory was short. But she knew she had to go meet her parents and couldn't take Evvy to such a public place. It was too risky.

"We're all going to handle it together," Taenya said. "I think we're a little more prepared this time around. The orcs filled me in on what happened this morning, and after my shift I read through some of the books on dragons down in the shop. It was helpful information. Plus, Theo and Arleta plan to drop by in about half an hour to make sure everything's going okay."

Doli let out a sigh of relief that Taenya was taking this so seriously. "I really appreciate your help." She held her father's blanket to her chest and hugged it, but deciding not to bring it after all, she placed it by the door.

Taenya's eyes softened as she lifted her spoon of lamb stew. "That's what friends are for."

12

As Doli stepped out onto the streets of Adenashire, pink spread out across the dusky sky like poured frosting over a blueberry cake. Soon it would be dark, and her parents would be waiting for her at the Tricky Goat for dinner.

The street was still quite busy, and a fairy flitted over her head, lighting the lanterns lining the road.

"Hello, River," Doli said to the pale-skinned fairy.

The two of them had shared multiple conversations since Doli moved to Adenashire.

River Goldendew stopped in midair with their wings fluttering like a hummingbird to keep them suspended. "Oh," they said in a high-pitched voice. "Hello, Doli. How are you this fine evening?" River wore a tight-fitting orange shirt and blue pants cropped just above their tiny brown leather boots. The blue was a shade darker than River's hair.

The dwarf had often imagined sewing a tiny wardrobe of clothing for the handful of fairies that lived in the village. But she'd never inquired whether they wanted such a thing.

Doli smiled, but it strained her lips and she feared River might pick up on her stress. "I'm well," she said. "Headed over to the Tricky Goat."

The fairy nodded, seeming distracted, and flew up to the nearest lantern. They held out their tiny pinkish hands, which emitted sparkling gold magic into the air. The sparkles floated to the lantern and fire burst inside the glass, not only lighting the street but also making it bright enough for Doli to see that the fairy had a different color painted on each of their fingernails, tiny as they were.

"The Goat is a lovely place," River said with an enthusiastic chirp and turned back to Doli.

Normally Doli would agree. The pub's atmosphere tended to be busy and jolly. But that night she would rather have stayed home.

"Yes," she said, instead of her true thoughts. "And I love your nails. Is that paint?"

The fairy turned their hands toward their face. "No, it's magic. Would you like something similar? You seem like the type of person who'd enjoy it."

Pure momentary happiness at the thought bubbled in Doli's chest. She hadn't treated herself to such a luxury as painted nails in quite a while. She was surprised that she hadn't considered the possibility of magical nail coloring since she was always on the lookout for new fashion. "I would!"

"Well," the fairy said, "you're in luck. My sister has recently started a new business manicuring nails." They looked at their hands again. "It's difficult to see in this light, but she's quite the artist. She can do most anything you might like."

"And where could I find her?" Doli asked.

"She's trying out a new booth at the outdoor market." The fairy nodded, indicating they must be off. "Tell her I sent you."

Doli looked down at her own nails, which had gotten a bit ragged in the past weeks. It wasn't like her. "I will!"

"Have a good evening at the Goat." With that River was off to the next lantern, conjuring magic between their fingertips and lighting the fire.

The dwarf waved and dropped her hands, still excited at the prospect of having her nails done. But she deflated, remembering that for now she was going to meet her parents. She took a right where all the lanterns had already been lit and took a deep breath of the night air. Up above, the sky was quickly turning dark blue with stars sparkling like diamonds in the sky.

It wasn't long before the streets led her to the inn. Out front, despite a slight chill in the air, the tables were lit with small brass lanterns and customers filled the seats. Some only held drinks, but most were eating enormous meals from wooden plates. There were heaping piles of roasted vegetables such as beets, turnips, and potatoes. One table had a large roast they seemed to share.

Doli's stomach rumbled at the sight, although she had no idea if she'd be able to choke down a single bite once she joined her parents.

The front door was ahead of her and past the patio. She steeled herself and put one small foot before the other. But a black, furry clawed paw caught her before she went more than a few steps.

"Hello again," the voice said.

Doli turned to see the same badger she'd met in the inn's lobby. His silver-handled cane rested on the back of his chair, and also seated at the table was a person Doli assumed might be his wife or partner. Her dark fur was slightly graying at the ears, and the woman badger wore a stylish, loose-fitting top embroidered at the neckline with a whimsical forest scene.

She glanced down at the folded and tattered *The Daily Lands* paper that lay next to his plate of half-shell snails swimming in garlic and creamy melted butter. His companion was dining on a heaping bowl of fruit salad, crispy, red-skinned apples, and ripened pears with walnuts.

"Unicorn Grievances Continue" read the headline of the discarded newspaper. Doli wondered if *that* was the topic she'd hear the most about that evening. That might not be such a bad thing, though, if it kept the conversation steered away from Doli or Evvy.

"Mister…?" Doli realized that they hadn't actually introduced themselves when they'd met before, and she didn't know his name.

He shook his head. "No 'mister' here. You can call me

Kliff." Kliff held out his paw to his companion. "And this is my wife, Hazel."

"Nice to make your acquaintance," Hazel said as she bared her teeth in what Doli was pretty sure was a smile. She'd met so few badgers in her lifetime that she wasn't entirely sure. But she seemed friendly enough to make the assumption.

"Yes, ma'am," Doli said. "Pleased to meet you too. I'm Doli."

The badger chuckled, and by that time Doli was certain the teeth-baring was indeed friendly. "Call me Hazel."

Kliff gazed around the outdoor seating area. "Have your parents arrived in Adenashire? I assume that's why you're here again." He leaned over to his wife. "She was booking a room the other morning when we met."

Doli nodded. "They did, this morning."

Kliff turned his attention back to the dwarf and raised his brow. "Oh, a little earlier than expected."

It was funny that he'd remember, but the badger had been right in the seating area in front of the check-in desk and had likely heard the entire conversation with Maven.

"Yes." The confirmation came out a bit too short and strained, but Doli quickly recovered. "How are you two enjoying your stay in Adenashire?"

Hazel clasped her small paws together. "It's been so lovely to get away for a few days. Kliff surprised me with the trip for my birthday." She gazed at him, her brown eyes sparkling in the lantern light.

Kliff shrugged. "All the cubs have grown and left the den. Now it's just the two of us. I figure why not travel the

Northern Lands while we can?" He eyed the newspaper on the table. "We'd only planned to stay three days, but this unicorn business has delayed our travels."

The lady badger leaned in and whispered, and somehow the words carried over the lively chatter of the other diners. "It seems serious."

"Do you think your parents will be delayed here in town as well?" Kliff asked.

Doli's stomach dropped into the cobblestones. *More than a week?* It wasn't even a possibility she'd considered until that moment. But she gave a smile. "Hopefully that situation will all be resolved soon."

The badger plucked the paper from the table and held it up. Below the story was an illustration of an angry-looking unicorn. But Doli still didn't know exactly what the problem was.

Doli eyed the front door. "Well, I must be going."

Hazel waved her paws out in front of her. "Oh, please don't let us keep you."

"Actually, I'd love to stay and chat," Doli said with a sincere grin. "But I'm sure my parents are waiting."

"Good evening to you then," Kliff said.

Doli bid her goodbyes and finally made her way to the door with the winking goat carved into the wood. She pushed it open, and immediately Maven flew past her into the main dining area with a tray full of meals in each hand. The woman's hair was sprouting from the back of her bun, and a trickle of sweat beaded down the side of her cheek.

The innkeeper was obviously short-staffed again.

Doli felt the urge to ask if the woman wanted some help, but before she could open her mouth, a cackling laugh came from the dining room.

Her mother.

The sound fully grounded Doli in reality. She needed to go in, have a seat, order something easy for Maven, talk about her uncle, and maybe get some answers about why he might have had a dragon egg. As for how the rest of the week was going to go, Doli had no idea. Would the unicorns' dilemma keep them in town longer? That was a problem for tomorrow.

Once inside the dining area, she had a full view of the bar stocked with ale, wine, and other harder drinks. Doli stayed away from those but loved an occasional red wine from the north with a meal, or an ale when tea wasn't cutting it. Each candlelit table was full of patrons, and there were two other humans serving meals.

She followed the laughter and found Maven unloading her large tray of food at her parents' table while her mother eyed each offering. Apparently they'd already done more than enough ordering.

"That doesn't look well-done." Gingrilin knitted her brows and pointed to a crusty steak on the plate before her. The dwarf was dressed in her finest and had her braids twisted in high style on top of her head. She looked like a queen. And was acting like one.

"I assure you, ma'am," Maven said with a hint of annoyance in her voice. "*This* time, the steak is guaranteed to be well-done. The cook made sure of it."

Gingrilin folded her arms over her chest, displaying the several gem-studded gold bracelets she wore on her wrist. "You were wrong about the last two."

Her father sat munching on what looked to be the same lamb stew Taenya had ordered, completely ignoring his wife's demands and the frazzled server before them.

It had been a while since Doli had "enjoyed" a meal out with her parents. She'd nearly forgotten her mother's record of sending food back at least five times before it was to her satisfaction.

Doli took a breath and edged in beside Maven. Then she put on her biggest smile. "That steak looks amazing," she got out. "Perfectly well-done."

Gingrilin's eyes flicked to her daughter. "Oh, my dear. You made it…a little late."

Doli's insides tensed, but she would not let her mother disturb her equilibrium, and she made sure her well-practiced grin stayed firmly in place. "I had to wait for Taenya to get to our apartment before I could leave."

While the dwarf matriarch was preoccupied, Maven quickly unloaded her tray and booked it out of the dining room.

Gingrilin looked around as Doli sat next to her father. "Where did she go?"

"I think we have plenty here." Doli surveyed what her parents had ordered, and she was pretty sure with the seven plates she counted it was most of what was on the menu, although there were no snails in garlic and butter.

The matriarch pulled the steak closer and grabbed her

fork and knife. She cut into the caramelized meat. "Might be a little *too* done."

Doli pinched at the bridge of her nose for a second, but then grabbed the honeyed pork loin with a side of mashed potatoes. "I have it on eminent authority that this meal is delicious." She couldn't help but remember Evvy's head with a blotch of potatoes on the top. Quickly she switched the pork for the steak. "I'll take this one. I love a well-done steak."

What she loved was getting her mother to move on.

Gingrilin eyed the plate hungrily. "The pork does look good."

Doli quickly sliced a piece of steak and stuffed it into her mouth. It was a little dry, but there was no way in the stars she was going to complain.

She grabbed a golden, flaky biscuit from a basket on her right and ripped it open, displaying layer upon layer of warm goodness. She slathered it with the Tricky Goat's signature whipped honey butter.

"Where's the dragon?" her father asked finally. Doli nearly choked on her steak and dropped her biscuit onto her plate.

"Shhh," she got out and scanned the room to see if anyone might have noticed. But everyone seemed engrossed in their own conversation, drink, or food. "I'm trying to keep that quiet."

"I don't know, dear." Gingrilin swirled the melted butter around in her mashed potatoes, dug in, and held up a bite in the air below her mouth. "Having a dragon in your home seems like quite a status symbol. I'd want to show one off."

Doli bit her tongue. Apparently her mother had forgotten all the trouble Evvy had caused in the bookstore. "Mother." Doli leaned both her elbows on the table and lowered her voice. "Dragons are people too. They don't exist for us to 'show them off.' How about you tell me why you think Uncle Thorras might have had an, um"—she paused for a blink and gestured an egg shape with her hands—"in the first place."

"I know you weren't well acquainted with your Uncle Thorras," Uldrick said. "But he was quite the collector."

Doli's stomach turned. She didn't want to think that Evvy was part of someone's "collection."

"But why would I end up with the box with the…certain something in it?" The dwarf looked around again. Still no one else really seemed to pay attention to the dwarves, and Maven was staying well away from the table.

Gingrilin shook her head. "You should regard yourself as lucky."

Doli didn't want it to be luck. The books she'd read had talked about hiding dragon eggs to keep them safe. If her uncle was a collector, that meant he'd been one of the people Evvy needed to be safe from. If it was more than that, maybe someone other than her grandmother had seen something special in her. She pinched her lips together for a moment in frustration since the conversation was going nowhere. She picked up the biscuit from her plate and took a bite to calm herself.

It was divine. Light and flaky…and the creamy butter accented the flowery sweetness of the honey. The biscuits were a masterpiece.

"How's your room?" she finally said.

"Oh," Uldrick mused. "It's not like guest accommodations in Dundes Heights." He shrugged. "But one can't expect other places to live up to dwarf standards."

It wasn't the worst answer he could have given. Doli assumed the room must be very nice.

"That elf friend of yours worked his magic and got us in early." Gingrilin took a bite of her juicy pork. "We just sat out on the patio and had a bite while he talked to the innkeeper."

And probably cleaned your room, Doli thought but kept her mouth shut.

"Very quaint. A little like camping," Doli's mother continued. "I did enjoy pretending I was a bookseller at the bookstore, though." She leaned in. "Exhilarating. I'm even thinking about reading a little more myself."

Doli didn't even want to go into their little selling escapade, but if it made them want to read…

"So, what are your plans while you're here?" Doli asked after gnawing on another bite of dry steak. She needed to keep eating it lest her mother try to send it back again.

"I'm so glad you asked." Her mother's eyes lit up. She reached under the table and pulled out a rolled piece of paper. "I've made a list of all the sights around and outside of town. I figured you could take us on a tour." The paper opened and rolled out onto the table.

Doli avoided looking at how many activities were on the page.

"And we want to meet the rest of your friends," her father added. "Make sure everyone is on the up-and-up."

Gingrilin reached across the table and scooped some greens from the bowl in front of her husband. "And then we can deal with this dragon business."

Doli sighed and ate another bite of steak.

13

Doli was up before the sunrise and had barely slept a wink before that. While the dwarf sat on her bed and adjusted the little dragon's sling, Evvy fluttered around the room lit by a single candle. She had improved it the night before after bidding her parents good night and heading back to her apartment. As Evvy slept, Doli had sewn several buttons along the opening so it would be easier to keep the dragon inside once they were fastened.

She leaned back on her fluffy pillows as her chest tingled. Her mother's words wormed their way around her mind: *And then we can deal with this dragon business.* Although she didn't want her parents interfering with her life, there *was*, in fact, dragon business to be dealt with. Even if Evvy had chosen of her own free will to bond with Doli, she couldn't keep her here in Adenashire. Evvy ultimately needed to be with other dragons, so Doli needed to figure out how to get word to Evvy's people on Mount Blackdon. She also knew Sarson was right that Evvy would attract attention, and Doli wouldn't be able to keep her a secret for long, no matter how many buttons she sewed on the sling.

"Want to go for a walk?" Doli asked Evvy as she flew around near the ceiling. "I'll bring a snack."

The dragon stopped and hovered in midair, lightly waving her wings to stay aloft. Then she darted to Doli's side, landed on the blanket, and rose on her back feet to lean against the dwarf's arm.

Doli gave her a pat on the head. "Come on. It's early, so there shouldn't be trouble." The dwarf opened the fabric sling to reveal the snug little fabric nest inside.

Evvy nuzzled her hand, crawled inside, and quickly twisted into a little pink ball, leaving her tail lolling out of the fabric.

Doli chuckled and tucked it inside. "I'm going to button these up," she said to the dragon. "But there's enough room for you to stick out your snout if you want to."

Evvy's eyes seem to enlarge with concern.

"I need you to stay in the sling if we're outside the house. I want to keep you safe until we figure out what to do with you."

The little dragon gave Doli a gummy smile, which the dwarf had to take as a confirmation of understanding. Evvy *had* behaved the night before with Jez and Taenya.

At least that was their story.

And when she'd returned, the apartment was the same as when she'd left it. Save for fewer dragon snacks. Meaning she needed to go to the market again.

And the ugly inheritance vase still sat on the kitchen counter. She wouldn't have minded if that had *accidentally* been broken.

With Evvy buttoned into the sling, some trout sticks in her pocket, and a bit of silver for the market, Doli snuck quietly from the apartment. Jez could be heard snoring through her closed door.

Doli knew Jez was tired of all the commotion lately. The fennex had a few health issues and needed more naps than the average person, but there hadn't been enough time with the dragon-sitting. So it was best if Doli could give her a peaceful, dragon-free morning.

Since it was still well before dawn, the bookstore below them was dark, and the rest of the town was mostly asleep.

There were, of course, a few early risers, including Mr. Figlet preparing for the market later that morning. And despite the CLOSED sign on the bake shop's door, the lights glowed in welcome.

Doli, with one hand raised to her eyes, peered through the glass of the empty storefront window. In the next couple hours it would likely be filled with baskets of herb bread, an intricately decorated cake or two, pastries, and delectable cookies.

Arleta still sold her baked goods at the outdoor market once a week as she had before the bakery, but generally Theo took care of those sales. The elf was charming and a fantastic salesperson, Doli would give him that. She was pretty sure he enjoyed selling everyone on his Fated's baking talents too, since he'd believed in her so strongly when she competed in the Baking Battle. Plus, he'd told the dwarf once over tea that it was nice to get away from tending the house for one morning a week since he did most of the cooking, cleaning, and taking care of Faylin and his horse Nimbus while Arleta ran her shop.

Beneath her chin Doli felt hot breath as Evvy's nostrils poked through the small opening in the sling and worked hard to sniff the air.

"She's baking bread, isn't she?" Doli could smell it too. The sweet, yeasty scent had wormed its way through the crevices of the door and out onto the street. Doli's stomach rumbled, and she could nearly taste the warm bread slathered with fresh butter.

The dwarf was pretty sure it was Arleta inside since she was an earlier riser than Taenya. The elf generally started working about an hour after the human but stayed to close the shop.

She tapped on the window in hopes that her friend would hear her.

And just then, Arleta came through the doorway from the kitchen while wiping her hands on a dish towel. Doli smiled and waved while Evvy gave a little whine of excitement from her cocoon.

Arleta unlocked the front door and swung it wide. "You're up early."

Doli blew out a big breath she'd been holding in her lungs. "Couldn't sleep."

"Well," Arleta said in a chipper tone, folding the towel and placing it inside her apron pocket. "Then come in and help. Taenya won't be here for a while."

Doli hadn't really expected to get put to work, but she didn't mind the distraction. "I do have Evvy." She ran her hand over the warm and now vibrating dragon in her sling.

The human placed her hand on Doli's shoulder and gently pulled her inside. "I have lots of pastries for her to choose from."

Evvy trilled with excitement.

Once inside, Arleta locked the door and Doli worked to unbutton the sling with Evvy nearly swimming around inside.

"Hold still." Doli fiddled with the buttons, but they were pulled tight by Evvy's wings pressing against her containment.

Finally, the buttons gave way, and the little dragon burst from the opening, flying directly up to Arleta and stopping in midair inches from the human's face. Evvy's tongue lolled out from her mouth like a dog.

A wide smile spread over Arleta's lips. "Let's go get you some breakfast." She gestured toward the back of the bakery, and Evvy didn't waste a second. She flipped around and buzzed off to the kitchen.

Doli reached into her pocket. "I have some trout sticks to round everything out." She held the sticks and followed them.

Evvy squealed and kept moving, her wings almost like a hummingbird's.

The dwarf and human raced into the kitchen after the

dragon, and to Doli's surprise, Evvy hadn't snatched anything from the assortment of cookies and pastries waiting on trays on the countertops. The little dragon floated above them with her hands clasped in anticipation.

"Choose whatever you like," Arleta said.

The dragon immediately took her cue and using her magic levitated a large bear claw covered in toasted almonds to herself. Gripping the pastry tight in her hands, she flew over to a small table in the corner with two chairs. Doli knew that was where Arleta and Taenya would often take breaks from baking.

Doli walked over and placed the trout sticks on the table. "Arleta and I are going to take care of some work right now. Enjoy your breakfast."

The dragon bobbed her head up and down, mouth stuffed with bear claw. Doli's mouth watered from the rich, almondy scent wafting from the flaky pastry.

She turned and grinned at her friend. "Shall we?" She gestured in a flourish at the waiting trays and loaves of bread behind them.

"All we need to do is get all these out to the displays." She tipped her chin to several naked cakes waiting on the other end of the counter. "Taenya will finish up those and take the next baking shift."

The thought of setting up the displays lightened Doli's heart. It was always her favorite job in the bookstore—next to actually reading the books, of course. There was an art to getting displays right that she couldn't quite describe.

The two of them carried the trays out into the bakery,

and Doli went to the window display. There were already plates and stands placed on multiple tiers so the goods could be seen easily. Before Arleta had opened the shop, the orcs had built and installed them.

"Some flowers from the market would look pretty in the window next to the baked goods," Doli said as she stretched to place a row of chocolate chip cookies in just the right order to show off the ones with the most chocolate first.

"That's a really good idea," Arleta said from behind the dwarf. "Maybe even some potted herbs from the types I use in some of them."

Doli chuckled. "You can put Theo on that job."

"Fantastic idea." Arleta laughed as she loaded pastries on her tray. "He picked all the lavender from our garden for this shortbread."

Doli turned to Arleta holding up a pretty cookie, golden on the edges with a tiny sprig of lavender baked right into the top for decoration.

"I haven't tried those yet," Doli said as she finished placing the stock on her tray in the perfect spots.

"They're delicious," Arleta said. "Orc-approved."

The dwarf laughed and walked back to her friend. "I'm sure the cookies are amazing, but Verdreth and Ervash like everything you make."

"They have good taste." Arleta winked.

Ervash had actually been the one to enter Arleta in the Langheim Baking Battle when she didn't have the nerve to do so herself. And it was a good thing he had—that kindness had changed all their lives for the better.

"That they do." Doli took her tray to the back, where thankfully Evvy had finished up her breakfast, trout sticks and all, and was curled up on the table grooming one leg.

Arleta took a large basket from the wall and loaded all her bread loaves into it, save for one. "I'm going to put these out. Why don't you slice that one up and make us some tea? The butter is on the counter, and the jam is in the cold box."

"What kind of tea would you like today?" Doli asked, more than glad to make it for her friend.

The human stood still for a moment and raised her attention to the ceiling as if in thought before she spoke. "Bergamot. Two lumps of sugar…and cream."

"Oh," Doli said, envisioning the creamy sweet tea with a slight kick of spicy orange. "I think I'll have that too."

The human left the kitchen with her basket and Doli retrieved bread, knife, butter, and raspberry jam.

The raspberries the jam had been made with grew wild, and she, Arleta, and Jez had gone out to pick them one hot day. Jez had eaten most of what she'd picked plus too many of Doli's before she'd caught the fennex with stained lips, napping under the shade of a bush.

But they'd picked enough for jam anyway.

By the time Arleta returned, Doli had the bread sliced and on plates for each of them, plus she'd grabbed a favored hand-thrown cup off the back shelf for Arleta and prepared her own teacup from her holster.

"That looks wonderful," Arleta said as she had a seat at the table.

Doli chuckled. "*You* made everything."

"Everything I make is delicious. Almost magical." She gave a sly grin and glanced over at the now-sleeping dragon. "But mostly I was talking about the company."

The dwarf's heart warmed. It was nice to share a few moments with a friend in the quiet of the morning. And always good to know people like Arleta had the time for her. Doli climbed up and sat in the average sized chair, so her feet dangled well above the wood-planked flooring.

Arleta picked up a slice of still-warm bread and smeared golden butter over it while Doli prepared to make their tea.

"What's it feel like?" Arleta asked before she took a bite. "I've never asked you."

"Feel like?" Doli knitted her brows.

Arleta set the bread down and nodded toward the cups. "To make the tea with your magic."

Doli bit her lip. She'd done it for so long that she barely thought about it anymore. So she placed her hand a few inches from the cup to start the process. "It's warm and kind of tingly," she said as she conjured the tea into Arleta's cup, the magic dancing over her hand. The warm liquid steamed against her skin, and she pulled back.

"That's it?" Arleta reached for the blue and gray glazed cup and took it by its large handle.

Doli thought for a beat and scanned her body. "No. Making the tea, especially for friends, calms me…almost lightens my mood." She thought for a moment more. "It's like being out in the sun on a just warm enough day."

Her friend leaned her elbows on the table and took a sip. "Then it's a little like your personality."

Evvy stirred next to them, but she didn't wake.

Doli leaned back in her seat, not having made her tea yet. "Is it, though? I haven't felt particularly like myself for a while."

"Nobody is one thing, Doli." Arleta put down her tea and took a bite of the fluffy bread. "We're all layered. And none of us are the same all the time." The human grinned. "I've even caught grumpy Jez laughing a time or two since she moved here. But in the end…she's still Jez. And we love her."

This made Doli chuckle, and she finally placed her hand over her own teacup. Tea swirled into the cup below. When it was done, she sipped the warm liquid. The spicy orange popped over her taste buds.

"You know," Arleta said, "we do like you just for you. Good days and…less good."

Tears pricked at Doli's eyes at the memory of very similar words she'd once spoken to Arleta on an incredibly difficult day.

And for a while they simply sat there in companionable silence, other than the lightly snoring dragon, drinking their tea, enjoying the bread, and waiting for the sun to rise.

14

Orange and gold magic sparkles danced up from the bakery's kitchen counter as Taenya finished decorating one of her stunning cakes. This one was small and two-tiered, and the frosting work was exquisite. The spotless white icing base was covered in what anyone would think were genuine orange lilies…which, of course, would not have been edible.

She spun it around on its wooden turntable for Arleta and Doli to admire. "There we go."

"It's for a wedding?" Doli placed her hand on her chest, then gulped at the potential romance of it all. She had a sudden hankering to read one of her books. She hadn't read in days. Not that a wedding was a necessary event to declare the love and commitment in a relationship. But she loved the flair of it all, and she'd had an extravagant, sunflower-themed wedding planned in her head since she was a little girl.

"If you can believe it, this is their *sampler* for the real cake." Taenya arched her auburn brows. "I like the bride, but she's a little tightly wound over her upcoming day."

Doli was on her fourth cup of tea, and Evvy was polishing off her third pastry. Arleta stood at the oven and took out her latest batch of cookies. The scent of oatmeal and coconut filled the kitchen, and Evvy sat up and took notice, despite the gigantic, gooey blackberry custard roll she held in her little clawed hands. Her lips were stained purplish red from the berry filling.

The dragon trilled again with excitement.

Arleta chuckled as she moved the cookies from the hot tray to a cooling rack. "You're worse than my dads, little one."

Before knowing Evvy, Doli wouldn't have believed that *anyone* could have a bigger appetite for baked goods than Ervash and Verdreth, but apparently a tiny dragon was on track to overtake them for the reigning title, her size taken into consideration.

When the cookies were on the cooling rack, Arleta plucked one of the goodies up with a cloth napkin and brought it straight over to Doli. "Now that's hot, but I think the two of you can share it."

The dragon quickly stuffed the last bite of the custard roll into her mouth, swallowed, and lolled her tongue out in anticipation of her next course.

"Thank you." Doli took the jumbo cookie and broke it in half while Arleta patted Evvy on the head and returned to the cookie rack. The home-baked scent of vanilla, coconut, and oats filled her senses as Evvy scurried across the table and stood up on her hind legs, her front hands leaning on Doli's arm. The dwarf looked over at her and giggled. "Patience."

The dragon whined, and Doli handed her half of the cookie, which she immediately took and began to devour, barely even dropping a coconutty crumb.

Still filled with bread and tea, Doli took a small bite, then melted a little from the mild but delectable buttery flavor. "Is this a new recipe?"

"Not really," Arleta said as she scooped dollops of dough onto a new tray to go into the oven. "But I only bake them every few months. Coconut is a little hard to get, but having it available at the Baking Battle party reminded me how delicious it is and how much my parents loved it. So when it's available, I try to stock up."

Taenya finished touching up her lily cake, set down her piping bag, and stood back to take a look at it. "She's making her father's favorite coconut cake next week." Taenya leaned in toward Doli as if she were sharing a secret. "I'm making sure to come in early so I can learn all her formulas."

"You know you could simply ask for the recipe, Tae," Arleta said matter-of-factly without looking up from plopping a cookie dough ball on the tray.

The human was the only person Taenya allowed to call her a nickname, and somehow it was fitting in their friendship.

Arleta and Taenya were a lot more alike than anyone could have imagined when they first met.

"It's more fun to be sneaky," Taenya joked and spun her cake around again.

It was satisfying to see the elf in such a good mood. Adenashire air—not to mention the people who lived there—had done her good.

"Do you think you'll ever have a wedding, Taenya?" Doli asked in between cookie bites.

The woodland elf startled a fraction, then whipped her attention to the dwarf and coughed. "What?"

"It's a simple question," Arleta said, snickering.

"Why are you asking *me*?" Taenya gestured at Arleta. "She's the one with the Fated."

Arleta laughed and shook her head. "Oh, I've had enough pomp with the Baking Battle to last me a lifetime. Theo and I are pretty happy with the quiet life. And my stress is finally under control." She stopped speaking for a second and then held her finger up. "But maybe we'll invite you all over for a little dinner and call it a wedding. Faylin can officiate in between naps."

"And spread the flower petals in your garden," Doli joked, imagining the forest lynx with a basket handle in his mouth and complaining that someone was making him do work.

"He'd love that." Arleta gave Taenya a wink and went back to work. "But you didn't answer her question, elf."

Taenya's pale cheeks turned a shade of red Doli had never seen on her friend before. It made her quite glad her own skin was much darker to better hide that sort of thing.

"If you're asking if I have a Fated," Taenya straightened and said, "I've never had the dreams that told me she was out there waiting for me." Taenya plucked her piping bag from the counter and quickly added more flourishes to the cake, even though Doli was pretty sure the project was complete.

"Plenty of people, elves included," Arleta noted, "have lifelong partnerships without being fated. Theo has told me all about it." Arleta giggled like she knew something that hadn't been shared with the rest of the group yet.

Taenya stopped her diversionary decorating and pulled her piping bag back from the cake. "I don't even have a *sometimes* romantic relationship at the moment."

Before Arleta or Doli could reply, the elf blurted out, "What about *you*, Doli? What about that gargoyle? He seems nice. Maybe *he* wants a wedding. Have you asked?"

Doli's heart fluttered at the mention of Sarson and let Taenya off the hook. "He does seem nice. But Jez doesn't like him." She popped the last bite of coconut cookie into her mouth.

"She...she mentioned that last night." Taenya seemed relieved to get the attention off herself and finally put the piping bag back on the counter.

"That fennex doesn't like anybody." Arleta leaned against the wall, her arms crossed. "It's not a reason to make life choices based on her *initial* opinion of a person."

"That's what I told her," Doli said, but just then the bell on the front door rang.

Evvy's head flicked toward the sound while she chewed her last bite of cookie.

"Seems we have customers," Taenya said. "I guess we should get to work out front."

As the words exited Taenya's mouth, the dragon's wings spread and she hunched down to prepare for flight. But somehow, that time, Doli was quicker. Maybe from all the tea she'd drunk. She reached out as Evvy had barely left the tabletop and grabbed her middle. The dragon squealed in protest.

A deep voice came from the front. "Anyone here?"

Doli stuffed the uncooperative dragon into her sling, nearly knocking over the two cups still on the table and spilling the leftover tea inside.

"I'll go," Arleta said and hurried to the front. "Ohhh, hello. How can I help you?"

"I know you're excited," Doli said to the dragon as Taenya grabbed something and hurried over to help.

The elf shoved another cookie at the dragon, who was still half hanging out of the sling. Evvy's eyes widened. She took the goodie and immediately stopped squirming to munch on it, slipping the rest of the way back out of the sling.

Taenya shook her head. "I'm not sure that's the best long-term strategy for keeping Evvy out of trouble."

"Me neither." Doli placed the temporarily calm dragon down on the table. She looked out the window at the risen sun painting the shops across the road in gold. "I really should go. There's so much I need to do this morning." She picked up and dried her teacup with a cloth napkin, then reattached it to her holster, snapping the cup in and making sure it was secure.

The dwarf reached out and plucked Evvy from the table as the dragon happily munched on her cookie, easily fitting the now-docile creature into the sling. Quickly she secured the buttons and gave Evvy a pat where the side of her belly should be.

"I suppose I need to get busy too," Taenya said as they walked toward the kitchen exit and onto the bakery sales floor. "That bride will come in soon to pick up her cake."

Doli laughed. "I hope she likes it."

"Ha. Me too."

But the second they entered the bakery, Doli saw the customer who had come in. Sarson. A smile curled at her lips, and flutterbees did a dance in her stomach.

"Look who it is." Arleta side-eyed the dwarf, her eyes crinkling.

Sarson's tail grazed across the wood floor, and Doli's eyes immediately locked to it.

"Oh." The gargoyle stuffed his hands into his pockets. "Hello, Doli." That day, he didn't wear a cloak, and his wings were out but tucked tightly behind his back.

"Hi." Doli gulped, barely even noticing when Evvy pushed her snout past one of the buttons that she hadn't quite secured.

He paused for a moment with his attention on her and then moved it to Taenya. "I'm not sure we've met."

"I'm Taenya." The elf leaned against the doorframe, placed her hand on Doli's shoulder, and gave her a gentle push. "Remember the wedding," she whispered with a dose of sarcasm to the dwarf.

Doli grunted and made it two steps, then stopped.

The gargoyle tipped his head in confusion and rubbed one hand over his left horn. "I'm sorry?"

The dwarf's eyes widened, and any words she might have said were caught in her throat while she stood frozen behind the counter.

Taenya waved her hand toward Sarson. "Oh, I'm sorry. Doli was just in the back helping me with a pre-wedding cake." The elf chuckled. "What are your thoughts on weddings?"

Doli almost died. She nearly keeled over right then and there of embarrassment. Dug her own grave and everything. In her mind she made a note to never be around while Arleta teased Taenya about her love life ever again. Her only consolation at the moment was that the heat burning at her umber cheeks and neck was not as obvious as it would have been on either Taenya or Arleta. That was something.

"Weddings?" he asked. The end of the word went up into a higher register of his voice. "Um. I've only been to a handful in my lifetime, but I guess I enjoyed them." He paused for a moment. "Unless the drunken speeches go on too long." Sarson gave a nervous laugh.

Before anyone could say anything else, another customer pushed open the shop door.

"Good morning," Arleta's voice rang out. "How can we help you?"

A human wore a blue dress down to her calves and a pair of laced up, calf-high black boots. She looked around as she entered and did a double take at the sight of Sarson.

She slowly gave him a once-over. "A gargoyle in Adenashire? That's not a sight I thought I'd see." She gazed around at the others. "Be careful. He's probably writing down all the current events for the history books." She chuckled lightly. "You hear about those unicorns?"

"No, ma'am," Sarson managed. "I haven't been here long."

"Oh." Her brows rose in surprise.

A sort of protectiveness toward Sarson bloomed in Doli's chest. The woman hadn't exactly been rude, but the dwarf didn't like her tone. "We have coconut oatmeal cookies right out of the oven," she got out while Evvy squirmed against her confines.

The woman's attention swung to Doli, then Arleta. "Those sound wonderful. I haven't had coconut in years."

While Arleta got to work bagging up a dozen cookies for the woman, Sarson leaned in a little and whispered to Doli and Taenya, "I just came in for some sourdough."

Taenya reached for a loaf behind her and quickly wrapped it up. "On the house." She winked at Doli.

The dwarf gulped and at the same time realized another button on her sling had come undone. This time, she wasn't quick enough. Evvy leaped from her nest, let out a shriek of excitement, and flew directly at the bag of coconut cookies being passed off to the customer.

The woman screamed and threw her hands at the ceiling. "What in the stars is *that*?"

15

"It's nothing!" Doli yelled and dove out from behind the counter. The dwarf reached up toward the dragon but grabbed unsuccessfully at the air.

Evvy turned around and hissed indignantly at Doli.

Doli stepped back, guilt filling her stomach for calling Evvy an "it."

"Your cookies, ma'am." Arleta held the bag out in a futile attempt to distract the woman, who couldn't take her eyes off the pink dragon.

"Is it going to bite me?" The woman yelped and backed into the counter as the baby dragon swooped over her head, hissing at her too. "It's not going to bite me, is it?"

Taenya tossed the bread bag to Sarson and came out from

the counter to help. "*She* doesn't have any teeth." The elf whipped her attention back to Doli. "Right? No teeth."

"But she has claws!" The woman tried to make for the exit, but Evvy swooped around her, flying close to the top of her head. "Help, help!" She threw her hands in the air, making everything worse.

"Please, Evvy." Doli snatched a pastry from the display next to the checkout and held it above her head to no avail. Something about the woman obviously had the dragon stuck in a one-track frame of mind, and it wasn't food.

To the side, Sarson had closed his eyes and raised his right hand. Small sparks of blue magic matching his skin rose from his palm and quickly turned to a smoky substance. Doli watched as he directed it toward Evvy, and it danced around her body.

Almost immediately, her wings stopped flapping and her eyes closed. But before she could drop to the ground, the gargoyle lashed his tail out and coiled it lightly around her.

The woman looked at Evvy, then the gargoyle. She sucked in a loud breath and said, "Never mind about my order. I'll just get something from the market." Then she ran out of the bakery as if she would never set foot in there again.

Doli wobbled as if her feet were going to give way beneath her, but somehow she stayed upright as Sarson approached and handed over the sleeping dragon.

"She'll probably be out for a couple of hours after that," he said. "I don't like using that magic without asking first. But…this seemed like an emergency."

"Thank you." Doli took Evvy and placed her inside the

sling again, this time making sure the buttons were completely secure. The dragon snored loudly from inside the fabric.

"Yes, thank you." Arleta plopped the bag of cookies on the counter and spoke to no one in particular. "So, you think that lady'll keep her mouth shut about the dragon?"

"Not a chance," Taenya said and eyed Doli. The elf shrugged.

Doli sighed and shook her head. "I've got to get this situation under control." She looked back at Arleta and Taenya. "I'm so sorry for costing you business." The dwarf felt tears well up in her eyes, but somehow she held them back. Falling apart all the time wasn't a good look.

"Doli," Arleta said, "this isn't your fault. It seems like you're doing the best you can."

"And dragons can be a handful," Sarson said with sympathy in his tone.

The dwarf looked down at her bulging sling with Evvy inside.

Sarson gazed at Taenya where she stood behind a large basket of muffins, lemon cranberry according to the handwritten sign in front of them. "Thanks for this," he said, gripping his bag with the sourdough inside.

The elf nodded.

"I guess I should go." The gargoyle looked around at the friends. "I really don't want to be in the way."

"Oh," Doli blurted, her cheeks heating again before the words barely escaped her mouth. "You're not."

He smiled. "I hope you all have a better rest of your day."

He turned and left the bakery before anyone else could object.

As if someone had thrown cold water on her face, Doli recovered from her blush. "I'll see you two later." And with that, she raced out the door after Sarson.

Either Taenya or Arleta said something to her on the way out, but she didn't catch the words.

Sarson was already halfway down the road, and Doli raced as fast as her dwarf legs could carry her while hanging on to Evvy inside the sling. But the dragon made no signs of waking.

"Wait," she called, raising her hand.

He turned and stopped walking.

Doli reached him and planted her hands on her hips while she took a moment to catch her breath. In the meantime, she noticed a few people staring her way. She wondered if it was simply the sight of a dwarf running to catch up with a gargoyle that had captured their attention or if they had already heard the news about the dragon running wild at the bakery.

News traveled fast in Adenashire.

"I do need to apologize again for using my magic on Evvy without her or your permission," Sarson said before Doli had caught her breath.

"Really…it's okay." Her breath and words were ragged. She blew out a quick puff of air and finally felt back to normal.

"That type of magic—sleeping magic—can be particularly off-putting," he said, clutching his bag. "I'm sure *that* will be talked about as well when that lady tells everyone what just happened. People don't like learning that someone has the ability to knock someone unconscious that easily without their consent."

Doli gazed up at his handsome, uneasy face. "I can see that, and thank you for your concern." His seemingly sensitive nature made him that much more attractive to her, and for a few beats too long all she could do was stare at him. She almost forgot all the trouble.

"Was there something you needed?" he finally asked.

"Oh! Yes." She gave a nervous grin. "You said you know quite a bit about dragons. I really need some help with this one."

He paused for a moment and gazed around the street, then back down at Doli. "Would you mind walking me back home? I've changed my mind about stopping at the market, so we could talk along the way."

Excitement at the opportunity bubbled in her chest. "I'm not working today. So I have as much time as you can spare."

The two of them, along with the sleeping dragon in Doli's sling, made it out of town before Doli really dug into her questioning.

"Jez and I read in one of the dragon books, I don't quite remember which," Doli said as she admired the tree-lined road to distract her from her nerves, "that certain dragons are bonded to their caregivers until they both fulfill some kind of destiny."

Sarson nodded. "This can be true."

"But what kind of destiny could that mean?" Doli ran

her thumb over the teacup in her holster. Just touching it calmed her slightly.

"I wish I could answer that," he said. "It seems like a question for the Fervour dragon people."

Doli clicked her tongue. "So, what do you suggest? A journey up Mount Blackdon to ask?"

The gargoyle shook his head vigorously. "Oh no, you'd likely be eaten before you got far."

Doli's eyes grew wide. She knew dragons weren't the friendliest bunch but didn't know they might actually *eat* a person. Would Evvy grow large enough to eat someone? "Eaten?"

He pursed his lips. "Only in the worst-case scenario, I suppose." Sarson switched his bread bag to his other hand. "Dragons are a private people and don't like intruders in their realm."

"Like gargoyles?"

He looked down at Doli and stated in all seriousness, "Gargoyles *never* eat people."

Sarson's answer took Doli off guard, and she giggled. "I meant the part about being private."

"Oh." His cheeks turned a slightly darker blue, and Doli realized Sarson was blushing. "Yes, we are quite private."

"But there's a good reason for that." Doli grazed her hand along Evvy's body inside the fabric sling. The little dragon let out a sleepy trill. Despite all her troublemaking, it was hard to believe she might grow up and want to eat someone.

Sarson released a long sigh. "Being the historians and librarians of the Northern Lands is a big job. Stressful. Even if it is self-imposed."

"I've read that the head librarian job is the most stressful of all," Doli said as she gazed up at the blue sky.

"That it is." Sarson paused for a moment.

Doli shrugged. "I think there might have been news about them in *The Daily Lands*. The headline was about head librarians, at least. I didn't get a chance to actually read the article."

"Ah," he said and wiped his hand on the side of his pants. "Whatever was printed was likely only rumor anyway. Gargoyles don't allow much information out of the Ridgelands, since too many times it's taken out of context. People try to use it against us for extortion to change the historical record. But gargoyles have good memories and a strong sense of doing the right thing. So it's hard to find one who'll go against our code."

At his mention of gargoyles' memories, she realized why he'd recalled her name so easily after they'd first met. Disappointment twinged in her stomach. "Truth and justice?"

"Pretty much," he said. "At least that's how it's supposed to be."

Something in his tone made her think there was more to the story, something more personal, but she decided not to ask about it. The fact was, they had only known each other for a few days, and it was far too early to ask something so personal.

Sarson's cottage came into sight, and although everything in Doli wanted to keep going, she thought it was best to turn around. "I guess I should go back…figure out what to do with this little girl." Doli gave Evvy a pat and looked up again as a flock of geese flew overhead, probably to a nearby pond.

"I...I thought possibly you'd be interested in coming to my place," he said. "I'm pretty sure I have one more book with some information on Fervour dragons specifically. Maybe you'd like to see it?"

Doli's heart leaped, but she kept her reaction under control. "Oh. That would be wonderful."

Sarson picked up his pace slightly to be the first to his front door. Reaching into his pants pocket, he pulled out a silver key and unlocked it.

"Most people around here don't even lock their doors," Doli said as she reached the front steps.

Sarson shrugged and opened the door wide for Doli to enter. "Old habits die hard...and one can never be too careful."

Jez's warning buzzed around at the back of her head. Did Sarson have something to hide and needed to keep his door locked? But she quickly cast that thought aside when she saw his library again. Somehow it seemed to have grown, but perhaps it was simply the effect of seeing it a second time. Besides, if she let Jez's warning scare her off, she'd have to go back to Adenashire and help fulfill her mother's lengthy activity list. She didn't know if she could stand one more story about the unicorn stampede and how it nearly ruined their entire trip.

"Come on in," Sarson said as he walked to the kitchen and set the bag of sourdough on a counter. "Would you like some?" He took the loaf from the bag and grabbed a large bread knife from a block. "I also have fresh butter."

Doli stood before the shelves and gazed up at the books. Most of the tomes seemed to be on serious topics—history, the study of the stars—but one book near the top caught her eye: *My Heart's Battle*. It was the romance book she'd been reading before her inheritance box had arrived. But since Evvy had hatched, she hadn't gotten to finish. In fact, she'd left off right at what looked to be the best part.

"That's a good one," Sarson said from right behind her. "Have you read it?"

Doli startled. She hadn't even noticed him coming into the library. How could such a large person move with such a light step? The dwarf gave a nervous laugh. "I actually have it on my bedside table. But I've been too busy lately to finish it."

"I can see that happening in your current situation. But I did find the ending particularly interesting." Sarson bowed his head slightly and gestured back to the bread. "Would you like some? I'm more than glad to share."

Doli remembered all the bread and jam she'd already had that morning and reached for her teacup holster. "Would you mind terribly if I just had a cup of tea?"

The gargoyle gazed around. "I'm afraid I'm fresh out of tea. I meant to get more at the market, but we came back here."

"That's not a problem." Doli unhooked the cup, held it out, and placed her hand over the top to conjure a fragrant cup of rooibos. As the tea appeared and began steeping for a spell, the scent of vanilla and caramel filled the space.

Sarson's eyes widened with pleasure as he watched her. "You wield tea magic?"

Part of Doli was embarrassed over the trifling nature of her magic, but at the moment she owned it. There was something about the word he'd used, *wield*. She'd never quite thought of it that way. She owned her magic, controlled it, and she was damn good at making tea. "I do. I can conjure any flavor or blend you might like, along with sugar, honey, milk, and cream. Would you like some?"

"That's amazing," Sarson said with no hint of sarcasm or disappointment in his tone. "And yes. I'd love some." He returned to the counter where the bread was laid, retrieved a cup with a handle, and brought it back to Doli.

"What's your pleasure?" the dwarf asked, holding her hand out, palm down.

"Surprise me." Sarson gazed down at her, smiling. "I can't imagine that your creation would be anything but delicious."

For the first time in a long time, since Doli's grammy had passed on, the dwarf felt completely seen. Like she might not have to hide who she was.

And she liked the feeling.

16

"You are getting Evvy exercise, right?" Sarson asked in a lazy tone.

The words startled Doli, and her eyes fluttered open. Apparently she'd been napping.

Sort of. Maybe. She wasn't fully admitting to anything.

Sarson's cottage was so warm and cozy. Several lanterns flickered on the wall, spreading a honeyed hue across the library and beyond. He also made her feel incredibly comfortable in his home.

The warnings Jez had given her were just Jez being Jez. Maybe she was even a little jealous.

The gargoyle still sat thumbing through a book and drinking what should have been his second cup of green matcha, but Doli's brain was foggy, so she wasn't sure.

He either hadn't noticed her dozing or didn't mind, because he'd said nothing about it. "It says here that baby dragons need several hours of entertainment and exercise a day."

The pair sat in Sarson's library chairs. Before they'd begun their research, he'd fashioned a snug little bed on the floor for the still-sleeping dragon. Doli was glad Evvy had been napping for so long, although she had a nagging annoyance in the back of her mind that she needed to get back to town. It was nearly the lunch hour according to the clock in Sarson's living room, and she was sure her parents would be looking for her to help check off all the boxes on her mother's list...

Another reason she hadn't minded drowsiness dragging her own eyes down. If only for a second or two.

Doli furrowed her brow and blinked away the languor. "Taenya and possibly Jez played some games with her, and then there's all that flying around the bakery...mostly eating, really." She paused for a moment. "But no. I'm not sure how to get her much exercise in my apartment or in town with so many onlookers. Plus, what if she escaped?"

"You could bring her here," the gargoyle offered. "There's plenty of space, and it's far enough away from town that I receive few visitors. And there's a nearby pond. I'm sure she'd love it since dragons are natural swimmers. We could have a picnic."

The dwarf hadn't read that dragons liked water. *Is he really asking me out here again? And is it like a date?* Her stomach gave a little shimmer at the possibility.

Doli thought for a second, then said, "Arleta and Theo have a fairly large property they share with the orcs too. I don't know why I hadn't thought of it before." She smiled, and the expression felt good. "Did you find anything else on Fervour dragons and their caregiver bonds?"

"While you were asleep?" He chuckled lightly without looking up from the book.

Apparently he *had* noticed Doli dozing.

The sting of awkwardness poked at Doli's stomach, but she used it as a prompt to sit straight and say, "Yes. While I was *napping*, did you find any other useful information?"

He looked up this time, and his lips quirked up halfway. The expression made Doli nearly melt right into her chair.

"I could watch you all day…and yes, I did. But the passage is vague."

The dwarf's stomach did a flop. Sarson was most definitely flirting with her, *and* he'd found something in the book. "Let me see." She held out her hand.

The book Sarson picked up from the side table and handed Doli was much smaller than the one he'd loaned her. Thin, really. She took it from him, put her thumb on the page he'd left open, and turned it over to view the cover. *Strange and Wonderful Stories Concerning Possible and Provable Magical Beasts*.

"This is fictional." Doli wrinkled her nose in disappointment. She thought Sarson might have been teasing her.

She flipped to the table of contents. It seemed mostly to contain unproven accounts about elusive magical creatures, like one large, hairy beast with gigantic feet that was occasionally spotted in woods all over the Northern Lands, but when anyone went back to look, there was no trace of them. Then a water-dragon-like creature who supposedly lived in a lake, some say for thousands of years. And then there was one section on various dragons.

She'd heard variations of these stories ever since she was a child.

"It is," he said. "It's why I didn't think of it right away, but I've studied and evaluated history all my life. And there are always kernels of truth in those types of stories, even if they are mostly fiction. At least we know that dragons are real." Sarson tipped his head to Evvy as she let out a loud snore.

"No doubt about that." Doli flipped to the page she had her thumb in, then Sarson leaned close and placed a large finger on the part about Fervour dragons.

"There," he said.

The gargoyle was so close to Doli that his scent seemed to envelop her. It was slightly earthy, which she expected from a being whose skin could become like stone. But there was also a hint of a floral aroma, maybe gardenia. She couldn't quite put her finger on it, but she knew she liked it.

And the only place she'd ever heard of someone describing another's scent like flowers and stone was in her romance books. She'd always thought it was a literary device. But maybe there was something more to it.

For a second she stared at him, inhaling the fragrance and wanting to lean forward a little more and place her lips on his. Her thirsty gaze roamed over the slightly curled horns on his head, and then she let out a big breath and compelled herself to look down at the page. She cleared her throat and scanned the passage.

"Says that this Fervour bonded with its caregiver until the 'prophecy' was fulfilled. When it was, the dragons appeared, and everything was set right." The dwarf put the book down on her lap. "That doesn't say much, does it? They don't even say what kind of prophecy it was. And it must not have been a very important prophecy if no one has heard of it outside this book." Doli held the book high.

"They don't," Sarson said as he leaned back into his chair and crossed one leg over the other. Well out of kissing—or anything else—range without a major effort on her part. "But there are other similar accounts in the book. Whether or not it's a real prophecy, the common thread is that at some point after the dragon hatches, it completes some kind of journey with its caregiver and then the other dragons appear. I wish I could tell you more." He looked back at his books longingly. "But when I…moved, I had to leave most of my library behind. And you're not likely to find much more information between your friends' bookstore and what I have here in Adenashire."

"But you would have it back in the Ridgelands?" Doli asked, suddenly more interested in Sarson's past again.

He paused before he spoke. "Yes."

That was all he said.

And Doli didn't want to pry. Well, she did want to, but didn't. Instead, she pinched her lips and patted the book cover. "Well, I sure hope I'm not expected to fulfill any sort of real prophecy. I wouldn't even know where to start." The dwarf looked to Evvy, who was lying on her back, all four legs in the air and wings tucked under her body. Every other breath, she'd let out a high-pitched whistle. "I'm not sure Evvy's up to it either."

"Not without a treasure trove of pastries," he joked, the humor crinkling the corners of his green eyes.

They both gave a hearty laugh, but then Doli blew out a big breath and brought her hands to her face in frustration, thinking over what little she'd learned.

"In the end, I think you need to allow your experience with Evvy to play out in your life," he said. "Maybe it will be less 'prophecy fulfilled' and more just getting you both to where you need to be." Sarson smiled as Doli looked at him between her spread fingers. "You seem to have supportive people around you."

"I do." She thought of her friends; she knew would prop her up every step of the way. "Everyone but my parents," she said, lowering her hands onto her lap.

"Do they live here in Adenashire?" he asked.

Doli shook her head. "In Dundes Heights. But they're here on a visit because of Evvy."

Sarson tipped his head in interest.

"Well, sort of. Evvy was actually part of a surprise inheritance from my uncle," she said. "No one even knew the egg was part of it." She rolled her eyes. "When they found out, they immediately wanted to take her back to Dundes Heights."

"Why?" he asked.

Doli bit the inside of her mouth. "Because they don't think I can handle her."

Sarson looked the dwarf up and down, from her toes to the top of her dark, curly hair, and then took another sip of his tea. "You seem like a completely capable woman to me."

Heat burned at Doli's neck and face. She recalled how she'd nearly fallen over two times and allowed Evvy to escape her grasp at least once in front of Sarson, and somehow he still thought she was capable.

And despite those things…she knew she was too.

"Thanks," Doli barely got out.

"Was there any information about why your uncle had the egg?" Sarson asked.

"None." Doli placed the book at her side. "There were a few other things in the box, but nothing like the egg. And no reason why he had it or willed it to me."

Sarson shrugged, holding up his clawed hands chest high. "Sometimes these things are without explanation. Magic, possibly."

"Magic?" Doli furrowed her brow.

"Maybe you and Evvy were written in the stars."

The edges of Doli's lips curled up at the corners. She actually liked the sound of that. Not everything needed to be fully explained. What if rolling with her experience with Evvy was the best plan?

Despite wanting to sit in it all day—and possibly do other things with Sarson—she hopped down from the comfortable armchair. She grabbed her cup from the side table, drank the last cold sip at the bottom, and secured the teacup in her holster.

"I should get going," she said. "Thank you so much for letting me ask questions and showing me the book."

The gargoyle leaned out onto his knees, and his wings extended slightly from the confines of the chair back.

Doli stared at them for a second. They really were lovely, with just a hint of blue iridescence and transparency in spots.

"And that picnic?" Sarson reminded her as she moved to pick up Evvy. She turned back to him, smiling. "I understand you are quite busy," he added, not taking his eyes off the dwarf. "But I would really enjoy spending more time with you, and if it could also help Evvy…"

"I'd love to," Doli said in her sweetest voice, beaming. "I've also enjoyed our time together." She gently deposited Evvy into the waiting sling. And that time she double-checked that the buttons were secure. When done, she looked back at Sarson. "How about tomorrow?"

The gargoyle's eyes lit with joy. "I'm free all day." He stood and towered over the dwarf as he gestured to the door. "I'll walk you out."

Doli nodded, suddenly feeling a little shy from the flutterbees doing a lap in her stomach. She managed a smile.

The pair ambled to the door, where Sarson reached for the handle and then opened it wide.

To Jez. Scowling.

"Where in the stars have you been?" The fennex growled, her fluffy tail flicking back and forth, right ear twitching. She didn't look at Doli at all but kept her narrowed gaze straight on the gargoyle.

17

A nearly silent growl fought at the back of Doli's throat. She looked from the angry fennex standing on the porch, then back to Sarson, and her tense expression softened. "Thank you for the lovely morning."

He nodded and she marched outside and right past Jez, leaving her with Sarson and not looking back.

Everything in her wanted to run, but she knew quite well that it wouldn't take much for Jez to catch her. Instead Doli kept her eyes trained on the tree-lined path and kept going. Even though she didn't actually want to get back to town. At all.

Jez shouted from behind her and quickly caught up as a murder of crows flew overhead. The black birds landed in a nearby oak tree as if settling in to watch a show about to happen. "What are you doing?" Jez demanded, but Doli kept walking.

Inside the sling Evvy was stirring. The commotion seemed to have woken her, and Doli realized she didn't have any snacks for the little dragon. All the more reason to hurry.

"What are you doing?" Jez asked again, this time more forcibly.

"What does it look like I'm doing?" Doli snapped, picking up her pace. But as she'd predicted, moving faster would not get her away from her friend. She would have hated to know if Sarson was still watching them.

Jez scoffed. "You know that's not what I mean."

Doli stopped and dug her boot heel into the road's packed dirt. She swung around to the fennex and planted both hands on her hips. "Then please be clearer what you *do* mean."

Jez nearly ran smack into Doli but stopped just short and crossed her arms over her chest. "I…I meant—"

"Yeeeess?" Doli stood up on her toes and leaned into Jez as Evvy squirmed and whined inside the sling.

"The others said you went off with that gargoyle." She thumbed toward the cottage, where luckily Sarson was nowhere in sight. "I followed your scent all the way out here."

"*And?*" Doli narrowed her eyes.

The fennex stamped her boot on the ground while the crows squawked and hopped from branch to branch of the old oak. It almost seemed they were taking wagers over who would win this fight—the fennex or the dwarf.

"And I told you what I think about him!" The fennex's words came out quickly, tumbling over each other. "I want you to be safe!"

Doli's already wide nose flared even further in irritation. "You know that I love you, and I will forgive you since you're saying this because you really do care about me." She paused for a second. "But for shit's sake, Jez. I am a grown woman and am perfectly capable of making my own choices about who I spend my time with!"

The fennex opened her mouth to speak, but Doli threw out her hand and shushed her. "I'm talking!"

Jez straightened and snapped her mouth shut, eyes wide.

"I am a *good* judge of character," Doli said. "And I am rarely wrong about people. Except Taenya maybe, but we were all wrong about her except Arleta. Even Taenya was wrong about herself for a while there." She shook her head at her babbling and got back on track. "Sarson is a good person. I have no reason to believe otherwise, and neither do you. Does he have secrets? Yes. But by the stars, we just met him. Do you tell everyone your life's story the second you meet them?" She stared at Jez for an answer. "Hmm?"

The fennex stood there pinching her lips together until she finally sucked her teeth. "No."

Doli folded her arms over her ample chest. "Do you like it when people judge you on your appearance?" She eyed Jez's tail flicking at the air. "Like how damn fluffy your tail is."

Jez pulled back her chin in offense. "What's wrong with my tail?"

The dwarf wrinkled her nose and gave a dramatic pause

before speaking. "Nothing! And there is nothing wrong with Sarson's wings—or his horns *or* his tail! You can't judge people by stuff like that."

"It's just—" Jez started.

"No," Doli cut her off. "There's no *just*. Simply because you think gargoyles are untrustworthy doesn't make it true, and it definitely doesn't mean Sarson is untrustworthy. A person has to have untrustworthy behavior for me to not trust them. And Sarson"—Doli pointed back to the cottage—"has done nothing of the sort."

Jez stuffed her hands in her pockets and dug randomly in the dirt with the tip of her boot as the crows took flight, squawking as they flew.

"I'm sorry," Jez said more quietly. "You're right. I don't know him. I guess I heard too many stories about gargoyles when I was growing up." She looked up at the sky and shook her head. "A few fennex might have sordid pasts they don't like highlighted in their books, I guess."

By that point Evvy was squirming in the sling as much as she ever had, and the buttons bulged.

Doli let out a huff. "I'd make you go back and apologize, but I really need to get her home." She gestured to the writhing sling. "So we'll have to take care of that later."

"Okay," Jez said, contrite, and briefly rested her clawed hand on Doli's shoulder.

The two walked about halfway to town before speaking again.

"You really should speak your mind more often," the fennex said. "I kind of like it."

"I honestly don't think you're ready for my mind." Doli picked up the pace. Although she held Evvy firmly, the dragon's pink tail had worked its way out of the sling and nearly flicked the dwarf in the face.

Jez chortled. "I don't doubt it, dwarf."

When they arrived at the bookstore, the street in front of it was packed with an enormous crowd: humans, halflings, a few elves, and a minotaur, to name a few. Several of them were pushing to get inside the door.

Several of them seemed to be speaking, but Doli was too far away to make out the words.

Jez sniffed the air. "They seem pretty excited, a little agitated, I think. Was there some kind of sale today we didn't know about?"

As much as Doli loved her books, she couldn't remember a time when a book had drawn such a crowd. Even ones on sale.

"There's no more room!" Verdreth boomed from inside. "This is a safety hazard!"

Doli looked at Jez and asked, "What's going on?"

The fennex shrugged. "It wasn't like this when I left." She pointed toward the back door and the two of them took the long way around to avoid the crowd.

But they didn't make it far.

"Dolgrila!" Her mother's voice carried high above the crowd, and seemingly everyone outside turned and looked at Doli. "There you are."

The dwarf froze, and Jez remained at her side. Her mother and father approached, but before Doli could say a word to her parents, some of the people rushed toward her.

"She's the one with the dragon!" someone shouted.

Doli's eyes widened, and she quickly whispered to Evvy, "I know you're hungry. But please settle down. I'll get you something as soon as I can."

Somehow the dragon listened and stopped fidgeting.

Both Jez and Doli turned to go the other way, but there were people behind them too. Jez drew closer in a protective stance, and this time Doli welcomed her friend's defensive nature.

The fennex held out her hand to block the mob. "Nothing to see here!" she growled while steering Doli through the crowd toward the bookstore.

Doli instinctively placed her hand over the dragon as she walked.

"Do you have it?" a woman shouted. "Or is it inside?"

"What do they eat?" someone else called.

But the fennex and dwarf kept moving forward.

"Let us through," Jez said loudly as she continued pushing them through the crowd. "Doli is not answering any questions."

Doli mostly kept her head down but lifted it once as they neared the shop entrance. She caught sight of the woman who'd seen Evvy at the bakery that morning.

She most definitely had not kept quiet about the baby dragon. Instead, she'd apparently gone to the market as promised and told everyone in sight.

Ervash appeared at the door and raised his brows. "You're both back."

Jez tightened her grip around Doli's shoulder. "Get these people out of here."

The orc's eyes widened, and he gave a curt nod. He reached around the back of the door, grabbed the wooden hand-carved CLOSED sign off the hook and held it aloft. "Sorry, folks. We're closed. Lunch break!"

Jez and Doli finally made it into the shop as Ervash, sign in hand, used it to wave people out.

Verdreth herded more out, saying, "If you want to come back and make a purchase later today, we'll be having a 10 percent off sale."

He was apparently trying to make a positive out of the unexpected foot traffic.

Several people groaned.

"We just wanted to see the dragon," a young adult faun protested but finally followed Ervash's urging.

When everyone was gone, the orc latched the door, hung the CLOSED sign on the glass, leaned against the wall, and let out a huge breath.

Standing near the checkout, Verdreth shook his head and pushed his crooked spectacles up on his green nose. "None of them even bought anything!"

Doli gazed around the shop and finally turned to the door where people had their noses pressed up against the glass, trying to get a glimpse of Evvy. She let out an exasperated breath when she saw that two of the faces were Gingrilin and Uldrick Butterbuckle.

"Oh, for stars' sake." Doli pinched at the bridge of her nose. "Let my parents in."

Verdreth flipped around to look at them, unlocked the door, cracked it open, and reached a massive hand through. He took them both by the arms and yanked them inside.

Before the door pulled completely shut, a human man with a mop of dark hair and a furrowed brow whined, "Why do they get to go in?"

Doli's mother gazed up at the orc and huffed, "Well, I *never*!" She smoothed down the front of her green silk dress, which was gathered with a wide leather belt with a yellow-jeweled buckle.

"You're in here, aren't you?" Ervash said and latched the door again.

Doli's father leaned closer to his wife and twisted one of his beard braids. "You can't expect much more from orcs."

"Excuse me?" Ervash frowned, and the skin on his neck turned a darker shade of green.

Doli let out a huff of annoyance at her parents. "Mother. These are my friends; can you please treat them with a little respect?"

Gingrilin muttered something under her breath before saying, "We were hoping you could show us around town today."

Jez stepped forward, but Doli stopped her.

"And you thought insulting my friends would help your cause? Can't you see there's a bit of an emergency, Mother?" Doli held her mother's gaze. "I didn't invite you to come to Adenashire. Maybe if you had given me a little more time to prepare, your experience would be different." Her voice was firm but exasperated.

"We thought you'd be happy to see us," Uldrick said, looking nearly as offended as his wife.

Doli's mind glimmered with the desire to appease them, apologize for being rude. But Evvy nudged her snout between the buttons and squawked loudly, shaking the dwarf out of her compulsion to people-please.

What she really wanted to do was march back to Sarson's and take him up on that picnic. That would be easier and much more enjoyable than her current situation.

She held her hands up and blew out a calming breath. "How about this? If—and that is a *big* if—I can figure out how to downplay Evvy's existence and people stop trying to break down the shop door to get a glimpse of her, then I might be able to take you to the end of the outdoor market and give you a tour."

Gingrilin raised one brow.

Doli continued. "I know of a booth where we can all get a manicure, courtesy of a talented fairy."

"That wasn't on our list, but—" Uldrick said.

"But it sounds good," Jez cut in. " Now, how about you two either grab a book here and relax or find something else on your list you can do without Doli?"

"We do have a long list." Doli's mother produced it again from her pocket.

"Then you definitely need to cross some things off." Ervash stepped toward them. "I'll see you both out the back."

Before they could even get in a word, the orc had already herded them down the hall. But he turned to glance back at Doli as he did it.

Thank you, she mouthed, then looked out the window at the throng.

Doli pushed Evvy's nose back into the sling and turned to Jez. "This little girl needs a snack."

18

After that fiasco, the dwarf decided that since the town knew about Evvy anyway, it was probably better to acclimate everyone to her presence rather than having people crowd the bookstore. Trying to keep the secret was futile.

Doli walked through the outdoor market with her parents. Unease had settled into her stomach, not only at the prospect of an outing with her mother and father but also because she had Evvy—with a full belly, of course—in her sling.

The only things that gave her some measure of comfort were the fact that people had calmed down slightly and that Ervash walked in front of them with his shirt off, displaying his back tattoos and large muscles. The orc was as gentle as a lamb, but his presence, particularly without a shirt, was commanding if he wanted it to be. Jez slunk behind them, growling at anyone who even seemed to look at Doli wrong or tried to approach or touch Evvy without permission.

Verdreth had stayed behind at the shop since a handful of people had taken him up on his sale.

The group did get plenty of stares. Doli had released one of the sling's buttons so Evvy's cute face could stick out and she could watch the market. But with Jez and Ervash acting as bodyguards, no one made the kind of fuss they'd seen at the bookstore a couple of hours before.

"What did you want to see, Mother?" Doli asked Gingrilin as she gave Evvy a pat on the head.

The sights at the market were like a rainbow. There were booths full of brightly colored fabrics that Doli had a hard time resisting when she had her mind set on sewing a new dress. Then there was the honey seller with their jars of golden liquid and beeswax candles, and the farmers' carts overflowing with sweet fruits and savory vegetables of all sizes.

As usual, the air was filled with the aroma of smoked meats, some of which could be enjoyed on a stick with an assortment of sweet and savory sauces.

"I'm actually a bit peckish." Uldrick gazed around at the offerings and homed in on a cart with giant smoked turkey legs. Before anyone could respond, his legs had already carried him halfway to his potential snack, and he'd brought out a few coins from his pocket to pay for it.

"Want anything?" He turned around, beard braids swinging, and shouted to his wife and daughter.

Evvy whined, but Doli shook her head. "I'll get you some trout sticks," she said to the dragon, not wanting to deal with the gigantic turkey leg.

The little dragon licked her lips and seemed satisfied with the offer.

"No, dear," Gingrilin called back to him. "I'm saving room." She rubbed her hand over her stomach, showing off the gold rings on most of her fingers, and Uldrick turned back to the seller and exchanged the coins for the turkey leg. As he walked back to them, the leg was so big the dwarf seemed to have a bit of trouble managing it, but somehow he kept upright.

"Your father." The dwarf matriarch shook her head but managed a toothy grin when he returned to her.

Doli was thankful that her parents seemed in a good mood. They hadn't said anything yet that had insulted her friends or made her cringe. She gazed around, looking for the fairy's nail art booth, and thought she might have spotted it in the next row.

"I think that's where we want to g—" Doli turned back to find her mother with a mouthful of turkey.

Gingrilin stood on her toes and looked in the direction Doli was pointing. "Yes, dear," she said, still chewing.

Doli caught Ervash's and Jez's attention and gestured to where they were going.

"Mind if we stop at Arleta's booth before you get your nails done?" Ervash asked. "She's supposed to have those blackberry custard rolls today." The orc licked his lips.

"Ooh, those sound like what I was saving room for," Gingrilin said through another mouthful of turkey.

"Save some for me." Doli's father took back the turkey leg from his wife's hands and gave her a little scowl. Half of it was already gnawed to the bone.

"It's on the way," Doli said, catching a glimpse of the A Little Dash of Magic Bake Shop booth. According to Arleta, it always had a much better location than it had before she had competed in the Langheim Baking Battle.

Thankfully, since the market was closing in an hour or so, the crowds had dwindled. But that didn't stop people from noticing Evvy.

"That's the dwarf with the dragon." A gnome carrying a basket full of colorful produce walked past them with a group of her gnome friends. They all craned their necks to look at Doli until Jez gave them a hiss. Then the bunch scurried off, dropping two apples in their wake.

By the time they'd reached A Little Dash of Magic, both Doli's parents had bought large bags of sweetened popcorn and munched away on the crispy treats. The stripped turkey leg had been discarded, but not before Uldrick had fed Evvy the last bite.

Of course it wasn't Arleta or Taenya selling at the booth, but Theo, with his back turned as he rummaged in the wagon for fresh stock. To Doli's surprise, Faylin had joined him, and instead of napping, the gray and white striped forest lynx stood on his hind legs with his front paws up on the table.

"Afternoon, Doli," he said with a yawn, looking at the dwarf and then at her parents. "And whoever the rest of you are." His dark striped tail swiped behind him.

Theo turned from the wagon to the group. Ervash had already reached across the display table with his long arms and was helping himself to the fresh blackberry rolls inside the wagon.

Evvy wailed at the orc while Jez stood with her back to the group, blocking anyone who might get too close.

The elf briefly looked the orc up and down. "Help yourself there, Dad. But save some for the dragon."

Ervash allowed his lips to quirk into a half grin. "You don't get to call me 'Dad,' elf." He stuffed a whole blackberry roll into his mouth, and a little bit of the custard on top oozed over his tusk.

"Yes, sir," Theo said, humoring the orc and bringing the tips of his fingers to his temple as in a salute.

"Better." He swallowed the roll and gave Theo a wink.

Doli knew it was all a joke between them. The orcs really loved Theo and found him a good match for Arleta, whom they did regard as their daughter. But it seemed they liked to play a little game as if they were very protective of her, which of course they were.

By this time Faylin had jumped up on the table between the two remaining loaves of sourdough bread and the sparse chocolate chip cookie display. He rounded twice, laid down on the tablecloth and curled his tail around his body.

Theo paused with a box of cookies in his hands and scanned the table. "I guess I'll find someplace else to lay these."

"Good idea," Faylin said, not even opening his eyes. "I'm exhausted from all this selling."

"What can I get you all?" Theo said as he arranged the cookies not too far from Faylin. "On the house, but I can't guarantee anything will be without lynx hair."

Faylin flicked his tufted ear and muttered, "All the more delicious."

"We're here for the custard rolls," Doli's mother spoke up and eyed Ervash, who had several of the pastries balanced in one hand and picked out more with his other. "If there are any left."

Theo grinned, turned, and gathered another box filled with custard buns. "I had Arleta send over extra because they've been such a big seller today. I didn't want to run out before the end of the market." The elf held it out to them and showed off the colorful spiral rolls with a generous dollop of creamy vanilla custard in the middle of each.

Gingrilin's eyes grew large, and her husband stepped up next to her. She still had her bag of popcorn tucked under one arm.

"We'll take two," Doli said before her parents could place an order, but Evvy squealed from the sling. She had wriggled one of her front legs out of the opening and was waving it toward the box of rolls. "Three," the dwarf conceded. "But to go."

The little dragon hissed and showed off her gummy mouth at Doli while Theo prepared the order.

"I agree with Evvy." Gingrilin sighed and returned to eating her popcorn.

"Don't want your fingers too sticky for the manicure," Doli said as Theo handed her the takeaway box of rolls. She looked down at the dragon, who was still hissing. "The trout sticks are right over there. I'll get you extra. *Then* you can have the roll."

Evvy gave her one last hiss and settled back into the sling.

"Thank you," Doli said to Theo as he handed her the box.

He bowed his head slightly. "You are always welcome." The elf saluted Ervash one more time as the orc stuffed another roll into his mouth.

"I'll be back for the leftovers," Ervash said, munching his snack.

Theo waved him away and said, "I'll just drop them on your porch."

"Even better." The orc grinned around his mouthful of pastry and gestured the group on.

As they were leaving, Theo handed Jez a cookie, and she gave Faylin a scratch on the cheek. The lynx purred loudly, then resumed his nap.

"He's nice," Uldrick said while sidling up to his daughter and eating a handful of popcorn from his bag.

"Theo is very nice," she said, maintaining a tight grip on the box containing the custard rolls. "We met at the Baking Battle."

Her father eyed the box. "You sure I can't have one of those yet? I won't tell your mother."

Doli could feel her mother's stare nearly burning a hole in the back of her head. She grinned and pointed to the smoked and dried meats booth. "I still need to get Evvy her snack."

At the booth, she bought a full bag of trout sticks for Evvy.

"She's adorable." The centaur gazed down at Evvy as he handed Doli her order. "Does she want anything else?"

The dwarf glanced down at the dragon, whose eyes seemed about triple their normal size. Doli threw her hand over Evvy's face. "I'm sure she does…but she's charming you."

"She most certainly is," the seller said in a dreamy voice as his horse tail swished behind him.

"As with magic!" Doli chuckled, keeping her hand over Evvy's face.

The centaur shook his head and glanced down at the little dragon again. "Well, stars." He shrugged and handed her a strip of sweet and spicy beef.

Which Evvy downed in three bites and licked her lips vigorously.

"Apparently she likes it. We'll get that next time," Doli said to the centaur. She took the bag and handed Evvy a stick from inside. "Pace yourself."

She didn't.

After the dried meat stop, where everyone else had also managed samples, they finally made it to the fairy's stall.

It was brightly decorated with green vines growing out of nowhere and covered with a rainbow of flowers. Doli inhaled the sweet fragrances of flowers she couldn't identify since they were either entirely magic or from a part of the Northern Lands she hadn't visited. The inside of the booth looked like an enchanted garden, where more flowers grew in the air and several large red and white spotted toadstool mushrooms waited for customers to sit on. Music wafted out even though there were no musicians to be seen. The sign, CHARMED ARTISTRY, sparkled with magic.

Despite the decadence of the booth, the fairy sat alone, perched on a small swing with the ropes made of the same vines growing everywhere else in the space. The fairy was dressed in a tiny pink, purple, and yellow chiffon dress.

Doli's mind was already at work trying to figure out how she might sew something similar for herself, juxtaposed with the desire to make the unhappy-looking fairy feel better.

"This is really something," Doli's mother was the first one to say. Her eyes roamed around the display as she finished up her last bit of popcorn.

"I'll say," Doli agreed.

The little fairy looked up, sadder than Doli had even expected. "I'm about to close."

"Oh," the dwarf said. "We were all hoping to have you work your magic on us." She held out her hands, displaying the tattered nails she'd been ignoring for several weeks.

"Oh," the fairy said in her high-pitched voice and ran her tiny hand through her rainbow-streaked hair. "Are you here for nails? Because I don't sell magic charms. People have been making that mistake all day."

Each of them, all but Jez, bobbed their heads up and down. Including Ervash.

"I'm just gonna watch," Jez said as she leaned against the side of the booth and munched her cookie loaded with chocolate chunks. But the glint in her eye told Doli that even the fennex might be interested in some nail art.

The little fairy clapped her hands together, flew off the swing seat, and hovered in the air. Her wings glittered as they swept back and forth to keep her in place. "I'm new and no one really understands what I offer. How did you know about me?"

"River Goldendew sent me," Doli said, and she smiled at the fairy's excitement. "I saw their nails and thought the work looked amazing."

"Oh, River," she said and waved her hand out. "They are the sweetest sibling. I'm Iris." She gestured to one of the toadstools. "Please, please have a seat." Then she looked up at Ervash. "I don't think I have quite enough room for you, though."

The orc shook his head. "I'm fine waiting out here." He took out another custard roll and popped it into his mouth. Apparently sticky fingers weren't a concern for him.

Gingrilin leaned in close to Doli and asked, "How come he gets to eat them now?"

Doli smiled and blinked several times. "Have a seat, Mother."

"Yes, yes." Iris flew down and patted the stool. "Let's get started."

For once the matriarch dwarf did as she was told without another word as Iris flicked her hand and produced a magical display of nail art options in the air. There were rainbows, sparkles, tiny flowers, and even some plainer designs. Each one was better than the next.

"So many choices," Uldrick said and pointed to one. It instantly displayed on his index finger as a sample. "Oh, that's fabulous!"

Doli's mother made her choice, as did the others, and Iris excitedly went to work. Each of them ended up with a masterpiece on their nails, even Evvy. The fairy had conjured the perfect shade of pink—and a shade darker than the dragon's body.

"After a week or so, the pattern will simply fade," Iris said, admiring her work. "And you can come back again."

Gingrilin took her daughter's arm as they both studied their multicolored nails. "Adenashire has turned out to be a pretty nice place."

Doli grinned. "It is, Mother. It is."

Ervash left the fairy with a generous tip and a custard bun…and that was a big compliment. "We'll be back and make sure to spread the word."

The five of them waved goodbye just as the market was closing, and even Jez was admiring her nails, which were black as coal with a hint of shimmer.

19

A cool breeze danced in the air as the group headed out of the market. They had barely passed the Tricky Goat, where the badgers sat out on the patio eating a late lunch. Evvy happily munched on another trout stick and admired her nails while half hanging from Doli's sling.

Doli gazed down at her own nails, happy with her choice and already planning another session to match a specific dress she owned. That day she'd chosen a delicate pink and yellow floral design that reminded her of spring. Something deep down inside hoped that she'd run into Sarson soon and he'd like it too.

Her parents walked ahead of them, chattering on about all the new foods they'd tried at the market. On the way out they'd filled a bag with fresh fruit and found a booth selling chocolate candies. Neither of them could resist a dozen filled confections. They'd already finished the custard buns after their manicures had been completed and of course fed Evvy hers despite Doli's insistence it was for after dinner.

"I think we can make it back to the bookstore," Doli said to Ervash, who walked beside her, still shirtless in the cooling air. The dwarf knew he had a meeting later that afternoon with a well-off halfling looking to commission a painting for his living room wall.

"Are you sure?" the orc asked, looking around. "I have time to stay with you."

They had been still getting a few looks from the people of Adenashire on the street, but no one was trying to crowd them anymore to get a peek at the baby dragon. It almost seemed as if they'd moved on to whatever the next piece of exciting news was that afternoon.

"Jez is with us," the dwarf said, glancing over her shoulder at the fennex. Jez was still examining her black nails, a near smile curling at the corners of her lips. "And if someone tries to bother us, I'll just get my mother going on the topic of unicorns again."

Ervash chuckled, the sound rumbling deep in his throat. "I do need to head home first to grab a shirt."

Doli nodded and eyed the orc's hairless and muscular chest. There was no doubt to anyone who looked at him that Ervash took good care of himself, despite all the pastry consumption. "Good plan."

With that, Ervash bid goodbye to Doli and the others,

patted Evvy on the head, and headed toward his and Verdreth's cottage.

Doli's father turned back to her, licking chocolate off his fingers. "What do you have for lunch?"

"Lunch?" Doli stopped in her tracks for a beat and then continued down the cobblestone street behind her parents. She'd hoped they had gotten their fill of snacks at the market and had forgotten all about a formal meal.

Gingrilin slowed her pace to wait for her daughter as she munched on an apple. "It's past lunchtime." The statement was a matter of fact as if *why would anyone forget about lunch*?

Doli blew out a slow breath while considering everything they'd eaten at the market. But they had not sat down and eaten an actual meal, so she supposed she was expected to serve one back at the apartment like a good host. She hoped her parents were at least not expecting anything too grand since back at Dundes Heights, that is exactly what the meal would have been.

She thought for a moment and deliberately kept her tone bland. "I suppose we have bread and some meat and cheese in the cold box," Doli said, half hoping they might decide to go to the Tricky Goat instead. "Nothing fancy."

But instead, Uldrick popped a chocolate in his mouth and said, "Sounds delicious. I'm starving."

"Yes, dear," Gingrilin agreed. "All this walking has made me positively famished."

Doli looked back at Jez, hoping for some kind of support, but received none. Only a shrug.

"I'm hungry too," said the fennex, not helping at all.

"Sandwiches it is," Doli said with a smile and bubbles in her tone. Her parents went back to chatting and polishing off the rest of their purchases.

It wasn't long before the bookstore was in sight. As the four of them climbed the steps, a tall, thin human came around the side of the building. He carried a basket as if he'd also been at the market.

Evvy stopped chewing on her current trout stick.

"A Fervour dragon?" he said in a surprised tone of voice.

Doli was instantly on alert. There was nothing unusual about the man, who had ash-blond hair graying at the temples, but she hadn't seen him around the village before, and she knew a lot of the residents, at least by face. He wore blue linen pants with fly stitching around the hem. If she remembered correctly, it was a popular fashion in the Lower Ocean area. Perhaps he was visiting someone.

Jez came right up behind Doli. The dwarf was grateful for her presence.

Her instincts urged her to run inside and lock all the doors, but someone asking a question shouldn't be a big deal. She gazed up at Jez. "It's okay." She turned back to the man and nodded. "She *is* a Fervour dragon."

He pursed his lips while looking over Evvy. The little dragon had finished her trout stick and pulled her head back slightly, as if she didn't really enjoy being stared at by the stranger.

"They're rare, right?" He raised his attention to Doli.

Doli took a step back, her discomfort intensifying. But the feeling wasn't just her own—it came from Evvy, as if she could sense the dragon's uneasy emotional state. "Yes…sir, they are."

Jez placed her hands on Doli's shoulders, giving the dwarf a start.

"We'd better be heading inside," Jez said and turned Doli toward the door again.

"Is she for sale?" the man blurted out.

Doli's eyes widened and she rounded on the man in shock. "No, Evvy is not for sale! Why would you even ask such a thing?"

He shrugged. "Everything has a price."

"We're going now." The fennex steered Doli firmly right past her mother, who'd been gaping at the exchange, and flung open the door. She pushed Doli into the shop and waved her nonplussed parents through. The man made as though to climb the steps and follow, but Jez bared her teeth and growled at him.

"Can't blame a person for asking," he called before the door shut in his face.

Gingrilin huffed. "The nerve of that man. We need to keep Evvy in the family."

Doli frowned. *What did she mean by that?*

But before she could say anything, Ervash came around the corner of a bookcase and pushed his spectacles up the bridge of his nose. "Oh, it's you all." He looked more closely at Doli. "What's wrong?"

Doli held Evvy, who was more than half out of the sling, tight in her arms and didn't say a word. Her stomach was roiling. *Was it too soon to take Evvy out into Adenashire?* She'd certainly made a mistake.

"Some guy out there tried to buy Evvy," Jez said while

leaning against the doorframe, pointing her thumb out the window.

Ervash strode quickly to the window. "Who?" He looked up and down the street. "I don't see anyone."

"And we were having such a pleasant time," Uldrick grumbled and held his empty market bag upside down. Nothing came out.

Doli gulped and lifted her hand from the dragon's back. Evvy wriggled her wings free of the sling then took flight, landing on the top of the highest bookshelf. She immediately stuck her back leg high in the air and began licking it.

"I hadn't seen him before," Doli said. "I think he might have been from the south."

Verdreth pursed his lips. "Well. He seems to be gone now."

The dwarf swallowed past a lump in her throat. All she really wanted, and even more than before, was to be alone.

"I guess it's nothing a hearty lunch won't solve." Uldrick draped his arm around Doli's shoulders and led her toward the stairs.

Steeling herself, Doli waved for Evvy to come, and thankfully the little dragon listened. She eyed Verdreth and said, "The human was tall, thin, blondish, and wore a pair of blue linen pants. If he tries to come in…"

Verdreth nodded. "I'll keep him away." He continued looking out the window.

Knowing Verdreth would keep to his word, she climbed the stairs with her parents and Jez tailing them up to the second-floor apartment.

"This is...*cozy*," Gingrilin said as the four of them entered. But the tone of her voice wasn't positive, and it set Doli's teeth on edge, especially after the strange man's offer to buy Evvy. Her eyes went to the ugly vase on the counter. "Was that Thorras's?"

Doli nodded. "It was in the inheritance box."

"Oh, lovely," Gingrilin said. She walked directly into the center of the living room and slowly spun around. "I suppose that's the tour."

"At least we can get to lunch more quickly," Doli said with a hint of sarcasm in her voice, but fully wanting to say something with more bite.

"Here, here." Her father either hadn't noticed Doli's irony or didn't care much since he was already in the kitchen scanning the space. "You said you have a cold box?"

Evvy perched on the edge of the counter and let out a long, squeaky chortle. Apparently she was ready for lunch too.

Jez slunk over and silently took out a loaf of bread and a knife. She pushed them into Uldrick's grasp. "You slice that." She drew Doli's step stool to the counter with her foot. "Stand there."

The dwarf stepped back and tipped his head in confusion, then quickly recovered and took the bread and knife. He climbed up onto the step stool and went to work as the fennex opened and dug through the cold box.

Doli turned back to her mother. "Yes, the place is small, Mother. But I'm happy here. Honestly, I'm happier than I've ever been in my entire life." But the statement was true and not true. In Adenashire Doli felt freer but still conflicted after so many years of having to hide who she was. Sometimes it still seemed like if she revealed everything about herself, people might not like her.

Gingrilin wrinkled her nose. "I'll admit, your father and I had a nice time at the market today." She gazed around again. "But how can this place make you happy long term? You know your sisters—"

"I *don't* want to hear about my sisters," Doli snapped.

Evvy raised her body up high and flapped her wings, shrieking loudly.

"Dolgrila—" her mother scolded.

"No." Doli stamped her foot. "I thought we'd had a nice day. But you had to come up here and ruin it. Everyone but me has lived up to your expectations, and I'm tired of walking around acting happy and pretending that I don't care what people think of me."

Her mother opened her mouth, but Doli didn't give her the chance to speak.

"I don't want to go back to Dundes Heights. I don't care what Brudela and Whurigret are doing, how they are following in the family footsteps in the gem business. I don't care how much gold they're making or how many grandchildren they've given you."

Out of the corner of Doli's eye she could see her father frozen in the middle of cutting the bread. Jez had retrieved a roasted chicken from the cold box and held it in her palm, not moving. And Gingrilin stood before Doli, hands on her hips, cheeks puffed out and looking like she was about to blow.

"Your father and I are just trying to help," Gingrilin said, finally managing to get a word in edgewise.

But the second the words exited her mother's mouth, Doli's chest burned with anger. She grabbed the hideous vase from her uncle with several wilting flowers inside and turned it upside down. The flowers fell out, and water splashed to the floor. She raised the vase up in the air.

"You wouldn't dare," Gingrilin said. "That's been in the family for years."

"Try me," Doli snarled, tightening her grip on the neck of the vase.

Jez scurried out from behind the counter, chicken still in hand, and faster than Doli had ever seen the fennex move. "I think lunch is over."

"But we didn't eat anything," Uldrick moaned.

Doli seethed. "Father, I think you've had plenty today."

"It's *to go*." Jez snatched several slices of bread and thrust those and the whole chicken into Doli's father's hands.

"Dolgrila!" her mother shrieked.

"To go?" Uldrick said, confusion peppering his tone.

But Jez quickly herded him and Doli's mother toward the door. She quickly picked up the blanket belonging to them and shoved it over his shoulder, avoiding the chicken.

His eyes lit up. "Oh, I'd forgotten about this."

"Everyone is so rude in this town," Gingrilin complained but didn't struggle against the fennex.

Doli, still wide-eyed and holding the vase in the air, turned to watch Jez open the door and escort her parents out, the chicken and bread slices still in her father's hands.

When the door shut, their complaining voices could be heard all the way down the stairs.

Frustrated and unable to help herself, Doli chucked the vase against the door. The glass smashed and rained shards across the wood-planked flooring.

"Damn it." The dwarf fell into a heap on the ground, sobbing. Evvy flew down to her, settled into her lap, and curled into a ball. The little dragon gently nuzzled against Doli's arm. The dwarf couldn't help but feel like things would never be quite right in her life.

That *she* wasn't quite right.

20

The rest of the day and night had been horrible. Doli had tossed and turned with the urge to run over to the inn and apologize to her parents…as a good people pleaser should.

But she didn't.

Instead, remembering her promise to Sarson, she snuck out with Evvy before lunch and went to see him. Each step made her feel a little bit lighter.

A little rebellious.

Doli wore her prettiest, frilliest dress that day. She wished she'd had time to sew a dwarf-sized version of Iris's fairy dress, but with Evvy there had been no time for sewing, of course. So what she had in her closet had to do.

The dress she'd chosen had a yellow daisy print on the

skirt and a solid butter-yellow top with flowy, off the shoulder sleeves. The neckline was cut a little low, but not too low for picnicking. A thick brown leather belt cinched her waist, and gold hoop earrings dangled from her ears. Doli had twisted her curly locks atop her head and allowed a tendril of hair to fall over each side of her face. She'd checked herself in the mirror before she left and spritzed herself with vanilla. The thought of spending an afternoon with Sarson had given her dark complexion a fabulous glow.

Plus, her nails looked amazing.

Just humming a tune from her childhood as she walked down the path to the gargoyle's cottage, something about the day seemed brighter, lovelier than the last time she'd been there.

"Now, you're going to be a good dragon, right?" Doli looked down at Evvy, who had her head poking out of the sling, one scaly arm playing with the necklace the dwarf wore.

Evvy didn't answer, but a sense washed over Doli that the dragon would do her best.

"I guess that's all I can ask." The dwarf ran her hand over the top of Evvy's tiny horns, which were sharp at the tips.

Her heart thudded in her chest as she got closer to his home. Part of her didn't know if she'd even be able to knock on the door, with her nerves roiling in her stomach. Picnicking could have just been what Sarson said it was: a way to help Evvy. It also could have been a date. Until she got there, she wouldn't know.

Whatever it turned out to be, it was a good way to avoid her family.

Over her arm she carried a bag containing a dozen of her jam spice cookies she'd stored in the cold box. It was her way of bringing a bit of the courage her grammy would have wanted her to have. She had been a great romantic as well—and probably would have had a few cheeky lines about Sarson and his physique.

The thought made her giggle and press on. The cute little cottage finally came into view, and something about it was simply so homey that Doli relaxed and picked up the pace.

The curtain in the window to the left of the door fluttered, and not a second later did the door open to a smiling gargoyle.

Doli's breath nearly left her upon seeing him. His dark hair was neatly combed, accentuating his two curved horns, and he wore a smart outfit of light purple linen pants held up by a mottled brown leather belt, matching shoes, and a crisp white cotton shirt with pearly buttons down the front. His dark blue wings were tucked neatly behind him.

"Hello," he said, a wide smile showing off his fangs as he took in her appearance. "You are so lovely."

"Thank you." The acceptance came out more softly than she would have liked, and she had the urge to admit she wanted to wear a different dress. But she wisely kept that fact to herself.

Evvy wiggled inside the sling and gave a high-pitched whine.

"Yes, yes," Doli said to the little dragon. "We're here to play." She looked up at the gargoyle and asked, "May I let her out?"

He chuckled. "As you said, that's what we're here for."

The dwarf carefully unbuttoned the sling, and Evvy immediately pushed through the opening, her iridescent wings unfurling right into Doli's face. She quickly threw up her hands to guide the dragon out into the air, where Evvy did four flips and dashed off to smell some flower bushes near the porch.

"I think she needed this," Doli said as she watched the little dragon dive after a tiny insect.

"It seems so."

Doli gave the gargoyle an appreciative look, impressed with his appearance and attention to detail. "I love the buttons on your shirt," she said as she stepped up onto the stoop to get a closer look.

Sarson grazed his fingers over the buttons, then bent his knee and gently lowered himself to be closer to Doli's height. "Would you like to see them?"

The gesture brought warmth to Doli's chest. "Yes, of course!"

The craftsmanship of the buttons was exquisite. Each one was hand-carved with its own unique design.

"They're made from shells from the Sea of the Somerdows," the gargoyle said, looking down at them. "They were my grandfather's…passed down to me. I sewed them onto this shirt myself."

Doli's attention slid from the buttons to Sarson's face. There was something especially tender in his tone. "Were you close?"

"My grandfather and I?" He paused for a moment. "You can say that. We were very much alike. I inherited his position."

Doli tipped her head in interest. "His position?"

Sarson cleared his throat as if he'd said too much. "Yes. But that's for another time." His lips pressed shut and he cast his eyes down just a little bit.

The dwarf bubbled with curiosity, but sensing his discomfort, she returned her attention to the buttons and reached out to touch one. "Well, they are beautiful. He must have had great taste."

"He did." Sarson gazed down at Doli's hands and his eyes brightened. "Your nails!"

Doli smiled shyly. "I had them done yesterday at the market."

He couldn't stop staring at them. "I love them."

"Thank you." Doli took the bag from her shoulder. "I brought you some more of those cookies…my *grandmother's* recipe."

Sarson rose and his eyes lit with excitement. "The jam spice cookies? Those were amazing."

"The very ones." Right as Doli spoke the words, Evvy was back on the porch with her hands clasped in front of her, tongue lolling from her mouth. Obviously asking for a cookie.

Sarson chuckled. "I have something for you, little one." He brought out a perfectly sliced apple wrapped in a fabric napkin and held it out to the dragon.

Evvy's golden eyes sparkled with delight. She flew up to his hand and took two slices, immediately stuffing the first entirely in her mouth like a chipmunk.

"There's plenty more," Sarson said, nodding toward the tree in front of his cottage. "Pace yourself."

Doli chuckled. "Good luck with that."

Evvy had already retrieved two more slices from his outstretched hand. She downed the first but took a bit more time munching the second.

"I read last night that Fervour dragons love fruit," Sarson said as he gestured both Doli and Evvy inside.

Doli followed his lead. "I don't doubt it," she said, thinking of all the fruit pastries the dragon had devoured in the last couple of days. Enough to nearly put Arleta and Taenya out of business if she didn't slow down.

Once they were inside, Sarson tossed Evvy the last of the apple and pocketed the napkin. "I have everything ready." He led them to the back of the house, where a large basket with a handle sat waiting on the counter next to a large bottle of expensive dark amber rum.

"Jez would love that." Doli pointed to the bottle.

Sarson chuckled, the sound rich. "I should hope so. She's the one who brought it."

The dwarf's eyes widened, and she looked around the space. "Jez has been here. When?" The fennex had said nothing about it.

"Oh…after she was on my porch to fetch you." He leaned against the wooden counter. "To apologize."

Doli's heart warmed for her friend, who'd come back without any extra prompting. "What did you make?" she asked, standing on her toes, eager to see what was inside, but the basket was too high up.

The gargoyle grinned and picked up the basket, along with a folded plaid blanket resting beside the back door on a wooden chair. "It's a surprise."

"Oh." Doli interlaced her fingers while Evvy buzzed around Sarson, trying to get a look inside the basket.

"It's a surprise for you too," the gargoyle admonished the little dragon playfully.

"Let's go," Doli said, barely able to contain herself, and left Sarson's spice cookies on the counter for him to enjoy later. "Don't keep us waiting."

Sarson bowed. "My ladies. I'm at your service." He righted himself and opened the back door. His outdoor kitchen looked like it had exploded with picnic preparations. There were dirty pots, dishes, and half a cut loaf of bread.

"Don't mind that," Sarson quickly said and walked in front of her before she could take in whatever else had been going on. "That's where all the *magic* took place." He hefted the basket and winked.

At this point Doli really didn't care what was in that basket. It was obvious that Sarson had put a lot of work into whatever it was…and had a lot to clean up later. "I'm sure it will be lovely."

"You get to be the judge," he said, leading them out to a path behind his cottage. Evvy flew in and out between the two of them, then raced on ahead.

Tall grass flanked them as they trod the dirt path, so Doli couldn't see much of what was ahead of her, but she had a full view of Evvy's display.

"She really is enjoying herself," Doli said as she watched the dragon flying high above them. Whenever she seemed to get too high, she would flip around and dive toward the earth, pulling up at the last possible moment.

"Dragons need their freedom," Sarson said. "Even baby ones."

Doli let out a long breath. "That's why she could never really stay with me forever."

The gargoyle shrugged. "It's true. But what you have now is meant to be. I have no doubt about that."

Not long after, the path widened and opened up to the pond, which was absolutely the loveliest view she'd seen in a long time. The water's banks were mostly clear of the grass, and several tall oak trees turning golden shaded the water. Floating on the surface were large lily pads, and several frogs croaked in the distance.

"I've heard about this place but have never been here," Doli said, her eyes taking in the beauty. "You're so lucky to have it right behind your cottage."

Sarson nodded. "I come out here to read, then watch fireflies when it gets dark."

The thought of it stretched Doli's lips into a wide smile. "I'd love that."

"Then you are welcome to come back some evening." Sarson grinned, his tail swaying behind him, and held up the basket. "That is, if you like my cooking."

"Oh yes. Only then." As she said it, Evvy skimmed across the water, snatched a dragonfly in her mouth, and swallowed it whole. "Speaking of lunch."

"You know *that's* not what I have in here," Sarson said with amusement and walked closer to the shore.

"What a shame. I was so looking forward to dragonfly sandwiches," Doli said, following him.

As he spread out the green and brown plaid blanket, he smiled. "Next time, then."

Overhead, unseen birds chirped in the trees while Doli helped Sarson arrange the blanket and smooth out the corners. They both stood and watched as Evvy dove under the water, came up with a small fish, and swallowed it whole, just like she had the dragonfly.

Doli shook her head and brought her attention to the basket sitting behind them. "So, what did you bring?"

The gargoyle brought up his index finger, sat on the blanket, and patted a spot, indicating Doli to do the same. She did and spread out her floral dress around her. For a second, the action seemed to catch Sarson's attention, but he quickly brought it back to the basket.

From inside he brought out two paper-wrapped sandwiches, one dwarf-sized and the other gargoyle-sized. Each was loaded with a thick slice of fresh, creamy white cheese, tomatoes, and what appeared to be basil leaves.

"I didn't know if you liked a particular type of meat or even ate it at all, so I went with this." Sarson held out the sandwich to Doli.

"I do—eat meat, that is—but this looks amazing." Doli took the sandwich, delighted by the vivid red and green colors.

"The bread is from your friend's bakery," he said as he unwrapped his own sandwich and took a bite before he laid it down and continued unloading the basket. "So, at least that will be good."

Doli took a bite, and the tangy, tomatoey flavor burst in

her mouth. "This tomato is delicious!" The sandwich also had a creamy basil spread on each side of the pillowy bread, making a decadent combination of flavors.

"I have a greenhouse on the other side of the cottage," he said as he brought out a green bottle of sparkling wine and two cups, along with a basket of cut fruit and two small chocolate candies in a tiny woven basket. "It still had a few tomatoes growing in it from summer, as well as the fresh herbs."

"What are those?" Doli's attention wavered between the sparkling wine and chocolate.

Sarson held up the wine first. "Well, I brought a few bottles with me from the Ridgelands. For special occasions." Then he eyed the chocolate. "And I've been working on my chocolatier skills. I'm new at it, but I enjoy the hobby. Other than myself, you'll be the first to weigh in."

Doli leaned in closer to the chocolate. The milky roasted aroma hit her nose and she immediately held out her hand. "May I?"

Sarson chuckled. "Who am I to tell anyone they shouldn't have dessert first? Be my guest." He leaned in closer to her and took a deep breath. The corner of his lips turned upward. "Is that vanilla?"

Doli gulped and brought her hand to her neck. "It's my perfume."

"It's my favorite scent in the Northern Lands." Sarson held out the chocolate to Doli, not taking his eyes from her.

A little flustered, the dwarf salivated as she chose the piece nearest to her, brought it to her mouth, and bit it in half. Inside was a chewy golden caramel that slightly stretched when she pulled it away. The slightly salty, sweet flavor complemented by the creamy chocolate melted over her tongue. "That's heaven." She popped the rest in her mouth and looked up at Sarson, who seemed pleased with himself.

She suddenly realized that either she had sat closer to him than she thought, or he'd somehow edged in without her noticing. Her heart pounded in her chest from both the sweet chocolate and her proximity to the handsome gargoyle. "Delicious," she managed.

He licked his lips, and Doli's head spun with dizziness as she was pretty sure he might be leaning in for a kiss.

This was it. She was ready.

Until something cold, wet, and flopping dropped dead center in the middle of her lap. She jerked back and screamed as the thing flailed and flopped its way onto the blanket next to her. It was a small golden fish, opening its mouth wide and gasping for air.

Doli flicked her wide-eyed gaze to Sarson and then up in the air, where Evvy hovered with a guilty look on her face and then dove off again like a fiend, completely unapologetic.

Sarson and Doli looked back at each other and broke into laughter. Sarson grabbed the fish and tossed it back into the pond. He wiped his hand on a cloth napkin from the basket and handed Doli a cup.

"How about a little wine?" he asked, still grinning.

She rolled her eyes at the silly dragon…and the possibly

ruined moment. But Doli's heart bubbled with the thought of the wine fizzing on her tongue. It had been so long since she'd drunk any. "I think I'm going to need more than a little after that."

Sarson obliged.

21

And for the next couple days, the stars seemed to align.

Doli's parents had been crossing off their to-do list on their own, and when they were with their daughter, they didn't mention the vase incident. That, and she was able to get away another time to Sarson's cottage to get Evvy some more exercise. The dwarf loved the challenge of being Evvy's guardian and for once thought everything might come together. Plus, her relationship with Sarson was blossoming, and spending more time with him was a joy. But she hadn't officially introduced him to any of her friends.

Or her parents.

That day at the bakery, Taenya had already gone home

and the CLOSED sign was on the door, but not before Doli and Evvy had stopped in to see her friends.

"I'm glad you stopped in since it saves me a trip to find you," Arleta said while wiping down the counter. "After I close up you should come over to the cottage. Tonight Ervash is cooking, and Theo and I are going to join them out in the garden."

Doli sat next to Theo, who'd arrived a few minutes before Doli to walk Arleta home. She looked up from the book she'd recently started, *The Minotaur and I*. So far it wasn't her favorite, but she was just glad to be reading again. A cup of steaming mint tea waited in front of her.

"Hmm?" the dwarf said, and Evvy barely stirred from her nap on the tabletop, seeming tuckered out from an afternoon of chasing and devouring winged insects.

"Dinner?" Arleta asked and leaned her elbows on the counter, eyebrows raised.

"Oh," Doli said, placing the book down on the table. "My parents are still here."

"Don't let that stop you," Theo said and laced his fingers behind his head while leaning back in his seat. "This is Ervash. That means there'll be enough food to feed half of Adenashire." He stood, walked over to Arleta and held out his hand. "There will be dancing." He seemed to still be addressing Doli but looked at his Fated, a twinkle sparkling in his eye and a trace of green and gold magic coming from his fingertips.

Theo sometimes basically sweated magic…particularly around Arleta.

She gave him a shy smile and tucked a stray dark tendril of hair behind her ear. "I'm covered in flour."

Theo's lips raised into a half smile. "You know I don't care about those things."

Arleta laughed him off, gave Theo her hand, and did one spin. Afterward she quickly let go, waving him away. "That's all you get. For now." She shook her head, grinning, and proceeded to load a bag with the leftovers from the day. "You could also bring Sarson. Jez and Tae are coming too."

"Sarson?" Doli's voice cracked a little at the end of the name.

Before she had a chance to say anything else, the shop bell rang, and each of them looked up from what they were doing, including Evvy.

"I'm sorry, we're closed for the day," Arleta said to the lanky man standing in the doorway.

From her seat, Doli looked him up and down. He was middle-aged, with hair to his shoulders and gray streaks among the darker brown waves. He looked human, but judging by the star pattern tattoo peeking out from the collar of his tan linen shirt, Doli was pretty sure he might be a wizard. To know for sure she'd have to see the entire thing. But as far as she knew, he didn't live in Adenashire.

The possible wizard pursed his lips and glanced at the sign in the window. "Apologies. I didn't see the sign. It's been an eternal day of travel, and I'm here to meet with a friend."

"Maybe your friend has something for you," Arleta said, putting the bag of leftovers below the counter since they were probably for the dinner party and the orcs.

The man gave Arleta a quick smile. "He doesn't know I'm coming. It's a surprise."

"Well, I'm sure the Tricky Goat is open for the evening," Doli said. "You can get a hot meal there."

His ice blue gaze went immediately to Doli and then to Evvy, still lying on the table, eyes half open.

"A Fervour dragon?" the man said, straightening his back and stepping farther into the bakery. "I haven't seen one of those in many years. Where did you get it?" His breath picked up slightly.

Heat traveled from Doli's neck into her chest at his question. "The stars smiled on me," she managed to get out. She kept her tone light, but remembering the other stranger who'd offered to buy her said, "She's not for sale."

"Oh. Of course," he said while shaking his head. " But you are very lucky indeed, then," the man said, and he didn't take his eyes off Evvy.

Theo walked from the edge of the counter to him. "Since we can't help you, let me point you the way of the inn." He placed his hand out toward the man's shoulder and gestured him out of the bakery. "What was your name again?"

"Oh yes. Zanzidore Sunfire." He followed Theo's lead, and the two of them exited the bakery.

Doli and Arleta looked at each other. Arleta's last name was Starstone, and she was sometimes mistaken for a wizard. It was only an old family name…and an adoption was involved. But odds were, it meant this Zanzidore was indeed a wizard.

"That was a little odd," Arleta said as she pulled the bag of leftovers back out and rolled down the top.

"Yes." Discomfort still pricked at Doli's chest, but she shook it off. The stranger hadn't really done anything besides looking for pastries and expressing curiosity about Evvy—which most people did. But she couldn't be too careful. "You know, I think I will accept your invitation to dinner." She hopped down from the chair, finished her tea, and attached the cup to her holster. "It's about time that everyone officially met Sarson."

Nerves buzzed at Doli's chest as she walked up the path to the twin cottages in a quiet section of Adenashire, one inhabited by the orcs, the other by Arleta and Theo. The last of the day's sunlight gilded the gray buildings, with their tall, pointed straw roofs and forest green shutters framing the crisscross design windows. Below the windows were rows of lovely rose bushes.

Evvy lay napping in the sling over Doli's chest. The little dragon lounged on her back with her feet sticking out of the opening, nearly scratching the dwarf's chin several times on the walk over.

Her parents had said little on the way after they'd found out Sarson was coming to the dinner party—concerned he wasn't a dwarf, or perhaps having their own thoughts about gargoyles. But they had worn the finest they'd brought with them…so that meant something. Her father was clad in a matching velvet shirt and pants embroidered down the legs and sleeves with golden leaves and vines. His beard was twisted with matching golden ribbons, and he seemed to be wearing every piece of jewelry he'd brought. Her mother wore a burgundy gown of mixed velvet and silk with her hair coiled in an intricate style on top of her head. She had rings on each finger and two chunky gold necklaces adorned with multicolored jewels.

With all the treasure on display, Doli had the distinct urge to ask if they hadn't been worried about being robbed on the trip to see her. But she kept her mouth shut. She suspected that if she asked, then the unicorn situation would have been brought up again.

"A gargoyle?" Uldrick finally said. "Why would a gargoyle be living here in Adenashire?"

"He needed a change of scenery," Doli said and shuffled the bowl of green salad she'd made for the dinner.

"But why would anyone leave the Ridgelands to come *here*?" her mother asked. Then she looked at Doli half apologetically. "This place *is* very nice. We've gone on several tours the last few days…like the winery. But leaving the Ridgelands? I've heard rumors that the place is pure luxury."

Doli didn't answer. She was too busy picturing her parents overindulging at the winery and the scene they might have caused.

"Maybe he was banished!" Uldrick said.

Doli scoffed and waved her hand in the night air, snapping from her thoughts. "Father! He wasn't banished."

"Now dear," Gingrilin said, shaking her head. "You haven't really known him for that long. At least that's what you said."

Doli gritted her teeth and fought against the urge to toss the salad at her mother. But she wasn't in the mood for another ruined evening. "You're right. I haven't known him for very long." She pursed her lips for a beat. "Why don't you ask him about his story yourself tonight?" She kept her eyes on her father so as not to miss his reaction.

Her parents were particularly nosy people, but they never wanted to look that way. For them it was better to find out information the old-fashioned way: gossip and conjecture.

As she expected, the dwarf bristled and puffed up his shoulders, which were already exaggerated due to the padding sewn into the shoulders of his shirt. "Well, uh." He paused, looking a mite put off. "I may just do that."

Gingrilin and Uldrick turned to the door, but Doli waved them around the back of the house. "They'll all be in the garden already."

Her parents gave each other a look.

"No greeting or announcement?" Gingrilin said, her eyes large with slight offense.

Doli faked a smile. "They all know who you are, Mother. And we'll simply stand here knocking with no one to answer the door."

Uldrick huffed but wrapped his arm around his wife's waist and followed Doli.

When they rounded the house, golden magic lights strung from the two houses' roofs and into the garden lit the space like stars. For a moment, Doli was so enchanted that she nearly forgot her parents were behind her. Then her eyes settled on Sarson, who'd already arrived. The gargoyle wore a fancy white shirt with a small amount of ruffling at the neck. Finding the look entirely pleasing, her heart bubbled until her mother cleared her throat, bringing Doli squarely back into reality.

She was going to have to navigate the gargoyle and her family that evening, and who knew how *that* would turn out?

That was the exact moment Evvy woke and decided it was time to play. The baby dragon squealed at the sights and launched herself out of the sling. She zipped across the lights and then made a beeline to Arleta and Theo, who, as the elf had promised earlier, were dancing.

"Evvy!" Doli called, nearly dropping the salad but somehow catching the bowl before everything fell out.

Her mother tsked from behind her. Doli had absolutely no desire to hear what Gingrilin had to say.

"Ervash!" Doli waved her free hand and stood on her tippy toes, still clutching the salad bowl.

The orc stood over the food, arranging it just so. He wore a smart, simple white shirt, unbuttoned several times, and a pair of pressed tan cotton trousers. He looked up and smiled around his tusks. "Welcome."

She picked up her pace and drew ahead of her mother and father to deliver the salad. "Would you mind distracting my parents?" she said in a low voice the moment she got to his side. "Until I can talk to Sarson for a bit?"

Ervash was in the process of wiping the edges of plates from any food splatters. "Sure. I talked to him for a few minutes when he arrived. A little close-lipped but seems like a decent guy."

Heat rushed Doli's cheeks. "I think he is too. More than decent." She glanced over at Jez and Taenya chatting against the back of the house. Faylin lay sprawled out in the garden on a bench, tail flicking in the slightest irritation at who knows what.

"All he could talk about was you," Ervash quipped.

"Me?" Doli placed her hand on her chest as she watched Evvy out of the corner of her eye.

Ervash chuckled. "Go talk to him. I'll divert your parents." He snatched a large tray of finger food up from the table and made his way toward the approaching dwarves. "Welcome to our home, my friends," the orc boomed.

Doli quickly made her escape to Sarson, who nibbled on a plate of the same finger food Ervash had brought to her parents.

"You made it," Doli said and hopped up on the wooden chair next to him. But her attention went back to her parents, where Verdreth had now joined Ervash.

"Of course I made it." Sarson picked up a roasted date stuffed with creamy cheese and bacon and popped it into his mouth. His eyes instantly lit up. "These are delicious." The gargoyle held his plate out to Doli.

But Doli's stomach was flopping, and it didn't seem like eating would be a good idea until everything was better settled. She opened her mouth to speak, but Sarson spoke first.

"I wanted to bring something up with you," Sarson said as he took the hint and pulled his plate closer to him.

"Yes?" Doli said, nervousness peppering her tone. She had no idea what he might say.

He finished chewing and swallowed the date. "Have you thought about doing any training with Evvy?"

Doli tipped her head in interest. "Training?"

He nodded and popped another date into his mouth. "I've done a bit more research and found that training can be useful for guardians and their dragons. Are you interested?"

Gingrilin released a loud laugh and the sound made Doli turn. Instead of answering, she gestured toward her parents with a tip of her head. "That's my family. Um. Are you okay with meeting them? We can talk about Evvy later."

Sarson stopped chewing for what seemed like an age to Doli but couldn't have been. "I think I am," he finally said.

The heaviness Doli had felt lifted suddenly, until she turned to find her mother approaching with a handful of the same dates Sarson had eaten. Uldrick trailed his wife and Ervash stood shrugging in the background as if the giant orc hadn't been able to contain the tiny dwarf couple.

Gingrilin stuck out her free hand at Sarson. "Pleasure to meet you."

Without missing a beat, the gargoyle took her grasp and bowed his head slightly. "All mine."

Doli's mother opened her mouth, in all likelihood to ask one of a thousand questions.

"Dinner's ready," Verdreth interrupted her and held up a half-carved roast on a platter. Then he proceeded to tell everyone the seating arrangement—with Doli's parents on the other end of the table from Doli and Sarson.

"We'll speak later, Mother," Doli said.

Doli's mother scowled. "Very well." But she made her

way to her seat, and as soon as the food was passed, Gingrilin and Uldrick seemed to lose themselves for at least an hour.

The feast was made up of roast beef, Doli's leafy salad, sourdough rolls with herb butter from the bakery, and a sautéed vegetable assortment. And there was more than enough for all.

It was heaven.

But just as Verdreth brought out an orange swirl cake that Taenya had brought for dessert, Doli realized something.

She hadn't seen Evvy since after they had arrived.

22

Doli shot up in a panic out of her seat. Her heart quivered as if it were going to burst from her chest. "Where's Evvy?"

Everyone looked around and Arleta's eyes widened.

"I haven't seen her at least since we started dinner." Arleta pushed back her seat and stood. "I thought she was asleep in your sling."

Picking up her empty fabric sling and throwing it back against her chest, Doli said, "Not with all this food around. What was I thinking? Evvy!" she called, desperation in her voice, and ran around to the other side of the table.

Where could she have gone? Doli's mind twisted and whirled with the possibilities. *Maybe back to the main street.* She strained to look past the darkness of the garden to the small pasture where Nimbus, Theo's horse, grazed in the moonlight. *How did I get so caught up in myself and being here with my friends and Sarson that I could forget about Evvy?*

"Evvy!" she called again, breath shortening, but there was no answer and no little dragon buzzing back to the table.

"I always say she lacks the maturity—" Gingrilin started to Doli's father, and not in a whisper.

Doli's eyes landed on her. "This is not the time, Mother!" But in the back of her mind she was thinking much the same thing. *Maybe I'm simply not cut out for this sort of responsibility.*

The matriarch dwarf threw her hands in the air while Uldrick simply stood there, biting his lip at his wife's side.

Nose twitching, Jez stood and whipped around. "It's faint, but I can smell her."

The corners of Doli's eyes burned with tears, but she didn't dare let them loose, not in front of her parents. "Please find her."

"She's not close." Jez sniffed and squinted as if she was having trouble finding the scent. Which wasn't like her.

"I can help too," Sarson added. "If Jez can smell the dragon, I can fly the two of you to find her." His wings shuddered behind him and extended slightly.

The fennex whipped around to face Sarson. "Fly us?" Her eyes widened, sparking from the magic string lights.

"Yes," he said. "I don't use them often because they can intimidate non-gargoyles, but my wings can be useful."

Jez stood there looking frozen.

"Damn it," Doli huffed and scurried back over to Sarson. "We're wasting time, fennex!"

Taenya gave her a gentle push on her shoulder. "Go!"

For a brief second Jez still didn't move, but eventually she growled, "It's only that I like to do these things myself. But fine."

At the word Sarson stepped back from the rest of the group and fully extended his wings like wind catching a sail.

"We'll keep looking here," Verdreth said. "Just in case."

The others agreed.

Doli ran over to him, and the gargoyle wrapped one arm around her waist and held her firmly against him. She turned slightly and clung to his massive chest.

Sarson held out his other arm for Jez. The fennex pinched her lips and reluctantly entered his grasp.

"Hold on tight," he said to both of them. Then to Jez: "I'm going to fly low so you don't drop the scent."

"Quickly," Doli urged.

He bent his legs, then launched into the sky with one powerful thrust. The wind rushed over Doli's face as her stomach seemed to be left on the earth.

"Oh shit, shit, shit," Jez said through clenched teeth with her eyes closed tight, looking like she was about to retch.

"Which way?" Sarson asked Jez while hovering in the air, wings flapping behind him.

But the fennex kept on cursing while she clung to Sarson.

The gargoyle gave Doli a look and the dwarf yelled, "Damn it, Jez! Use your sniffer. We need to find Evvy!"

Jez's eyes popped open. "Um…um…"

"Are you afraid of heights?" Sarson asked calmly.

"Yeeeesss!" Jez said through chattering teeth and quickly closed her eyes again.

Doli was a ball of empathy mixed with anger at her friend and worry about Evvy. She dug her nails into Sarson's back and chest but managed not to say anything.

"Okay." Sarson tightened his grip on the fennex. "I'll take us down even lower. But when I do that, you have a job to do before I can put you down. Can you do that?"

"I...I think so." Jez's voice was much higher than usual.

Sarson slowed the pace of his flapping wings, and the three of them dropped slightly.

The fennex still had her eyes closed.

Doli was about to burst. "For stars' sake, Jez." She looked down at the ground. "Even I could jump from here." It was a bit of an exaggeration, and Doli knew it. "You can do this."

Opening one eye, Jez gazed down and released a long breath. Without another word her nose twitched, and she pointed north. "That way." Realizing she was only hanging on with one hand, she grappled for Sarson again.

Sarson didn't waste a moment as he flew them north along the outskirts of Adenashire. Jez had been right: Evvy had somehow gone a substantial distance from the cottages.

"Evvy!" Doli called along the way while Jez directed them. The moon was bright that night, but it still wasn't that easy to see the ground with all the trees and plants below them.

"The scent is getting stronger." Jez gestured slightly east. Her voice had slowly gained more confidence.

Suddenly a white flash bounded after something.

"There," Jez said.

"It's Faylin." Doli shifted to get a better view while her heart picked up even more speed. "Was he gone too?"

"Slow down, you foolish imp," Faylin called from below.

"Faylin!" Doli shouted, and the lynx turned and looked at them.

"You need to get this troublemaking dragon," he growled. "I'm getting too old for children." The lynx's tail swished wildly as he resumed the chase.

A flicker of motion could be seen ahead of him, and Sarson dove toward it.

"Shiiiit!" Jez had her eyes closed again.

The moment before he reached Evvy, he let go of the fennex. She plopped less than half her height to the ground, but she still shot the gargoyle a string of expletives that Doli did her best to block from her mind.

"Right there," Doli said, pointing to the twirling dragon.

Sarson dove and caught her with one hand. "Got you." Then he immediately landed and handed her off to Doli.

The dwarf took the dragon with two hands and first hugged her, then held her out almost at arm's length, exclaiming, "What in the stars were you thinking?"

Evvy blinked at her twice, let out a long breath…and fell asleep.

Faylin bounded up beside Sarson and Doli. Jez still sat where Sarson had dropped her, arms crossed over her chest in a huff.

"At first we were taking a little walk," Faylin said, his tongue lolling out, panting. "But then she stopped listening."

Still holding Evvy and shoulders sagging, Doli said, "She has a hard time listening sometimes."

"Yes, but—" Faylin started.

"Can you just take us back?" Doli asked Sarson, looking at their dark surroundings. "I really want to go home." She kept her hand tight over the snoring dragon.

Boot steps clomped behind her in the dirt. "No way in the stars I'm doing *that* again."

The dwarf turned to see a bedraggled-looking fennex, running one hand through her mop of white hair that seemed to glow in the moonlight. She quickly pulled out what looked to be a flask from her inside her shirt and took a swig.

"I'll walk home." Jez coughed, turning on her heel and heading through the grass, tail flicking back and forth behind her.

Sarson peered down at Faylin, who sat on his haunches, grooming his paw. "How about you? Want a ride back?"

The lynx slowly looked up, keeping his paw hung in the air. "Pass." He gave the paw a few more deliberate licks, then trotted off to catch up with Jez.

The gargoyle turned his attention back to Doli. "This might not be the time, but I *had* mentioned that training session for Evvy back at the party."

Exhaustion settled into Doli's limbs, and she didn't really want to think about it. "Yes. Tomorrow, perhaps? For now, would you mind taking me back to the cottage so I can tell the others what happened, then to the bookstore? I'm so very tired."

Without a word, Sarson picked Doli up and allowed her to settle in comfortably. Finally he said, "Ready?"

She nodded, but her eyes drooped. The dwarf barely remembered the trip, vaguely recalled telling the others what happened and her parents being slightly perturbed by the whole evening…but she did remember how Sarson tucked her into bed and pulled the blanket up tight around her. He patted Evvy, who lay on the dwarf's pillow snoring after her adventure, then ran his hand gently along Doli's forehead and cheek. "I'll be here at ten in the morning."

After that, she drifted off.

Doli scooped scrambled eggs from a cast-iron pan onto two plates, one for her and one for Evvy. She had barely sat at the dining table and picked up her fork to enjoy her first bite, when Evvy levitated the last bite of egg in front of her mouth, snapped it up, and then licked her plate clean on the counter.

Seconds later, the door to Jez's room cracked and the fennex emerged. Her white hair stuck out in several places, and her ear twitched in irritation.

Still with eggs in her mouth, Doli said, "Oh, I didn't know when you'd be up. Would you like—"

"We're not going to talk about it." Jez held out her hand, not looking at the dwarf.

Confusion knit Doli's brows. "We're not going to talk about—"

"It." Jez growled. "We're *not* going to talk about it!"

"The eggs?" Doli barely got out.

"Ugh." The cranky fennex threw her hand out. "Shit, no. Not eggs. What's wrong with you?"

Doli didn't know whether to laugh or be completely offended by her friend's behavior. So she just stuffed another bite of eggs into her mouth. "I don't think anything is wrong with me."

Staring at her wide-eyed, Jez finally spit it out. "Last night."

"Oh, that. I am glad you made it home safely." Doli kept her attention on Evvy, who was playing with a bit of string she'd found. "So you're afraid of heights?"

Jez hissed and went for the pan Doli had cooked the eggs in. "I'm not going to talk about it." She held the pan in the air by the handle.

Doli threw her hands up, as if in surrender, but snickered. "Talk about what?"

The fennex was most definitely afraid of heights and flying.

Grumbling, Jez nearly slammed the pan back onto the stovetop and grabbed the matches to relight the fire. "I am glad we found Evvy," she finally said while swirling butter around in the pan.

The dragon landed on the edge of the counter and watched Jez crack her own eggs into the hot pan. Her neck straightened when the eggs sizzled and popped.

Doli let out a breath after she finished her last bite. "Thanks for helping."

Jez nodded but didn't look up from her breakfast making.

"Sarson wants me to come over for some dragon training." She picked up her plate and brought it over to the basin.

The baby dragon flapped her wings in excitement.

"She needs it," Jez said flatly as she flipped her eggs with the yolks still intact.

"He said he's coming at ten." She checked the clock and gave a start when she saw it was already 9:45. "But I'm going to meet him out front before he gets here."

"Then you better get moving," the fennex said as she plated her own eggs and grabbed a hunk of sourdough bread off the loaf sitting on the counter. She held it up and examined it for a second as if deciding whether to heat it up, then shrugged and tossed it on the plate.

Doli smoothed down her pink gingham dress and adjusted her leather belt.

"You look fine." Jez groaned as she plopped into her chair at the table. "You always look fine."

"I don't want to look fine!" Doli shot back and checked that she'd put earrings in that morning. She had. The little gold hoops.

Jez glared at her friend. "Personally, I don't care much about those things. But to everyone else you probably look…" She paused as if to choose her words. "Very fashionable."

Doli's lips pulled into a thin line. But she was actually quite pleased to hear Jez say such a thing. "You did like your nails, you know. You aren't completely opposed to fashion."

The fennex scoffed and stuffed a big bite of sourdough into her mouth. "Fo met yur grguyl." She tossed Evvy a piece of bread. The dragon caught and ate it, then crawled into Doli's sling.

Before leaving, Doli made sure to put a couple of trout sticks in her pocket to keep Evvy happy on the trip over to Sarson's.

Downstairs, the bookstore was packed again, but she quickly made it past the crowd and outside. It was not much better out there.

Was there some kind of festival she hadn't remembered? Jez hadn't mentioned anything. The people milling about didn't seem to be interested in Evvy today. No one was paying attention to her even though the little dragon was more than half hanging from the sling.

And nearly everyone seemed to be a stranger. Sarson was nowhere to be seen.

But across the street from the bookstore, someone leaning on his cane with a newspaper in hand caught her eye: Kliff the badger. He wasn't exactly a resident of Adenashire, but Doli felt like she knew him, and he had seemed to know what was going on in the world around them.

"Mr. Badger—Kliff!" she called and held her hand up in the air.

He looked around as if to see where the voice was coming from. When he saw Doli, he waved her over with the newspaper.

"What's—" she started, nearly yelling over the noise of the throng.

"I'm so glad Hazel and I decided to stay one more day." He gazed around at the crowd, brown eyes bright. "We had no idea you had someone so important living here."

"Important?" Doli asked. "What are you talking about? What's going on?"

He didn't seem to quite hear her, but he leaned in and whispered, "That and the *scandal*. Or potential scandal. No one really knows."

The dwarf placed her hand to her chest above where Evvy panted and gazed around from her spot in the sling. "Scandal?"

But he didn't answer. He simply flung open the newspaper, where a large image of Sarson's face took up most of the page. The headline read "Runaway Head Librarian Found in Small Village; Questions Still Unanswered."

"Sarson?" His name slipped out of her mouth, and she flicked her attention around, looking for him again.

"Do you know him?" Kliff asked and looked down at the paper. "I don't think that's his name, though."

But as he did, the crowd hushed and parted, revealing the gargoyle walking down the street toward the bookstore with a completely bewildered look on his face.

Doli wanted to go to him, but her feet stayed frozen to the ground.

Kliff leaned in. "That's him," he whispered.

But the second he spoke, someone in the crowd shouted a question. "Why did you leave the Ridgelands?"

Sarson furrowed his brow and stopped walking.

Then the barrage of questions ensued.

"Was it a cover-up?"

"Did you take a bribe?"

"Is there a love child?"

"Were you kicked out?"

The questions didn't seem to stop, and Doli stood there and watched as Sarson's shoulders grew tense. Something in his eyes had changed.

"I'm not interested in answering any of your questions," he said, holding his hands in the air. His eyes landed on Doli, and his brows furrowed.

But his refusal to answer simply egged the questioners on further, and people began rushing at him, shouting questions.

Doli stood stunned. All she could figure was that many of the crowd must be reporters from newspapers around the Northern Lands. But why were they all in Adenashire now? What had brought them? She quickly stuffed Doli completely into the sling and despite the dragon's squeaky protests, the dwarf buttoned it up.

"Not right now, Evvy." She stuffed a trout stick in between the buttons to keep her quiet.

She wanted to go to Sarson, but the crowd had built up around him, and Doli had no idea what to do. He looked over at Kliff, but he was too focused on the goings-on to be any help at all.

"Coal!" someone from the crowd called, trying to get his attention. And then several more people shouted the name and more questions.

Doli's brow furrowed. Had he called Sarson "Coal"?

The gargoyle's breath was ragged and sweat beaded down the sides of his face. He turned and tried to leave, but of course they followed him.

"Leave me alone!" he shouted and raised his hands. Blue magic sparked from his fingers, and as he turned and roared at the crowd, his skin crackled and hardened. "I'm leaving. If any of you follow me, you might find out exactly what happened back in the Ridgelands." He held up his hands in a threatening manner and bared his teeth. "And you might not like it."

At that the crowd backed off and parted, allowing him to leave. Sarson gave one more growl, turned, and marched down the street.

Doli started to run toward him, but Kliff caught her arm.

"What are you doing?" he asked, alarm in his voice. "He seems dangerous."

"I have to go." Doli pulled from the badger's grasp.

"Hazel and I are leaving tomorrow," he called after her.

"It was nice meeting you," Doli said, still walking the way Sarson left. "I hope we see each other again."

"Me too," Kliff said.

But Doli didn't stop walking.

23

Finally she made it out of town and saw him. No one had followed.

"Sarson," Doli called after the gargoyle as he trudged back toward his cottage. Doli's legs were much shorter than his, and the dwarf struggled to keep up.

Evvy wriggled free of the sling, shot into the air, and darted past the gargoyle. She stopped in midair in front of him and held out a tiny hand.

Sarson groaned and stopped walking, allowing for Doli to catch up with him.

"Why are you running away from me?" Doli asked, panting for breath.

The gargoyle's tail flicked behind him in either irritation or frustration. Doli's stomach tightened, not sure which it was.

"I should have kept to myself," Sarson muttered. "That was the plan all along."

"But you didn't." Doli fiddled with her belt, anxious about what he was going to say.

Sarson ran his hand through his wavy brown hair and then over his right horn. "No. I just had to go to the bookstore to browse. I couldn't seem to help myself." He brought his gaze sheepishly to the ground. "And then I met you first thing."

"Me?" Doli drew her hand from the teacup to her exposed collarbone. Her breath picked up the pace.

Evvy squealed and did a flip, but Doli ignored the dragon as best as she could. She didn't want to jump to any conclusions.

He shook his head and then brought his gaze to the dwarf's face. "Yes. You." His voice was gravelly, deep. "After that, I felt like getting to know people in the village might not be such a bad thing, rather than getting deliveries or meeting people at their back doors for supply pickups before closing. I got to thinking maybe I could go into Adenashire myself." He glanced away. "Plus, I wanted to see you. Mostly the last part."

Doli gulped and stood there a bit too long without saying a word. After a while Evvy descended, landed on her shoulder, and wrapped her tail along the back of Doli's neck. Instinctively the dwarf brought her hand to the baby dragon for comfort and scratched at the side of her chin.

Evvy made a purring sound.

"I enjoy seeing you as well," she admitted softly, keeping her hand on Evvy for a smidge more emotional support.

"But it also meant there were going to be more questions about who I was," he admitted. "When I left the Ridgelands and my position as Head Librarian and Historian, I was told not to be a public figure. For privacy reasons."

Doli shifted her feet. "And then those reporters showed up in Adenashire wanting to know more about you."

"If I had simply played the hermit as I intended for a few years," he said, "then everyone would have moved on. There is always something new for people to obsess over."

"And with Evvy here too," Doli said. "Everything was getting out of control."

"That and the unicorn stampede," Sarson added.

Doli chuckled. "Who could forget the unicorns?"

They stood there in the middle of the path for a moment and then broke into light laughter over the joke.

"What were you going to do to those reporters?" Doli asked, genuinely curious.

Sarson lifted his hand and allowed the blue magic to form in his palm. "Make them go to sleep, I suppose. That's kind of the extent of my magic abilities."

Doli laughed. "But they don't know that?"

"Apparently not." His eyes crinkled with humor.

"You know…" The dwarf eyed Evvy and gave her another scratch on the chin. "I think this little one would still like to do the training you promised. If you're still willing."

Sarson's eyes twinkled, and he blew out a long breath. "It would be nice to get my mind off today."

Evvy squealed and launched from Doli's shoulder high toward the sky, twisted around, and dove back in between

Sarson and Doli, stopping again in midair. Her wings vibrated with excitement.

"I have the book with the training exercises at my cottage," Sarson said, pointing toward his home.

Evvy immediately took off down the path and was quickly out of sight.

The dwarf and gargoyle glanced at each other, and Sarson raised his brow.

"I guess we'd better get going," he said. "Don't want to keep her waiting."

A few minutes later they caught up with Evvy, who had already entered the house and was throwing books off the library shelves, apparently looking for the right one. At least ten books lay splayed out and scattered on the floor.

Doli's eyes widened in horror at the mess. "Evvy!" she scolded.

The baby dragon stopped what she was doing and hung her head, then held her hands in the air to conjure magic. One of the books levitated itself back to the shelf.

Sarson chuckled. "You're so eager," he said and picked up a book from the table next to his library chairs. "This is the one."

Still a little embarrassed by what Evvy had done, Doli reached for one of the books on the floor, picked it up, and held it, not knowing where it belonged on the shelves.

"Don't worry about the rest of those," the gargoyle said and walked to the counter, where a bowl of apples waited. "I'll get them later. I've shelved a lot of books in my lifetime." He picked up a shiny red apple and tossed it to Evvy, who caught it easily.

While holding the fruit in her claws, she bit into the skin, leaving tiny tooth marks.

"Oh," Sarson said, grinning. "Looks like those are coming in. I'm sure her fire is next."

"But it's supposed to take a month!" Doli protested. "It hasn't been that long yet." Her mind whirled with images of the dragon doing more damage than throwing books off shelves.

"Apparently you've been taking excellent care of her," Sarson said. "I've read that quick development can happen for dragons when they feel very safe and loved."

The dwarf flushed with pride.

Beside the apples was a bowl of the same sparkling candy Doli had seen and wanted at the market but didn't have time for. The dwarf reached out her hand and plucked a blue piece.

"I saw you eyeing those at the market," Sarson said.

Doli smiled at him and popped the sweet, fruity candy into her mouth. She wanted nothing more than to kiss Sarson at that moment. But Evvy, having already devoured the apple, flew to the front door and began squawking.

Doli shrugged as she looked at Sarson. "We should get moving on this, then."

"Let me find the page," Sarson said, flipping through the book.

When he'd found the right page, they all went into the front yard. Sarson and Doli spent several hours guiding Evvy to perfect many of the things she was already doing, like quick turns in the air, avoiding and overcoming obstacles, chasing and catching. Evvy loved every minute of it.

Finally the little dragon seemed ready for a break, and Sarson brought her a large bowl of water while Doli pulled out her remaining stash of trout sticks. Evvy eagerly grabbed the entire bunch and began attacking the first one. As she ate, Sarson held up the book. "The last thing we need to work on includes you too," he said to Doli.

She furrowed her brows. "What do you mean?"

He pointed to and paraphrased the passage in the book. "As her guardian, you have a mental bond with her."

The dwarf pursed her lips. "When she was first hatched, she told me her name. And I've experienced the connection a couple of other times, but it wasn't as clear."

"Says here that it takes practice," Sarson said as he sat down on the edge of his porch. "And that's what we're here for."

Evvy flew over to Doli and hovered, lightly flapping her wings and wringing her hands as if in anticipation.

"What do I do?" The dwarf's stomach fluttered with excitement at the prospect of actually communicating with Evvy.

"Hold out your hand," Sarson read from the book.

Doli did as he said and the little dragon landed on her palm, resting her warm belly against the dwarf's skin.

"Close your eyes."

For a moment the dwarf gazed into Evvy's golden irises but then closed her own eyes and felt the small creature in her hand.

"Now wait."

"Wait?" Doli's eyes flickered open.

Sarson chuckled. "I think you have to stay focused."

The dwarf shook her head and let out a long breath. "Okay. I can do that." She closed her eyes again, feeling a bit silly. This time Doli focused on the dragon's weight and how Evvy's body fit perfectly in her hand. And waited. Just breathing in and out.

Until something happened. A golden thread of magic sparked in Doli's mind, and without opening her eyes, Evvy appeared there.

Her eyes were bright, and she smiled, her mouth full of brilliant sharp teeth. "Greetings, Doli Butterbuckle." She bowed low. "We haven't fully had the chance to introduce ourselves."

The dwarf gasped, not knowing what to think. Evvy was larger and older than Doli knew her as, and her scales had deepened in color. She was gorgeous, radiant.

"Uh…hello," Doli managed, nervous at being near such a beautiful and somewhat terrifying creature—especially after remembering that dragons might eat people.

Evvy straightened and paused for a moment as if to think. "My full name is Evengeline, Protector of the Dawn Order." She lowered her head humbly. "At least, I will be as I grow." A pink aura spread out from around Evvy, and she held her regal head high. "And I chose you to be my guardian to start my life," Evvy said. "It's been a long voyage over hundreds of years. But I've known you for that time. Even before you existed in the Northern Lands I saw and chose you. I waited, guided by magic."

The dwarf gulped. "But…but why?" Within her mind she took several steps back in shock. "Me?"

"Why not?" Evvy gazed deep into the dwarf's eyes. "You are important, and our journeys are intertwined. Without each other, our destinies can't be fulfilled. It's been written in the stars since the beginning of time."

With those words and without time for any of Doli's questions, the vision ended. Doli snapped back to the present, Evvy still in her hand. And back to her regular size.

The dwarf's eyes widened, her mind jumbled with confusion.

"What happened?" Sarson asked.

Before Doli could answer, Evvy's small voice met her mind.

Do you think I could get a nap? The dragon blinked sleepily. *That was entirely exhausting.*

Stunned, Doli walked right past the gargoyle still sitting on the stoop, took the little dragon inside, and placed her on the bed Sarson had made for her in the library.

When she was done, she came out and leaned on one of the wooden columns holding up the porch. "That was… interesting."

"And I have an impression it was only for you and Evvy," he said. "At least for now."

Doli agreed and she and Sarson just sat there for a long time, looking out at the view. A flock of cranes flew overhead across the lightly clouded sky.

"I really hated keeping anything from you about who I am," Sarson finally said and cast his emerald eyes to the ground beside Doli. He fiddled with a forming splinter on the wooden step with one hand and ran his other over his right horn. "It felt wrong." His shoulders grew tense as his tail flicked behind him on the wood, making a thumping sound each time it hit.

Doli's stomach burned with the desire to comfort him. She really hated seeing *anyone* sad.

"You weren't allowed to." She placed her hand on his shoulder, and the powerful muscles quivered beneath the fabric of his shirt. A shiver ran down her spine as she did so, but she did her best to remain focused. "I understand that."

"But it felt wrong anyway," he said and pulled the splinter off the board. "I wasn't lying, but it seemed as if I was. And I never want to keep things from you."

Doli placed her hand on her chest, unsure of what he was telling her. *Does he really want to be with me as much as I do with him? Am I that important that keeping a secret like that from me truly bothers him?*

"Then what happened?" Doli asked.

Sarson sighed. "It might not sound like it, but my job was extremely stressful. I couldn't take being approached by people offering gold—or a myriad of other things, even magic and power—for me to somehow change what had been logged in the records of the Northern Lands. It was never-ending." He looked down at her, shoulders sagging and lines pulling his forehead. "Truth is important, you know."

Doli's heart hurt for him. It was obvious that leaving had not been easy. "Who's handling the position now?"

He bit his lip. "Someone less tired. But I trust them. I wouldn't have left otherwise."

"Then how about going forward, we don't keep things from each other?" she asked. "That is…if you are staying in Adenashire."

"I'd like that." The gargoyle's wings, which had been tucked at his back, extended slightly. "And yes. I plan to stay."

"Did I hear one of those reporters call you Coal?"

"Coal is my first name," he said. "Sarson is my middle name, and my grandfather's. I've always gone by Sarson with my family. But professionally I was Coal."

"I like that name too." Unable to help herself, Doli's eyes roamed over the edges of his gorgeous blue wings.

"You can touch them," he said quietly. His deep voice was even huskier than normal. "If you like."

Doli's breath hitched. She brought her hand up to one silky wing and grazed her fingers against the edge. He quivered under her touch, and out of the corner of her eye she saw the skin on his neck ripple and harden like stone, then quickly return to normal.

He stretched them out fully, and the sound was like that of a boat sail raising against the sea wind. They spanned the entire porch, and the sight made Doli gasp.

Whatever Jez thought, Doli was pretty sure a wingspan like that *was* a good thing. He'd proven that the night before.

And he liked her. She was sure of it.

The dwarf bit her lip, placed her other hand on his cheek, and turned it toward her. The pair gazed into each other's eyes for what seemed like an age.

"You're the most beautiful woman I've ever known," Sarson

whispered as he brought his wings tight against his back again. "And not only your outside, but—" He hovered the tips of his fingers over her heart. "But inside too. You care and feel so strongly. I've adored everything about you since the moment I laid eyes on you in the bookstore." His eyes drank Doli in. "Your elegant browned skin, your curls, your curves… The clothes you choose that not only perfectly accentuate your beauty but express the sunshine beaming from your soul." He grinned, showing off his fangs. "You've captured me every moment and refuse to let go. And I don't want you to."

Doli gulped and thought she might die happy right then and there. She hadn't heard such romantic words spoken—especially concerning herself—outside of some of her favorite books.

And she'd staked her dreams on some of those words.

But instead of expiring, since that would have been a waste of a perfect moment, she cupped Sarson's face and brought her lips to his.

They were unusually soft, and she inhaled his earthy, floral scent as he enthusiastically returned the gesture. Dizziness spun in her brain as the gargoyle took her into his muscular embrace and gently pulled her onto his warm lap.

"You taste like sunshine on a summer day," he murmured between kisses and, in Doli's opinion, some particularly skillful hand-roving. "Exactly how I imagined."

"How many times have you imagined kissing me?" Doli asked, eyes wide and her heart pounding.

His chest heaved with heavy breath. "Every exquisite second since we met."

Her breath hitched and Doli wove her fingers into Sarson's thick hair and pulled the kiss in deeper, not wanting to waste any of their first time.

It both wasn't long *and* passed like an eternity before Doli giggled, leaned in close to Sarson's ear, and whispered, "How about we give Evvy some snacks to keep her busy if she wakes up, and we go inside for a while?" She traced one finger down the center of his chest. "There are a few book scenes I've been dying to reenact."

He leaned in to kiss her briefly. "Are you sure that's what you want?"

Doli's breath picked up. "I've never been surer of anything in my entire life."

Sarson's lips turned up in a wicked half grin and he said, "I thought you'd never ask. I have a couple of my own bookmarked I believe you'll enjoy."

"Oh, stars," Doli breathed, her mind and body aflutter.

"Yes." Sarson stood with Doli in his gentle arms, kissed her again, and took her inside the warm, cozy cottage.

And there were stars indeed.

24

The next day, Doli's head was in the clouds. And then the stars…and then whatever might have been beyond them.

She leaned her hip against the bakery counter with one hand stuffed into her pocket and the other hand twisting at the pink stone necklace around her neck. Evvy half hung from the sling on Doli's chest.

"You're coming today, right?" Taenya teased slightly as she loaded three gigantic cranberry muffins into a bag for Doli. "Or are you heading back over to Sarson's?"

The bakery wasn't open to the public that day, but Taenya had come in anyway to prepare the weekly spread for her friends, and the place smelled of caramelized sugar and rosemary. They tried to all get together in the shop for a meal or snack as often as possible to make sure they didn't miss any of the goings-on.

The words sounded almost muffled to her until Evvy screeched and grappled at the folded-over bag held out in front of the dwarf. "What?" She giggled and took the bag, keeping it away from the hungry little dragon. "No…I'm bringing him with me."

"Oh. That's nice. I didn't get to talk with him much at the orcs' dinner party the other day. I'd love to get to know him better." The elf gazed outside. "Plus, a bunch of those reporters left this morning. So something else must have caught their attention. Maybe they won't bother him again." The elf bit her lip.

Taenya had her own reasons she'd left behind her home, Langheim, and the life she'd led there. So it seemed she empathized with Sarson.

Doli nodded absentmindedly, unfolded the bag, and took a muffin out. She broke off a small piece from the rough top covered in sugary streusel topping and speckled with bright red dried cranberries. Evvy snapped her jaws at the muffin, and Doli could make out more teeth pushing through her little pink gums.

"Is she teething?" Taenya leaned over the counter, her eyes wide. "Already?"

"Apparently." Doli popped a small piece of the muffin top into her mouth and gave the other half to Evvy, who grabbed the morsel with her tiny hands and stuffed it into her mouth. "It's my excellent guardian skills apparently. Even with losing her once." She sighed, proud of her accomplishment in making sure Evvy was loved and cared for but concerned about the future. "It will be fire next, and I have no idea how I'm going to deal with that."

Taenya gave a slight grimace before she smirked. "Well, at least you won't need matches anymore."

The dwarf half scoffed, half laughed as she chewed her muffin piece and swallowed. "That's one way to look at it." She held the bag up in the air. "Well, I'm meeting my parents with these. Kind of a peace offering. They're finally leaving tomorrow."

The elf raised her brows in question. "That's a good thing, right?"

Doli released a long, deliberate breath. "Yes. I wish we could have gone out on better terms." She held up the muffins again. "Maybe these will help. But I'm not sure we'll ever see eye to eye."

Taenya nodded with understanding, but said, "Baked goods never seem to hurt." She winked. "I'll see you later."

Doli thanked her for the muffins and headed over to the Tricky Goat with Evvy. On the way she was glad to see Taenya had been right. The streets were much less crowded than they had been the morning before.

Humming a little tune, Doli smiled up at the sun and focused on the fact that it was a new day. And since it would be her parents' last day in Adenashire, she might as well make the best of it.

But when she got to the walkway in front of the inn, there sat Zanzidore Sunfire eating breakfast on the patio. Seeing him made her chest tighten, and Evvy gave a whine, likely sensing the dwarf's emotions since they'd been working on their connection.

"It will be okay," Doli said, the encouragement as much for herself as for the dragon. But the man made her feel slightly off balance, and she put her hand over Evvy while picking up her pace.

"You again?" He leaned back in his seat and peered slightly over his shoulder to speak to Doli.

Time seemed to slow. Everything in her wanted to keep walking and pretend she hadn't heard him, but she didn't. Instead, she braked.

"Um, yes," Doli said, keeping her hand across the little dragon's body. But Evvy managed to pull herself up over Doli's hand and peer at the man with her golden eyes. "I live here." It was a silly thing to say.

Zanzidore's brows furrowed in confusion. "At the Tricky Goat?"

A nervous laugh came from Doli's lips. "No…in Adenashire."

"Oh, of course. How silly of me," the man said, and his eyes dropped to Evvy.

"Did you find your friend?" Doli didn't know why she'd asked. What she really wanted to do was excuse herself and find her way to her parents' room.

"Not yet," he said and took a bite of the scrambled eggs on his plate. "I'm not sure if I will see him after all. My plans have changed a bit since my arrival."

Doli stood there for a moment, her mind trying to help her form the words she intended. "Well, I must go." She gestured to the door. "Enjoy your breakfast and the rest of your time here. However long." Her voice was chipper even though her inside felt quite the opposite.

Zanzidore smiled and bowed his head slightly. "A good day to you."

As fast as she could, Doli uprooted her feet and made her way through the front door and to the front desk where Maven stood hunched over her guest book. The woman's hair poked out from her messy bun, and one of the buttons on her wrinkled shirt hung by a thread. She finished scribbling something down and looked up at Doli. "Oh." Her eyes grew wide. "You look about how I feel."

Doli ran her hand along Evvy's bumpy head and horns to calm herself. "I'm just looking for my parents' room."

"You haven't been to it yet?" Maven asked, her head tipping in surprise.

Doli realized in all the commotion, she hadn't. The dwarf looked down at Evvy, who was eyeing a bowl of wrapped hard peppermint candies on the desk. "It's been a week."

The innkeeper nodded. "I can't argue with you there." She gave Doli her parents' room number and pointed the way.

"Thank you." Doli grabbed one piece of candy, unwrapped it, and gave Evvy the contents. "Don't ask for more. We'll have plenty of snacks for lunch with the group."

Evvy bobbed her head up and down as she munched the candy. *Fine.*

After a left, then a right down a hallway behind the check-in station, Doli came to room 120. Just like the inn's entrance, a goat eating grass was carved onto the door. She raised her hand and knocked. A few seconds later, footsteps sounded across the wooden floor inside. The handle rattled and the door flung open. It was her mother.

"Oh," she said with surprise in her tone and a droop of disappointment on the corners of her lips. "I thought you were room service."

Doli raised her brows, then shrugged. "Just me."

"Is that the food?" Uldrick called from somewhere in the room.

Gingrilin, wearing a dark blue velvet robe with gold piping along the edges, swung the door wider to reveal what was a very nice room. "It's our daughter. She doesn't have our breakfast."

There was a wooden four-poster bed covered in a fluffy white duvet. Sunlight streamed in from two large windows facing a garden courtyard at the back of the inn where they grew some of the produce for the pub's food. Coming into cooler months the growth was sparse, but there was still some color.

Doli's father sat on a rather large red brocade chair with carved maple legs complete with lion feet at the bottom. The thing looked as if it might suddenly come to life and walk around the room. He had been in the middle of reading a book plucked from the bookshelf behind him. "Oh, come in." He set the book down on a side table and smiled at her. "Come to visit us on our last day?"

A tiny bit of guilt twinged at Doli's stomach as Evvy wriggled free of the sling and flew up to balance atop a bedpost.

Her parents were no doubt difficult to get along with. That was a fact. And she hadn't made it any easier by not establishing proper boundaries and communication with them.

"Yes," she said walking into the room. "It is your last day, and I'm here to invite you to lunch with me and my friends at the bakery."

Her mother closed the door behind her. "Well…after the other night—"

But Doli held out a hand to stop her and Gingrilin closed her mouth. "Mother. We need to talk."

The matriarch planted her hands on her hips and threw a look at her husband.

He shrugged. "It's probably a good idea."

Doli bit her lip and walked over to the bed. She crawled up onto the end and faced her parents. Everything in her wanted to stuff her true feelings down and say everything was fine. But it wasn't. She glanced up at Evvy, who was still perched on the very top of the bedpost licking her hands, probably from the sugary candy. The dragon gave Doli a little wink.

I can do this, Doli thought, then opened her mouth to speak. "We are very different," she started and then made the mistake of looking over at her mother, who was still near the door with her arms crossed. Her cheeks were puffed as if she held air in them. Doli quickly looked instead at a painting behind her mother of a serene pasture with a herd of grazing sheep. For whatever reason her mother had not interrupted, so she continued.

"And I don't know if you are really okay with that…but I

am. I was never interested in taking over the family business, but you have Whurigret and Brudela to do that. And they seem to love mining and gems and typical dwarf magic and all that. On the other hand, I like being here in Adenashire. I liked competing in the Baking Battle. I love sewing and fashion. I *love* romance books, and I'm not afraid to admit it!" She ran her hand along the teacup snapped into her holster. "I like my tea magic. It's part of me… It's part of who I am. And I'm tired of pretending to be someone I'm not. I am a cheerful person, but not always. Sometimes I'm frustrated and angry. And I don't want to pretend that I don't care when you or anyone else puts me down, or underestimates me." She finally looked up at her parents. "I feel like I can love *you* for who you are—imperfect people—and I simply want that returned."

Gingrilin stuffed her hands into her robe pockets, looking…humble, something Doli couldn't recall seeing before.

"Your mother and I were just discussing something related," Uldrick said as he hopped off his chair. "There was a reason"—his eyes averted to Evvy, still up high—"for you to avoid us this week. And it was more than only being busy with that little one."

"As much as I still wish you'd have followed in our footsteps and stayed in Dundes Heights," her mother said, "you've made a life here. And that Sarson fellow seems interesting. He spared no time helping you when little Evvy went missing."

Doli gulped. She'd never expected this impromptu conversation to go so well. "I like him too. Getting to know someone who loves books as much as I do has been amazing."

Uldrick gazed at the book he'd laid down. "I found reading a few chapters of that book quite relaxing."

The spine read *There and Back Again*. Doli hadn't read that one yet, but she'd heard about the adventure story.

"Maybe Maven will let you take it with you," Doli said, sliding off the end of the bed.

"Could be." Her father shrugged. "I'll have to ask."

Doli gritted her teeth about the last thing on her mind. "And I'm sorry I broke Uncle Thorras's vase." She wrinkled her nose, not sure how they would react.

Her parents gave each other a look, then Uldrick said, "It always was ugly."

Gingrilin chuckled. "Probably for the best."

They were all quiet for a moment. During that time Doli wavered between letting the nice moment stand and finishing what she had to say. Finally she spoke again, "The next time you plan to come to Adenashire, please give me more advance notice." She gestured around the room. "That way I can plan for your arrival. Book this room again…get time off work at the bookstore. That way I can devote time to you with none of us ending up resentful."

"Resentful?" Her mother huffed.

But Doli didn't back down. "Yes, Mother. You know it's true, even if you don't want to admit it." She kept her gaze on the dwarf, who relented with a nod. "Coming here on short or no notice doesn't work for either of us. I'll do the same for you when I visit Dundes Heights."

Gingrilin's brown eyes brightened. "So you do plan to visit."

"Yes. Of course I plan to visit." Doli walked to her mother and opened her arms. "I love you both."

"We love you too," her father said and joined the hug while Evvy flew down to the back of the chair and chirped.

A knock came at the door and the group separated.

"*That* must be our breakfast!" Uldrick said and made his way to the door.

Doli sighed as the dwarf let a man in with a large and loaded tray in hand.

"Where would you like this?" the man asked, looking around the room.

"Over here, over here," Gingrilin said, pointing to the side table by the chair and bookcase.

Waving to Evvy to come, Doli said to her mother, "You enjoy that. But you will come to the bakery for lunch, right? At noon."

Before the man even had the tray of eggs, bacon, buttery toast, scones, fruit salad, orange juice, and coffee on the table, her parents already had loaded plates.

"Yes, yes," Uldrick said right before biting a scone. "We'll be there."

Evvy landed on Doli's shoulder, and the two of them made their way out the door.

Her parents weren't perfect. But who was? Doli was simply relieved the conversation had gone better than expected.

25

Doli left the inn, and her heart lifted again. That strange wizard, Zanzidore, was no longer eating breakfast on the patio, and her parents would be leaving the next day. Life was about to return to normal.

She looked down at the little dragon asleep in her sling. Except for that.

But maybe Evvy was the new normal. That, along with figuring out where her relationship with Sarson was going. Fairy dust whirled in her stomach at the thought.

So she went home and spent the next few hours lost in a book to pass the time.

After finishing chapter 15 of *The Minotaur and I* (still not her favorite), she realized it was almost noon; time to meet her friends at the bakery. So she gathered up Evvy and rushed out the door and down the stairs, only checking herself once in the mirror before she left.

Just a right, then a left around a flower shop to the bakery, she spotted Sarson, who must have been on his way as well. But he was not alone.

Instead, he was speaking to Zanzidore.

Her stomach dropped as she stood there on the cobblestone street. Neither of them had spotted her, so she quickly stepped back in front of the flower shop and hid beside a barrel of tall ferns, her chest suddenly heaving with nervous breath.

Her brain whirled with recent conversations: Jez not trusting Sarson, her father wondering whether he'd been banished from the Ridgelands, the reporters with all their questions. But Sarson had explained that all to her—that he'd left because the job was too stressful.

What if there was something more to the story?

She peeked back around the corner. They were still there. Still talking.

"May I help you?" came a female voice from her side, and Doli's attention went to a light-skinned woman who she thought was named Bonnie, the owner of Floral Fantasies, the shop Doli was hiding in front of.

As she turned, her face went directly into the ferns. "Um," Doli managed, blowing fern leaves out of her mouth. "These are so lovely!" Her voice came out squeaky as she grabbed one of the stalks and held it up.

Evvy squawked from the sling, and Doli threw her hand over the dragon's mouth.

Bonnie's eyebrows raised in confusion. "Yeeess. But why are you in the middle of them?"

Sarson's voice had gotten louder, but Doli still couldn't hear what he was saying. Instead of answering the florist, the dwarf whipped her head around the corner to try to see what was going on. But when she did, both Sarson and the lanky wizard were gone.

"Um," Doli said to Bonnie without looking back at her but still holding the fern. "Sorry, I have to go." She started off, but a hand caught her sleeve.

"Are you going to pay for that?" Bonnie demanded.

Doli shoved the fern back into the woman's hands, and with a look of surprise, the florist let her go. Not wasting a second, the dwarf headed straight to the bakery. When she got to the door, she could see that Sarson was inside with the others. The sign read CLOSED, but she knew the lock would be open.

The baby dragon whined, but the dwarf ignored her.

Doli's hand hovered over the door handle as she peered through the glass. Was Sarson the friend that the wizard was in Adenashire to see? It wasn't as if the stranger had done anything to her—it was just a bad sense about the man. What did that say about her judgment concerning Sarson? Doli had no idea what to think, but Evvy's wiggling around in the sling brought the dwarf back to the present. She flung open the door, making the bell on it ring several times.

Doli scanned the room for her parents, knowing she was a little late, but they weren't there. Quickly she blew out a breath and steadied herself. What she wanted to do was pull

Sarson aside and ask what was going on, but Evvy launched from the sling and flew up to Taenya, nearly making her drop the tray of sandwiches in her hand. Then Evvy turned and flew back to the closed door, scratching at the handle.

"Evvy," Doli scolded. It came out too harsh, and she immediately regretted it. She gently turned the dragon back to the room, and she flew back to Taenya.

"It's fine." Taenya recovered and placed the sandwiches on the table while shooing Evvy off. "They're not ready yet."

Evvy relented, flew up to a high shelf, and perched on the edge, gazing at the door.

Doli gave her a "stay out of trouble" look and the dragon started to groom her back leg.

Theo, who was standing next to Arleta near the checkout, turned to the dwarf. "Hello, Doli." His tone was friendly but the space between his brows wrinkled in concern. "Are you okay?"

Instinctively Doli smoothed her skirt and put on a smile. "I'm fine. Just a little hurried." She gazed around again, this time spotting Faylin asleep in the corner. "My parents aren't here?"

He shook his head.

Since they had known that lunch would be served, Doli found it strange that they weren't on time, particularly with the conversation they'd had.

Sarson's eyes drew to her, and he raised his hand to wave. She forced a smile but then settled her attention on Jez, who sat at a booth by herself. Doli slid into the booth next to her, saying nothing.

Jez didn't even look her way as she poured rum from a glass bottle into a mug. Her nose twitched. "What's wrong with you?"

Doli winced at the question. She hated that Jez could smell strong emotions. "Nothing." The word came out too quickly.

"Bad meeting with your parents?" Jez picked up her mug.

"No. Actually, that went surprisingly well." Doli gave Sarson a quick eye but brought her attention back to the table. He'd been looking at her. Of course he had. She ran a trembling hand over the teacup in her holster and unsnapped it, hand already warm and tingling with magic. She placed the cup on the table and hovered her fingers over it. Steam rose and traveled between her digits. She grabbed the handle and chugged the hot tea inside, but she barely tasted it or felt it go down. She didn't even know what kind of tea she'd made.

Jez twisted her neck toward the dwarf. "Are you avoiding Sarson?" Thankfully she'd kept her voice in a whisper.

"No." It came out as a squeak.

"You are!" This time, the fennex spoke a bit louder. "Do you need my help? You need me to kick his ass? Did he hurt you?" She began to rise from the booth, but Doli blocked her.

"No!" Doli grabbed Jez's arm and yanked her to sit again. "I don't know," she whispered.

"Lunch is ready," Taenya called, making Doli jump.

"It's fine, really," Doli said while climbing out of the booth and hopping to the floor.

Evvy swooped above the small buffet table loaded with egg salad as well as cheese sandwiches. There were chocolate chip and sugar cookies and a vegetable tray, along with a pitcher of freshly made lemonade.

Jez picked up a plate and placed two chocolate chip cookies on it.

"You've really outdone yourself this time, Tae," Arleta said, throwing her arm around the elf's waist and pulling her friend in close.

Doli had to admit it all looked delicious. She glanced from the table to Sarson, who had a furrowed brow. He had to have noticed her distance. Had she overreacted? How was she supposed to know if she didn't even talk to him? That's what she'd said she needed from her parents—communication. And here she was doing the exact opposite. A pit grew in her stomach as he approached her.

"Are you okay?" Sarson said, his voice gentle. "Do you regret—"

The shop door flung open, and Doli turned to it, expecting her parents. But it was Maven. The woman looked directly at Doli and put her finger in the air. "I have a message for you." She panted as if out of breath.

Doli furrowed her brow and walked over to the innkeeper. "Are my parents okay?" She didn't even know why that was her first thought.

Maven waved the question away. "I think so. But they asked me to tell you they left."

Doli's face contorted in confusion. "What? Today? Why?"

The innkeeper nodded, then shrugged. "I don't know. All

I know is they checked out about an hour ago and asked me to tell you they'd gone." She turned and glanced outside the window. "I need to get back to the Goat." Then she turned around and left, but as the door swung back behind her, a rock got caught and prevented it from closing.

Doli's shoulders sank. She didn't know why she was sad. She should have been happy that her parents were gone. But she wasn't. Their talk that morning had given her hope that things could get better between them. And here they were taking off without even telling her why.

A blue hand settled on her shoulder, and Doli startled.

Sarson immediately pulled it back. "What happened?" he asked quietly, but his flicking tail betrayed his concern.

Doli shook her head. "Nothing. Let's just eat." She walked over to the table and grabbed a plate. Not even hungry anymore, she still placed one of each offering on her plate and then sat at the long table that was made up of several tables pushed together. The group had grown too large to all sit in a booth, particularly with Sarson.

Someone made Evvy a plate, and she sat on the end of the table happily eating, finally settled down.

Doli was able to get down a few bites of her cheese sandwich, but she barely tasted it as the others talked about their week.

"Please talk to me," Sarson finally said after they'd sat for at least twenty minutes in silence.

A flurry of thoughts went through Doli's mind, but her resolve firmed and she turned to him. "Why were you talking to that wizard?"

Sarson leaned back in his seat. "Zanzidore?"

"Yes." Doli kept her voice down. "He's been around town the last couple of days and mentioned coming here to see a friend."

"He talked to you?" The skin along his jaw hardened.

"He came into the bakery the other day at closing," Doli said. "He noticed Evvy." She looked around for the dragon but didn't see her.

"Zanzidore is not my friend," Sarson said, his tone firm. "He's one of the reasons I left the Ridgelands."

Doli tipped her head. "Oh?"

"He was here trying to convince me to go back." Sarson shook his head. "His offers never worked before. I don't know why he thought they'd work this time." The gargoyle paused. "I'm pretty sure he was the one who told the reporters where I was…to encourage me to go back. But I told him I wasn't going to, and he needed to leave. Hopefully he will."

Doli breathed a sigh of relief over the whole thing. "I'm sorry I doubted you. I don't regret our relationship at all, but I saw you with him and panicked. Then this whole thing with my parents."

"What thing—" Sarson asked, looking slightly relieved.

But Doli didn't hear what he said next because she was still looking around to find Evvy. The little dragon was nowhere to be found. "Has anyone seen Evvy?" Doli pushed back her chair and stood as panic buzzed in her chest. She'd let Evvy out of her sight. Again.

Everyone stopped talking and looked around.

"She was right there eating a few minutes ago," Taenya said, pointing to the empty plate.

But Doli knew Evvy was a fast eater, and the dragon had tackled her lunch before Doli herself had even sat down. More than a few minutes. The dwarf turned to the door and saw how it was propped open…not a lot, but enough for the little dragon to have squeezed through. "She was acting strange when we got here, trying to get out the door. But I was too distracted."

She called for Evvy again with no response. The next minutes were a complete blur for Doli as they searched the bakery and then made their way out to the street, all calling for her.

She didn't answer.

And right when things didn't seem like they could get any worse, a voice came from behind her.

"Dolgrila," her mother called.

For some reason, her parents were back. She let out a long sigh and turned. This was the last thing she needed right then—her parents getting in the way.

"I know we left in a hurry," Uldrick said, panting with sweat running down the side of his face. He looked as if he'd been running.

Doli's mother looked about the same and plopped her luggage down on the dusty cobblestone street. She huffed and puffed, apparently lacking breath for anything else since she'd called Doli's name.

"You did leave in a hurry!" Doli threw her hands on her hips. "You barely give me notice that you're coming, then you leave with nothing more than sending Maven to tell me you'd gone."

"We got word," Gingrilin said, still panting, "that the whole unicorn situation was in negotiations and the road was clear. But it could change anytime."

Her father continued. "It was either leave right then or stay here for stars know how long."

Doli's heart gave a jolt at the thought.

Uldrick crossed his arms over his chest. "Anyway, we did tell Maven this."

"She was very busy though," Gingrilin said.

At that point Doli didn't care anymore. "Mother! Evvy is missing. I don't have time for this, so thank you for coming back and telling me why you left. But I have more important things to do!"

Both parents pulled back, staring as Doli started to turn away.

"We know," Doli's mother said. "We saw a wizard with her at the carriage station."

Doli flipped back around. "What? What did he look like?"

Gingrilin thought for a second. "Tall…taller than most men…lanky. With a tattoo mark on his neck."

"Zanzidore?" Doli asked, shaking.

"We didn't exactly ask his name," Uldrick said, pulling at the lapels of his coat. "But he was fiddling with a birdcage, and when he lifted the fabric over it, both of us were sure she was inside."

The others had joined Doli, and Sarson had come up beside her.

"This is my fault," Sarson said. "When I told him to leave town, I mentioned where I was going. He must have seen you and Evvy go in as well. He could have cast a spell on Evvy to get her to come to him before you even reached the bakery. You said she was acting strange."

Doli shook her head. "This is no one's fault except the wizard's." She turned back to her parents. "Was he still there when you left?"

"Yes," Uldrick said. "He was headed north on a different carriage than we were supposed to take. It doesn't leave for another hour."

"We have to go find her," Doli said to the others, and they all agreed.

Doli hugged both her parents. "Thank you. For coming back to tell me."

Gingrilin placed her hand on her daughter's dark cheek. "And we'll stay until you return. To make sure you and Evvy are okay."

After another hug, the friends were off to the carriage stop to rescue Evvy.

26

Huffing and puffing, Doli, Sarson, Taenya, Arleta, Jez, and Theo finally crested the hill and saw Zanzidore waiting for the next carriage out of Adenashire. His back was turned to them, but Doli immediately spotted the fabric-covered birdcage he held in his hand, and she knew Evvy was inside.

"We have to get her," Doli said, her stomach tightening with anxiety. She started to march toward the wizard, but Sarson put his hand on her shoulder.

"I know him," the gargoyle said. "He's not kind and won't give her up easily." He looked around at the group.

Jez and Taenya stood next to each other, balling their fists and both looking as if they were about to bite someone's head off.

"What if we offered him a trade?" Theo said. "We have some gold saved up."

Arleta furrowed her brow as if the gold was probably saved for something important to them, but then said, "Yes, we should do that."

Sarson glanced toward the wizard and kept his voice down. "Evvy is not about gold to him. Having her is likely about power."

"Then what do we do?" Doli's voice cracked with stress as she wrung her hands. Her tea magic zipped between her fingers, and more than anything she wanted it to go away. What good was making tea in a moment like that? "Maybe you could make him go to sleep with your magic, and then we can take Evvy back."

Sarson's brow furrowed. "It's probably the best we can do at the moment. But he'll come after us." The gargoyle let out a long sigh. "We're going to need a distraction."

The only people from the group that Zanzidore had not seen with Doli were Jez and Taenya. So the others stayed behind watching from behind some bushes as the elf and fennex made their move. Probably not the move they'd imagined a few moments before.

"What a lovely day to travel!" Taenya had threaded her arm with Jez's as they walked toward the carriage stop. "Isn't it, dear?"

Jez flicked her tail slightly in irritation, but since they were both facing away from the group, Doli could only hope the fennex's expression didn't give her away.

Doli could barely hear what was being said, and her heart

thumped in her chest. Arleta placed her arm around her friend's shoulders.

"When they have him distracted," Sarson whispered, "I'll swing around the other side. That should be close enough for me to use the sleeping magic on him. I don't know how long it will remain in effect." He looked around at the group. "I can carry and fly only two of you out of here. The rest will need to run."

Doli and the others nodded as if they all understood the risk.

At the carriage station, Jez and Taenya continued acting the part of an old married couple.

Taenya clasped her hands together and brought her gaze down to the covered cage. "I just *love* birds. What kind do you have there?" Her voice was higher than normal, possibly acting the part or maybe because she was nervous.

Jez clicked her tongue. "Don't bother the gentleman…dear." The last word came out uncertainly, nearly a question.

Zanzidore looked up at them and rested his hand on top of the cage. "It's a simple canary. But she's asleep right now. You know." He leaned in a bit. "For the trip. Can't have her chirping the whole way."

"Yes," Taenya said with a sweet smile and turned back to Jez. "What time does the carriage get here again?"

"Why don't the two of you have any luggage?" Zanzidore asked, eyeing the fennex and the elf.

The question made Doli's heart pick up as Sarson quietly made his way around to the back of the station.

"The second the wizard is asleep, we need to be ready to run to her," Doli whispered under her breath.

Theo would be the most likely to reach Evvy first with his quick, long legs. Doli knew this, but it didn't mean she wouldn't try.

Sarson was finally close enough and conjured his magic, directing it at the wizard. The blue sparkles wove through the air and met with his back.

"You didn't answer my question," he said, yawning, his voice heavy with sleep.

Jez and Taenya each took a step backward, as if waiting to see what was going to happen.

The wizard slumped and immediately Jez threw off the fabric, revealing Evvy gagged and tied up inside.

"Evvy!" Doli shouted and ran toward her. Theo and Arleta followed.

By the time they had all reached the cage, Jez had pulled the little dragon out and released her from the bindings around her body and mouth.

Evvy squawked, spread her wings, and took flight.

"Let's go," Doli said, but a sound made her turn back. The wizard had righted himself and was blinking his eyes open.

Magic sparked in his palm, and before any of them except Evvy could move, he'd shot it out at Jez, Arleta, Theo, and Taenya. "I knew there was something going on with you two."

The magic surrounded them like a bubble. They were trapped.

Zanzidore spun around to Sarson and gritted his teeth. But Sarson spread his wings and launched into the air. The wizard raised his hands as though to cast a spell at the gargoyle, but Doli had already begun running. She rammed into the wizard like a bull—a small bull, but a bull nonetheless.

Somehow she managed to knock him over, but he was up in a flash, directing his magic with one hand into the sky and the other at Doli.

Sarson crashed to the ground. Doli opened her mouth to shout a horrified protest, but as she did, the weight of the magic impacted her chest, sending the dwarf tumbling backward through the dirt.

As Doli lay dazed on the hard ground, she could barely make out Zanzidore's sparkling red magic swirling in the air. Sarson lay not too far away, but out of her reach. She was pretty sure he was either unconscious or on the edge of passing out.

"Doli," a voice she thought might be Jez's called from far off in the distance. "Get up." But it couldn't be, because Jez was trapped in Zanzidore's magic with the others.

She tried to lift her head to see where the voice came from, but it felt like a stone.

Thoughts spun through Doli's discombobulated brain, and she tried to forced them to coalesce. *Has Evvy escaped?* She was pretty sure that she had, but if Sarson's magic was useless against Zanzidore, would any of them make it out alive? And if they didn't, he would go on the hunt after the dragon. She wouldn't be safe anywhere.

The gargoyle propped up on his side and turned his attention back to Zanzidore. He bared his teeth, growling.

"You bastard." In one motion his wings unfurled. The wind they displaced washed over Doli's face and somehow cleared her mind.

Zanzidore clicked his tongue. "Let's not bring family history to this fight unless you want to discuss yours as well. What's in the past is just that."

Sarson growled, deadly serious but for some reason unable to harden his skin for protection against the magic. "I will end you."

"Oh, will you?" Zanzidore chuckled and gazed at his hands. "You tried that a moment ago." He moved his hands in a spiraling pattern, and the magic floated from his fingertips in sync with the motion. "Your magic isn't very strong, gargoyle." Zanzidore raised his brow. "This dragon means little to you. If you value your life, I suggest you turn and fly away. Leave the troubles of these useless people behind." He paused for a second. "I won't give any more warnings, but I do feel as if I owe you for stumbling onto something valuable to me. Have the freedom you desire…a life with little meaning. But leave me to my business."

Slowly Sarson moved onto his hands and knees, staring at Zanzidore. "If trapping a being that should be free is your definition of a meaningful life, I want nothing to do with it."

Doli's heart rate picked up as she envisioned what was going to happen next. The reality was that none of them were a match for Zanzidore's magic. He was a powerful wizard, and he wanted Evvy. Sarson was going to get himself killed trying to protect the dragon. And it wasn't even his job to do so.

It was hers.

This realization sparked something in Doli's chest, and her fingers buzzed with frenetic energy. Evvy had chosen her. If they were indeed destined to accomplish something together, then it was Doli's responsibility to fulfill that fate. Even if she had to die trying. As ridiculous as the whole thing sounded—that a dwarf specializing in tea magic would somehow save the day—it didn't matter.

Nothing else mattered at that moment.

Her side ached from Zanzidore's magic blast, but Doli ignored it. She needed to get up. She needed to help her friends; she needed to find Evvy and get her out of there so she could grow up to become Evengeline, Protector of the Dawn Order.

She needed to take down that wizard. Even if bergamot tea was the best weapon she had.

As Doli rose, Sarson lunged at Zanzidore with his wings fully spread, fangs bared and claws fully extended as his skin hardened into an armorlike texture. She gasped. The gargoyle was terrifying. But Zanzidore's magic was faster than Sarson's brawn, striking him in the chest and enveloping his entire body. Red magic twisted around him, sparkling and squeezing. Howling in pain, he fought to stay upright. His skin was normal again.

"You were always a fool," the wizard sneered. "Your entire line has been weak."

"You mean we wouldn't give in to people like you." Sarson had to fight to get the words out.

The world went into slow motion for Doli. Filled with

rage, she gritted her teeth, and her arms prickled with electricity that flowed down to her hands and into her fingers. Magic wove between her digits. The sensation was exactly as if she were about to make tea but a thousand times stronger. The dwarf struggled to breathe.

Steeling herself, she planted her feet in a fighting stance she'd only read about in books. On instinct she hadn't known she possessed, Doli threw her hands forward. Before they were even fully extended, the energy was so strong she thought it would blow her backward. But she focused as she never had before in her life, and the awesome power burst from her palms and hurtled toward Zanzidore.

The wizard was swept off his feet and slammed against the trunk of a massive tree a considerable distance from where he'd stood.

"Touch him again and die!" she screamed, burning with rage. She stalked toward the downed wizard, who was struggling to talk.

"You shut your mouth. You have no right to speak here!" she yelled. She shot more of the invisible force from her hands and bound his entire body with it. "I will not let you harm anyone I love!"

"Doli," Sarson said weakly behind her.

The dwarf felt the power surging in her body as she came closer to Zanzidore, and part of her really wanted to end him. But she knew it would be wrong. Working again by instinct, she somehow tied off the magical bindings to keep the wizard confined, then lowered her hands. She'd find all of her friends again, and they'd figure out together what to do with him.

"Doli!" Arleta's voice rang out, and the dwarf spun around to see her friends running toward her.

Theo helped Sarson up, while Taenya, Jez, and Arleta, followed by Evvy flying over their heads, crashed into the dwarf.

"What happened?" Jez wrapped her long arms around her friend. The others joined in a group hug while Evvy spun around them.

"I…I don't exactly know." The power still buzzed in Doli's hands. She squeezed each of them tightly and then wriggled away to check on the others.

"Are you okay?" she yelled as she ran toward Theo and Sarson.

"I'm fine." Theo smiled as he directed the dwarf to the gargoyle.

Doli collided with Sarson's massive frame, and tears rolled down her cheeks. "You could have died!"

Sarson picked Doli up and hugged her tightly. "I could say the same for you, my lady. You're the most breathtaking woman I've ever met." He looked deeply into her eyes. "Thank you."

She was about to kiss him when something else happened.

The dragons came.

27

The dragon clan gloriously appeared out of thin air in a puff of magic and mystery.

As Sarson put her down and held on to her hand, Doli gasped at the sight of their long, graceful necks, powerful muscles, and jewel-toned scales in a myriad of dazzling colors. Each had a long tail and iridescent wings that sparkled in the sunlight. And just like Evvy, they had curled-back horns, though theirs were much longer than the baby dragon's. They were not the largest dragons Doli had ever heard of in the Northern Lands, but they were at least double Sarson's height, which was substantial, so to take in the full view she had to crane her neck.

She was pretty sure the situation was safe, but when it came to dragons, one never really knew.

Little Evvy, still no bigger than a kitten, zipped in and out among them, radiant joy on her face at seeing those that looked like her.

Happiness also bubbled in Doli's chest at the sight. But mixed with the happiness of knowing their destiny had been fulfilled was sadness. She knew that if the dragons were there, then it was time for Evvy to go.

She looked back at her friends, all standing together as if in shock at the dragon clan's arrival.

A red dragon blew fire into the air and let out a trumpeting sound as if in celebration. The friends moved closer to surround Doli, and she found their support comforting.

A medium-sized dragon turned to Zanzidore, who was still bound by Doli's magic.

With all the excitement she'd almost forgotten about Zanzidore. Almost.

"You'll be coming with me," the golden dragon said in a deep, musical voice. He lowered his head and narrowed his eyes as if he already knew exactly what had happened. Golden magic emitted from his claws and encircled Zanzidore. In a flash, they were both gone.

Doli didn't even bother to ask what Zanzidore's fate would be. She gulped and brought her attention back to the largest of the dragons. The scarlet dragon held out her palm to Evvy, and the little dragon immediately flew and landed on it.

The large dragon examined Evvy for a beat and then twisted her head to Doli, her golden reptile eyes widening.

The dwarf froze, gripping Sarson's hand tightly.

"Doli Butterbuckle," the dragon said in a gentler, warmer tone than Doli had expected.

"Yes," the dwarf squeaked.

"Please step forward, guardian," she said and gracefully launched Evvy back into the air.

Doli released Sarson's grasp and somehow took a step forward, despite her wobbling knees. The bravado she'd had a few moments before had all but disappeared. Evvy descended and landed on the dwarf's shoulder. Doli automatically placed her hand on the baby dragon's back and ran her fingertips along the bumpy scales. A calm that felt like it came from Evvy swept through her.

As Doli approached the scarlet dragon, the large being bowed her head low to the ground, as did all the others. The dwarf gulped and glanced back at her friends, who urged her on.

"I don't deserve—" Doli started.

But the lead dragon righted herself and stated, "Of course you deserve this. You were given a challenge and rose to the occasion, my dear." She paused momentarily. "But I do appreciate your humility." Her eyes flicked to Evvy. "You chose well."

Evvy lowered her head and nuzzled her snout along Doli's cheek.

The lead dragon continued. "The strength inside your mind and body is great. It has always been there...*brewing* until the right time." She winked.

And the pun, all the funnier coming from the enormous, dignified being, made Doli laugh.

"Your magic lies in protecting those you love and making them feel warm and safe. The tea-making was only the beginning; becoming Evvy's guardian fulfilled your fate." She gazed around at the other friends. "From here on out, the magic will grow because of those you've chosen to be in your life." The dragon straightened. "Doli Butterbuckle. You are a gift to everyone around you. Never forget that."

"Thank you," Doli managed.

The scarlet dragon brought her attention to Evvy. "And now for you."

Evvy rose to her tiptoes on Doli's shoulder and glided a short distance, landing on the grassy turf in front of the adult dragon.

"Your journey is only beginning as well." The scarlet dragon raised her clawed hand, and a puff of magic enveloped Evvy.

Before Doli's eyes the little dragon grew larger and larger. Her wings unfurled like those of a flutterbee emerging from her cocoon, and she soared into the sky.

Doli and all her friends gasped in awe. And a tear may have rolled down Doli's cheek.

Evvy blew out a long stream of fire, did three flips, and descended to the ground, landing directly between Doli and the scarlet dragon with a thud.

"You are ready to take your place among us, Evengeline, Protector of the Dawn Order."

All the dragons bowed low. "Hail, Evengeline," they said in unison.

Evvy bobbed her head slightly. "I think casually I still prefer Evvy."

The leader bowed her head once more. "When you are ready, Evvy." The scarlet dragon waved to the others as if to give Evvy some privacy, and they all retreated.

The grown version of Evvy immediately turned to Doli. "Thank you for everything."

Hearing her new voice, Doli suddenly realized that it was Evvy who had encouraged her to get up and confront the wizard.

Doli's instinct, of course, was to tell Evvy that it was nothing and anyone could have done it. But she stopped herself because it wasn't true. "You're welcome."

The dragon brought her enormous head close to the dwarf's and whispered, "The necklace in your inheritance box—"

Doli brought her hand to the jeweled charm hanging around her neck.

"It binds us," Evvy said. "Use it to contact me whenever you'd like to see me. And if you see it glowing, I'd like to see you. Just accept the magic and we'll be together."

"Is tomorrow too soon?" Doli asked, a lump rising in her throat.

Evvy shook her head as her golden eyes glistened with tears. "No."

Doli threw her arms around the dragon's neck and squeezed. When Doli released her, Evvy turned her attention to her other friends.

"And you all were also very brave. You supported Doli

when you could have turned back to save yourselves." Evvy raised her regal head. "Every one of you has become honorary members of the Fervour dragons. If you ever ask one of us for help, it will not be denied to you." She raised her hand in the air, and pink magic enveloped the group.

They took turns giving her a hug and wishing her the best on her passage. No one had dry eyes as they excused themselves to give Doli and Evvy their last private moment.

"Oh, and I wanted you to know," Evvy said to Doli with a twinkle in her eye. "While I was waiting for you on the other side of the stars, I met someone who you were very special to."

Doli tipped her head in interest. "I don't understand."

Evvy bowed her head slightly and flapped her wings. "The other side is like that…difficult to understand. But I met a dwarf very much like you—beautiful and equally kind."

"Who?"

Evvy gazed up at the sky as if recalling a pleasant memory. "On multiple occasions, she made me lavender tea, always with two portions of sugar. And those same jam-filled spice cookies you make so well."

A lump instantly formed in Doli's throat. "You knew my grandmother?"

"Yes. Grazigrett." Evvy paused for a moment. "Lovely woman. I hope to see her again. I have no doubt that I will. And you will too, someday. Because love is eternal."

Tears rolled down Doli's cheeks, and Evvy's tail came up and wiped them away with the tip.

"Next time we meet, we shall have tea and cookies, and I'll tell you more about my conversations with your grammy." Evvy brought her friend in close with her tail and tapped the necklace around Doli's neck. "Call on me anytime. Even tomorrow—if I don't call you first."

The dwarf wrapped her arms around Evvy's long neck. "It was a pleasure knowing you, Evengeline, Protector of the Dawn Order."

The dragon bowed her head low. "The privilege was all mine, Doli Butterbuckle."

With that, Evvy rejoined her dragon clan and Doli's friends returned to her side. Both Jez and Arleta placed their arms around her, and the three original bakers watched the dragons take flight to return to Mount Blackdon.

Sarson, Theo, and Taenya stepped up beside them, and no one took their eyes away until the dragons were completely out of sight.

When they were, Doli stepped forward, turned to the group, smiled and said, "Let's all go home."

And they did.

Epilogue

Jez

It was a bright, sunshiny day, but a slight chill on the breeze gave Jez a taste of the months to come.

And she didn't like it. The fennex didn't really like much of anything, but she particularly didn't like cold weather and the musty aromas that came with it.

She grumbled as she lugged the heavy lunch basket down the brown grass-lined path to the pond. It was her own fault really that she was carrying it. The fennex had volunteered to do it even though she hadn't even wanted to come to the picnic, let alone tow around a heavy basket.

But it was likely the last time before snow came, ushering in the Yule season, and Doli insisted that all her friends come and enjoy the end of the fall season. Including Jez.

She'd wanted to take a nap, but Doli was difficult to refuse.

The fennex wasn't used to the cold that living in Adenashire brought. All her life, she'd lived in the Southern Desert where it was warm most of the year, and there was definitely no snow.

In fact, Jez had never even seen snow before.

The rest of the group—Arleta, Theo, Doli, Sarson the gargoyle, and Taenya—were far ahead of her already as her feet slowed. Even so, their individual scents permeated her nose. Floral, spice…several others. With her powerful sense of smell, Jez mostly blocked out her friends' scents lest they become overwhelming, but her scent magic didn't always allow it.

Doli spun around and waited, her arms crossed over her chest. The dwarf wore one of her completely impractical, overly frilly dresses with a long blue cape draped over her shoulders. She'd stayed up all night making it for this occasion.

Doli usually smelled of vanilla and sunshine.

So with a huff and her fluffy tail flicking behind her, Jez picked up the pace and finally caught up.

"You didn't have to carry that." Doli's brown eyes lowered to the basket hanging from Jez's clawed hands. "Sarson would have carried it, you know."

"I'm fine," Jez said gruffly, wishing she'd worn a warmer coat rather than her thin one made of cotton. But she didn't have one.

Doli scowled, keeping her arms crossed over her chest. "You look cold."

"I'm not cold!" The fennex flicked her ear in irritation, hiked up the basket, and edged her way past Doli. "It's just not the best day for a picnic." Over the grass she spotted the pond and the others laying out the blankets they'd carried.

"Well, we're almost there," Doli confirmed, although the fennex was pretty sure Doli couldn't see a thing with the grass several inches over her head. The dwarf looked Jez up and down for an uncomfortable second. "And you need to stand for a fitting. I'm going to sew you some new wool pants and a shirt."

Jez wrinkled her nose. "For a what?"

"A fitting," Doli said, raising her brow. "All the clothing you own is far too thin for the upcoming weather."

She meant snow.

The fennex looked down at herself, taking in her ivory linen shirt, black cotton pants, and of course the too-thin coat. "My clothes are fine."

"Yes," Doli agreed. "For warmer months. It will snow soon."

"Damn snow," Jez scoffed.

"Yes, damn snow," Doli said with sympathy in her tone and waved Jez on. "And...our group is getting bigger. That's difficult for you."

Jez's chest tightened. She hadn't mentioned that to Doli, but even without scent magic the dwarf was intuitive about people and their feelings. "You know I don't like *anybody*," she muttered.

Doli nodded. "I know. Not even me."

"I like you," Jez admitted.

"I know," she said with a half smirk. "And Arleta…and Theo, Taenya…and Sarson is growing on you." Doli ran her brown hand across the wall of grass beside her as they walked.

"I like Faylin," Jez admitted, knowing that she probably had the most in common with the aloof forest lynx. "And Evvy is cute when we get to see her."

"Oh, definitely Evvy." Doli bobbed her head in agreement. "Everyone likes Evvy."

"It's hard for me to…people. And I get tired," Jez said as the path opened up wider and she got an unobstructed view of the pond. Which was, in fact, nice.

If you liked that sort of thing.

Doli reached up and placed her warm hand on the fennex's elbow. "I know. Thank you for coming."

Warmth filled Jez's chest at her friend's touch. Sometimes she forgot how much she really did love Doli…and her other friends too.

The last of the golden leaves were barely clinging to the oak tree branches, and the breeze made ripples in the pond, which was larger than she'd imagined from Doli's description.

"Did I tell you about when Evvy dropped a fish in my lap from the air and ruined Sarson's plan to kiss me?" Doli giggled.

"Multiple times." The fennex rolled her eyes and let out a sigh as Doli chattered on, retelling the story anyway. Jez was pretty sure the size of the fish got bigger each time.

But thankfully, Sarson looked up from spreading out a

blanket and came over to them, and Doli stopped talking. He held out his hand. "I can take that if you like."

For a moment, Jez fought the impulse to say no and handed the basket over. The gargoyle gave her a smile, then looked down at Doli and held out his free blue clawed hand to her.

"My lady," he said gently as she took his grasp.

"Yes." Doli sighed, and they walked on ahead, hand in hand.

Jez rolled her eyes and shook her head but picked up the pace to join the others.

"We were just talking about the Yule Games." Arleta came to Jez's side and threaded her arm in the fennex's, leading her to sit with Theo and Taenya. Doli and Sarson spread out the buffet of sandwiches, fruit, cut vegetables, and of course multiple types of cookies.

"Yule Games?" Jez said. She immediately regretted asking and rubbed her arms to warm them.

Theo passed Jez a plate. "Arleta has been telling us all about it. Every year after the first snow of Yule, the entire village holds a competition."

"A scavenger hunt, snow sculpting… There's an ice maze," Arleta said as she plucked a roast beef sandwich from the tray.

"Ugh," Jez scoffed, thinking about the ice maze.

"You didn't say what the winner receives." Taenya scooped some apple and walnut salad onto her plate, poked a piece with her fork, and took a bite.

Arleta shrugged. "Mostly bragging rights, but businesses

pitch in prizes. Oh…and did I mention that it's in teams of two? Because of that, I've never taken part before, but Ervash and Verdreth have. Even took first place about ten years ago."

"You can compete this year, though," Theo said, rubbing her arm.

Arleta's eyes lit up with delight. "You mean it?"

Theo nodded. "Wouldn't miss the chance to hang out with you all day." He waggled his eyebrows.

The fennex scoffed and stuffed her hands into her coat pockets.

"Doli and I would give it a go too," Sarson said as Doli nodded enthusiastically.

Taenya pulled her knees up to her body. "I'd do it if I could find a partner."

"Sounds terrible," Jez said as her teeth chattered. She grabbed a sliced lamb sandwich with mint sauce and stuffed a bite into her mouth to stop the clacking.

The group all turned their attention on the fennex and stared at her. Jez stopped chewing and frowned at the others.

"Oh, stars in heaven." Taenya wriggled out of her coat and held it out to Jez.

"What?" the fennex said, her mouth still full of food.

The elf scowled and pushed it farther at Jez. "Just take it, you silly fox. I'm more used to the cold."

Jez wrinkled her nose for a second as she finished chewing but then considered the woolen coat lined with sheepskin. She put down her sandwich, grabbed the coat, and threaded her arms through the padded sleeves. A perfect fit. Warmth enveloped her torso and arms. The scent of the coat was nice too. Scents of the woods, piney and warm and a hint of sweet icing sugar…like Taenya…enveloped the fennex with a sense of safety and caring that she hadn't experienced before. But she quickly shook the feeling off.

"Thanks," she muttered, not looking at the elf and taking another bite of sandwich.

"I'm making you a new coat too," Doli said and leaned her head on Sarson's muscular arm. He pulled the dwarf a little closer with his wing. "You aren't allowed to say no."

"Because I want mine back eventually," Taenya quipped.

Jez grunted and chewed on her sandwich, enjoying the sweet and savory combination. She was warm again, and it wasn't only from Taenya's coat but from the people in her life that she'd never trade for all the riches in the Northern Lands—even if she didn't always want to admit it.

Interrupting her thoughts, Sarson popped the cork of a bottle of sparkling wine he'd brought and poured a portion into each of their glasses. "To friendship." He held his glass high.

All smiles, the others did the same. Even Jez managed to curl up her lips halfway. "To friendship," they all called in unison. They drank the bubbly wine and enjoyed the food and the pleasure of each other's company.

And it was indeed a special occasion on which this Fellowship of Librarians and Dragons planned many more adventures together.

Bonus Chapter

Favorite Things

The scent of spice swirled in the air, filling Doli's eight-year-old senses as she burst through the dark stained wooden front door of the uniquely modest dwarven home. Everything about being there made the realm better for the young dwarf. From the cozy lived-in, perfectly sized furniture as well as the oil paintings hung too high on the walls of family, some long gone and some still with them. The entire place held cherished memories for Doli. The cottage was nothing like her home, which was too big, loud, and always bustling with activity. Upon her entrance, comfort and peace instantly took hold of Doli's little body, even with the contrasting buzz of excitement twirling inside her stomach at the thought of seeing her grandmother.

Grazigrett Butterbuckle was Doli's favorite person in the Northern Lands.

And for good reason.

"Grammy!" Doli shouted as the weighty door clicked shut behind her. But calling out wasn't truly necessary since, by the delicious scent filling the place, the eight-year-old had known at once where her grandmother likely was.

In the kitchen.

"In here, my love." Grammy's familiar, rich voice reminded Doli of both music and cinnamon twirls.

Doli smoothed down her favorite rose-colored velvet dress, then grazed her fingers over the little pink-and-black flutterbee she'd embroidered on the left side of the sweetheart neckline to make the dress her own, then ran from the front door toward the kitchen. The well-worn path on the oak floor easily led the way, although Doli needed no directions.

The cozy kitchen was a den of delight where Grazigrett stood at the heirloom worktable in the middle of the room, her wrinkled umber hands pushing a rolling pin into a disk of tan dough to form a large sheet. Her gray micro braids were pulled up onto the top of her head and secured into a near-perfect bun that reminded Doli of a cinnamon roll. The dwarf glanced up from her work and a wide smile stretched over her lips, revealing a set of pearly teeth, despite her age.

"You're early," she said, voice rich like molasses.

Grammy's sleeves sat rolled up on her upper arms that still bore dwarven strength, not so much from working the earth with an axe or pick—although the woman had done her share in her day—but from a lifetime of rolling dough, stirring cake batters, and kneading delicious breads to serve to those she loved. Over her head hung a rack of copper pots and pans used for the cooking she also seemed to revel in nearly as much as baking.

"Are we making spice cookies?" Doli's voice filled with hope as she clasped her hands together in front of her in anticipation. But she already knew they were since a batch lay cooling next to the cast-iron stove.

"They're your favorite, aren't they?" Grammy winked in affirmation and returned to her work.

"Yes!" A squeal left Doli's mouth, and she skittered around to the other side of the worktable where a worn and chipped white step stool already waited for her to stand on. The small dwarf was about to step onto it when Grammy spoke.

"Wash your hands?" she asked, not deterred from the cookie dough.

"Oh, yes." Doli turned toward the familiar basin behind her grandmother and poured water from the pitcher beside it over her palms. The young dwarf quickly scrubbed her hands and under her fingernails with the gently scented vanilla soap her grandmother loved. Doli quickly finished the rest of the job, dried her hands on a waiting cloth, and threw them in the air in presentation. "All clean!"

Grammy chuckled, and the skin at the corners of her eyes crinkled like skirt pleats. "Well, let's get them dirty again."

Already salivating, Doli was more than ready to oblige her grandmother's offer. She hopped up on the stool and

Grammy quickly thrust the rolling pin into her granddaughter's hands.

"You finish rolling that out and I'll get the jam." Grammy turned and shuffled slowly to the cold box, her feet dragging slightly across the floor.

Doli eyed her briefly before returning to the dough in front of her. Even she had noticed her grandmother was slowing down, but anytime anyone asked about it, the woman would simply wave her hand in the air and say, "When you've lived as long as me, there's no need to rush anymore."

And truly…that didn't sound too bad to Doli. But something tickled the back of her mind, telling her there was more to it. It was part of the reason she never missed their weekly baking sessions. That and Grammy was the only person who truly got Doli.

Grammy's home was her safe place.

"When the cookies are baking, you'll make us some tea. Won't you, love?" Grammy clutched the jar full of red plum jam she'd retrieved from the cold box and placed it on the butcher block worktable.

Doli's tea magic tingled in her palms at just the mention of tea. The rest of her family couldn't understand why Doli's magic revolved around the drink. In the end, she didn't understand either, since most dwarven magic centered around gems or the earth. But tea magic it was. And at least her grammy loved it.

"What would you like to try today?" Doli stopped rolling for a moment.

"Hmm." Grammy squinted in thought. "How about that lavender cream you made last time?"

Doli's brain and hands buzzed with excitement. She'd spent hours trying to perfect the lavender cream tea and was so pleased Grammy had actually enjoyed it enough to ask for it again. "Really?" The question came out a little squeaky.

"I've been thinking about it all week." Grammy popped opened the jam jar and plucked a spoon from a drawer behind her. "Two lumps of sugar this time."

Warmth seeped through Doli's chest, and she placed the rolling pin aside as she reached for the round metal cookie cutter. She began cutting the dough into circles and moving each onto the baking sheet.

Grammy spooned a small amount of scarlet jam into the center of each round, folded over the dough to seal it and pinched each into the shape of an apple seed.

"You know," Doli said as she cut the last of the dough. There was a small amount left over, but not enough for a full cookie. She rolled it up under her fingers. "It would be much easier just to make a ball and then push it down in the middle. You could fill it with jam. The cookie would taste just as good."

Grammy chuckled and stopped what she was doing. "My love, you are entirely right, and I have. But years ago, I once made them in the shape of an apple seed and your father—" She stopped speaking for a blink. "He must have been just about your age."

Doli couldn't really ever picture her father as her age, but Grammy always told her the truth, and so it must have been true.

"He enjoyed them so much I never made them in any other shape." She grinned. "Sometimes love is worth a little extra effort."

A smile crept its way over Doli's lips as she studied every earned line on her grandmother's beautiful face. Doli couldn't wait for the time in her life when she was just as stunning and wise. But it did seem a very long way down the path of life.

When the cookies were complete, Grammy placed the tray into the hot oven. It wasn't long before the air filled again with spice while the two dwarves, young and old, sat at the small, lace-cloth-covered table in the corner of the kitchen enjoying cups of steaming magical tea from the special dainty cups Grammy kept in her cupboard.

Doli gazed down at the plate of frosted spice cookies between them, then up at Grammy.

Grammy took one from the pile and handed it to Doli. The young dwarf took it and immediately bit into the spice cookie. A blend of sweet spice and tart jam flooded her taste buds, reminding her of her favorite things in life, one of which was her grandmother.

And even at only eight, Doli Butterbuckle couldn't agree more that sometimes love *is* worth a little extra effort.

RECIPES
of
ADENASHIRE

Developing the recipes for this book series has been such an honor. I hope you make and love each one of them.

Jam-Filled Spice
COOKIES

These cookies have a history in my family, and I've attempted to make them since I was about eighteen—don't ask me how long ago that was.

My husband's Mennonite oma up in Canada had long made them, along with an orange-flavored cookie, and both were family favorites. When he and I were dating, I'd go over to his house, and his family would have those one-gallon ice cream buckets full of both types of cookies that his oma had made for them. They'd been sent down from Canada at some point to be frozen and eaten. I'd say they typically showed up around Christmastime.

No one else in the family made them, so I asked for the recipe and decided to give it a go.

It was pretty much a miserable failure.

Not only are the spice cookies a very old-fashioned recipe with ingredients like lard, but they are also notoriously difficult to shape. The cookies have an oblong, apple seed shape that I've never seen before—and believe me, I've scoured the internet. They are not there.

At eighteen there wasn't much internet to scour in any case—don't think about how long ago that was. So with nothing but Oma's handwritten recipe, I had to go it pretty much alone with my attempts at making the cookies.

In the end, if I remember right, they tasted pretty good, but I never got the shape right. I ended up making a lot of them into thumbprint cookies. And while my husband, then boyfriend, liked them and was grateful for my efforts, he was still nostalgic for the stuffed apple seed–shaped version.

So, after that? I kind of gave up and left it to the cookie care packages from Oma. Although I did hang on to the handwritten instructions for all these years. (It got wet at some point and was very difficult to read.)

Fast-forward to 2023, and Oma passed away.

I knew at this point I needed to give the cookie recipe another go, otherwise, there would be no more spice cookies and my husband's family tradition would die. So I asked around to family members who live up in Canada if I could get a readable version of the cookie recipe. Soon after I was texted another handwritten version as well as a similar recipe printed in a Mennonite cookbook. I also finally found a version on the internet from a woman who also had a Mennonite oma.

But once again, the recipes were all very old-fashioned to

some degree. Some of them called for ingredients like lard and baking ammonia.

I went ahead and made the recipe from Oma's original handwritten one. The only thing I changed was halving the recipe because it made so many cookies—and I didn't have any one-gallon buckets for the freezer.

The result? Even following the recipe to a T (other than the halving part), the dough was incredibly soft and nearly impossible to form the "required" apple seed shape. I started having flashbacks to my eighteen-year-old self and remembered why all those cookies ended up as thumbprints.

So I spent a few days rethinking the recipe. There was a lot of liquid called for, so I reduced it to see if I could get an easier dough to work with. Still too soft. I couldn't help but wonder how Oma had made all those cookies for all those years when the dough was so incredibly difficult to work with. And why had she chosen such an unusual shape (that my husband was clinging to) for the final product when it only added to the difficulty?

At that point I started doing more research on cookie dough to figure out how to retain the intent and flavor of the cookie while using more modern ingredients and methods.

The dough has a similar flavor to rolled gingerbread cookies but without the gingerbread, of course. So my research headed in that direction. I mapped out the ratios used for soft, chewy gingerbread cookies and gave a version based off those a go.

And that was my most successful cookie so far. The texture was good. The cookies were much easier to roll out.

And that right flavor was there. I'll admit my apple seed shaping skills still needed work. But the process was easier.

My husband really liked them, although he found them sweeter than the originals.

For the final recipe I ended up reducing the sugar ratio and called it a day. For now.

I have a feeling that these jam-filled spice cookies are a work in progress. But they are still a delicious tribute to a hardworking, so much more than cookie-making, woman.

Ingredients

COOKIES:
- 1 cup softened unsalted butter (277 grams)
- ¾ cup granulated sugar (150 grams)
- 1 large egg
- ¼ cup molasses (60 mL)
- 1 tablespoon apple cider vinegar (15 mL)
- 2 teaspoons vanilla extract (30 mL)
- 5 cups flour (600 grams)
- ½ teaspoon salt (6 grams)
- 1 teaspoon baking powder (4.8 grams)
- 1 teaspoon cinnamon (4 grams)
- ¼ teaspoon ground cloves (1 gram)
- ½ teaspoon allspice (2 grams)
- ⅛ teaspoon star anise (.5 gram)
- 1 cup plum jam (or your favorite flavor) (320 grams)

ICING*:
- 3 cups powdered sugar (345 grams)
- 2 tablespoons corn syrup (30 mL)
- 2 tablespoons water (plus more for thinning) (30 mL)

Note

* I chose an eggless royal icing because I don't love to work with raw eggs, and corn syrup is easy to keep on hand. But a traditional thinner royal icing with eggs would also work very well with this recipe.

Instructions

In a stand mixer with a paddle attachment, combine the butter and sugar on medium-high until just combined. Then add the egg, molasses, vinegar, and vanilla and beat on medium speed.

In a medium-sized mixing bowl, combine the flour, salt, baking powder, and spices.

Add the dry mixture to the butter, sugar, and molasses mixture and mix on low speed until it forms a soft but not sticky dough.

Form the dough into a ball and cut into three equal pieces. Place one piece between 2 approximately 10.7×13.6-inch sheets of parchment paper, then roll the dough out to the edges. Repeat with the other two dough balls. Stack the dough sheets and place in the refrigerator for 30 to 60 minutes. (If you leave it longer, you will need to allow the dough to warm up for a few minutes before cutting.)

Preheat the oven to 350°F.

Prepare a baking sheet with parchment paper.

Remove one sheet of dough from the refrigerator. Cut twelve pieces using a 3-inch round cookie or biscuit cutter, then place onto the prepared baking sheet. (You may need to reroll the dough between the sheets of parchment paper to achieve 12 pieces.) Place any excess dough back in the refrigerator.

Place 1 teaspoon of plum jam in the middle of each dough piece, fold the dough over the jam into a half circle, and pinch the edges shut. (For a simpler method you can use the tines of a fork to finish crimping the edges, then skip the next instructions and proceed to bake.) Turn each cookie so the sealed edge becomes the bottom of the cookie. Make any adjustments to form the "apple seed" shape. The cookies should have approximately 1 inch of space between each other on the cookie sheet.

Bake for 11 to 13 minutes.

Cool the cookies on the baking sheet for a few moments, then transfer to a cooling rack. (For easier cleanup later when icing, place paper towels or parchment paper under the cooling racks to catch drips.)

Repeat steps 7 through 10 until all the cookies are baked and cooled.

After the cookies are cooled, make the icing. I like using a small 6×6-inch baking dish for this because it makes dipping the cookies easier.

In a small to medium bowl or a 6×6-inch baking dish, combine the powdered sugar, corn syrup, and water. Stir, then thin it to the desired consistency by stirring in an additional 1 teaspoon of water at a time.

Dip each cookie in the icing and return to the cooling racks to dry completely.

Note

These cookies can also be shaped as thumbprint cookies. For these, you can skip the rolling and cutting instructions; instead, scoop 1 tablespoon of dough and roll between your hands into a ball. Place onto the prepared baking sheet. Make a depression in each cookie and place about a ½ teaspoon of jam into each depression. Bake for 11 to 13 minutes at 350°F. Allow the cookies to cool, then drizzle the glaze over each cookie.

Original Recipe
FOR JAM-FILLED SPICE COOKIES
BY OMA PENNER

Keep in mind if you try it that this is definitely not a complete recipe and not all steps are clear.

Ingredients
- 1 cup lard
- 2 cups sugar
- ⅔ cup molasses
- 3 eggs
- 1 cup milk
- 1 cup sour cream
- 7 cups flour (plus up to 1 more cup)
- 2 heaping teaspoons baking powder
- 1 teaspoon baking soda

- **1 teaspoon cinnamon**
- **½ teaspoon ground cloves**
- **½ teaspoon allspice**
- **1 teaspoon ground star anise**

Instructions

Cream the lard and sugar, then add the molasses.

Beat the eggs, milk, and sour cream into the lard/sugar/molasses mixture, then gradually add the flour mixture. Mix well and add up to one more cup of flour to make a fairly stiff dough. Add the baking powder, baking soda, and spices and mix well.

Chill the dough in the refrigerator overnight and take out only a little piece at the time to make the cookies. The dough has to be kept cold for handling.

Let them harden overnight, then ice them with whatever you prefer to do.

Blackberry Rolls
WITH VANILLA CUSTARD

These rolls are a wonderful alternative to cinnamon rolls, particularly for those who enjoy fruity flavors. The lightly sweet and creamy vanilla custard pairs perfectly with the blackberry filling.

And because they are not as sweet as cinnamon rolls, my goal was to infuse as much flavor into the bread as possible. So you might notice some unexpected ingredients like buttermilk and lemon zest, plus lots of butter and some extra sugar used during the rolling process. Each of these enhances the other flavors and makes for a wonderful finished product.

To give the bread a richer texture, I used a technique called lamination in which you layer butter into the dough by folding it over itself multiple times. Lamination is the same process used to create the flaky texture of croissants (although the version in this recipe is greatly simplified). It adds an extra step, but finding those layers in the finished product is so satisfying and delicious.

I tested multiple types of fruit jams/preserves in this recipe and liked blackberry the most. But honestly, if you have a favorite jam or preserve, feel free to use it. It will likely be delicious—and orc-approved.

Ingredients

CUSTARD*:
- 2 cups whole milk (480 mL)
- 4 large egg yolks, at room temperature
- ⅓ cup granulated sugar (65 grams)
- 2 tablespoons cornstarch (20 grams)
- 2 tablespoons flour (18 grams)
- ⅛ teaspoon salt (.75 gram)
- 1 tablespoon vanilla extract (15 mL)

Instructions

Heat the milk in a medium saucepan over medium heat, but do not boil.

Combine the egg yolks, sugar, cornstarch, flour, and salt in a heat-safe bowl and whisk until combined and smooth.

Pour about 1 cup of the hot milk into the bowl in a slow, steady steam while whisking with the egg and sugar mixture. Add the remaining milk and return to saucepan.

Whisk on medium heat until the mixture comes to a boil and begins to thicken (2 to 3 minutes). Continue whisking for another minute.

Remove from the heat and whisk in the vanilla extract.

Transfer to a heat-safe bowl, cover with plastic wrap (push it all the way down to the custard to avoid any skin), and store in the refrigerator until you are ready to use in the rolls.

Note

* There will be approximately double the amount of custard needed to bake into the rolls. I like to serve mine with a dollop of custard on the side.

DOUGH:
- 4 cups all-purpose flour, plus a few tablespoons if needed (480 grams)
- ½ cup sugar, plus ¼ cup more for laminating (100 grams + 50 grams)
- 1 teaspoon salt (6 grams)
- 1 packet instant dry yeast (7 grams)

- 2 eggs, room temperature, plus 1 extra egg for wash
- Zest of 1 lemon, grated finely
- 1 tablespoon vanilla extract (15 mL)
- ¾ to 1 cup buttermilk or buttermilk substitute* (see below), warm (235 mL)
- 6 oz room temperature unsalted butter, cut into pieces (170 grams)
- 4 oz melted butter for lamination (113 grams)
- 1 cup blackberry preserves or jam (for filling) (320 grams)
- 1 tablespoon milk or water (for egg wash) (15 mL)
- Powdered sugar for serving

Instructions

Combine the flour, ½ cup sugar, salt, yeast, eggs, lemon zest, and vanilla in a stand mixer with a paddle attachment turned on low for about one minute to combine.

Begin adding the warmed buttermilk to the mix. I recommend adding no more than ¾ cup while the dough comes together for about one minute. More can be added if it's too dry.

When combined, increase the speed to medium-low and allow to mix for 18 minutes. Scrape down the bowl occasionally with a rubber spatula.

Add 6 ounces of room-temperature butter and mix on medium for approximately 2 minutes until fully incorporated. Allow the dough to mix approximately 5 more minutes until it pulls away from the sides of the bowl and is no longer tacky.

Prepare the inside of a medium-sized bowl with cooking spray or butter.

Form the dough into a ball and place into the prepared bowl. Lightly cover with plastic wrap and let the dough rest for 1½ hours in a draft-free location.

For the rolling-out process I like to measure out 15×10 inches on my counter and tape off with painter's tape (but this is not a necessary step).

Lightly flour the rolling surface and use a rolling pin to roll out to approximately 15×10 inches. (Do your best with this. If the dough won't quite roll out this much, the final product will still be delicious.) Make sure to keep the dough moving a little to make sure it's not sticking to the counter.

When the dough is rolled out to your satisfaction, melt 2 ounces of butter and brush over the dough. (This is the lamination part.)

Sprinkle 2 tablespoons (⅛ cup) of sugar over the butter.

Fold the dough using the envelope method. Take one of the short ends (the 10-inch part) and fold it to meet in the middle. Then fold the other end over the top. The dough should look like a piece of paper folded to fit inside an envelope.

After folding, rotate the dough 90 degrees (flour the surface again if necessary) and begin rolling out again to 15×10 inches.

Brush once more with butter and fold in thirds again using the envelope method.

Cover with a tea towel and allow the dough to rest for 30 minutes.

Reflour surface if necessary and roll out dough to a thin 15×10-inch rectangle.

Spread with blackberry jam.

Cover two baking sheets with parchment paper.

Cut the dough into 15 to 16 equal strips, tightly roll them up, and place on the baking sheets with an inch or so between.

Cover lightly with plastic and allow the rolls to rise for at least 1 hour.

Preheat the oven to 350°F.

Beat 1 egg with 1 tablespoon milk or water in a small bowl.

Brush the top of the rolls with the egg wash. Using a spoon, press open the middle of each roll at least an inch, then fill with about one tablespoon of jam each.

Bake one tray in the lower third part of the oven for about 18 to 20 minutes or until golden on top. Repeat with the second tray.

Allow to cool slightly.

Sprinkle with powdered sugar and serve with extra jam.

Note

* Buttermilk substitute: Add 1 tablespoon of either white or apple cider vinegar to a 1-cup liquid measuring cup. Fill to the 1-cup mark with regular milk.

The Tricky Goat's
FLAKY BUTTERMILK BISCUITS

These ultra-flaky biscuits are simple to make and pair wonderfully with honey butter (like at the Tricky Goat), your favorite jam or preserves, or a simple slather of creamy butter.

Ingredients
- ½ cup grated butter (115 grams)
- 2 cups all-purpose flour (240 grams)
- 2 tablespoons cornstarch (20 grams)
- 1 tablespoon baking powder (14 grams)
- 1 teaspoon salt (6 grams)
- 2 teaspoons sugar (8 grams)
- 1 cup buttermilk or buttermilk substitute* (see below) (236 mL)

Instructions

Place the grated butter in the freezer for 10 minutes.

Preheat the oven to 425°F.

Prepare a baking sheet with parchment paper.

Using a metal strainer (or flour sifter), sift the flour and cornstarch into a large bowl two times. Discard any large or hard bits.

Add the baking powder, salt, and sugar. Stir to combine with the flour and cornstarch.

After 10 minutes in the freezer have passed, add the grated butter to the dry mixture and stir. Make sure all the butter is well-coated with flour.

Add most of the buttermilk. (I leave a few tablespoons in the measuring cup and only add if needed.) Then lightly stir until the mix comes together and is slightly sticky.

Turn out dough onto a lightly floured surface and bring together in a loose ball. Fold the dough over on itself ten times.

With a floured rolling pin, roll the dough out to 1-inch thickness.

Use a 2-inch round cookie or biscuit cutter to cut each biscuit. Press the cutter straight down and pull directly up. Do not twist the cutter.

Handle the leftover dough as little as possible but reroll it out and cut the biscuits. I ended up with 9 full-sized and 1 half-sized that I formed by hand.

Place the biscuits on the prepared baking sheet.

Bake for 15 minutes.

When done, remove from the oven and transfer the biscuits to a cooling rack.

Enjoy warm.

Note

* Buttermilk substitute: Add one tablespoon of either white or apple cider vinegar to a 1-cup liquid measuring cup. Fill to the 1-cup mark with regular milk.

KEEP READING FOR AN EXCERPT
OF THE NEXT BOOK IN J. PENNER'S
CHARMING ADENASHIRE SERIES

A Fellowship of Games & Fables

"Damn sssnow," Jez grumbled to herself through chattering teeth as she passed the florist on Adenashire's main street. She picked up the pace and burst into A Little Dash of Magic Bake Shop, flinging open the door so hard it slammed against the wall. The attached customer bell rang with a vengeance.

She ran her hand over her pointed, furry ears as a heady concoction of sweet and musky lavender, bright piney rosemary, and dried cherries mixed with sugar, flour, and vanilla hit her nose. The scent was completely different from the acrid wood smoke from the Adenashire chimneys she'd taken in on her trudge from the lake nearby, which harbored silvery rainbow-colored fish under its blanket of winter ice.

The aromas coming at her from all directions overwhelmed her brain. Baked goods, smoke, lingering evidence of the morning customers...not to mention the scent of Taenya Carralei, a woodland elf and part bakery owner who was also one of her best friends. She was nowhere to be seen but had to be working there somewhere...probably in the back. The elf usually smelled of icing sugar and relief.

And that day was no different.

Being a fennex meant that Jez had an extraordinary sense of smell, but she had an extra magical edge to hers. She could smell people's emotions, their intentions.

And some days, she wished she hadn't been born that way. A regular sniffer would have been fine. Easier.

The gift mostly caused engulfment and exhaustion. So over the years, Jez had learned to control and repress the magic, but doing so made her tired...and cranky some of the time.

Most of the time if she was honest with herself. But the occasional shot of rum helped with that. And so had moving to Adenashire, where she didn't have to be reminded that she'd never lived up to her potential back in the Southern Desert.

Her foxlike ears twitched, and her nose burned as she chafed her hands over her arms, shivering despite the coat she wore. A light sprinkling of snow fell to the floor and looked like scattered salt. Another of her best friends, Doli Butterbuckle, had handmade the woolen coat for her before the season's first snowstorm. Of that, at least, Jez was grateful.

But for the snow? Not at all.

The snow and cold made the hair on her uncovered tail stand on end. And she hated that.

On her back perched a pack of winter fishing equipment, including an ax, a pole she'd bought from the local outdoor market, and a handful of other odds and ends. Two good-sized trout were nestled inside a double-lined cotton bag clipped to her brown leather belt.

Jez already had lunch plans for the fish—sautéed with butter, dried herbs, and a sprinkling of preserved lemon. Her stomach growled at the thought.

And although the lunch would be nice, she never went fishing for the fish. It was chiefly to get a break for a few hours. She loved Adenashire and her friends, but at least once a week, she needed time to herself at the quiet lake to think. Snow or no snow.

Almost three quarters of a year ago, she'd moved to Adenashire, right after the Langheim Baking Battle. She'd decided on a whim to apply for the competition after a disagreement with her father. Jez had always been a good baker, and the hobby had offered her solace in what was always a noisy, bustling household.

But even after she received her invitation and snuck away to the Battle, she'd never honestly intended to win (and she didn't, but that's a story for a different day)—doing so would have brought her more attention than she could afford. Competing was only a diversion.

Then, to avoid returning to the Southern Desert, she'd followed her new friend Doli, a dwarf (who had also been running from a challenging family, and that too is another interesting story), to live in Adenashire.

Overall, the village was a peaceful home with minimal responsibility, unlike the place she'd come from. Always churning in the depths of her brain was the question of whether her family missed her. But she hoped they thought life was easier without her and would let her absence be.

She had left a note. Not a detailed one but a note, nonetheless, which told them where she'd gone and that she needed space.

That said, all the snow in Adenashire had recently been making her regret her decision. Sand and sun were far more to her liking than the cold. But the discomfort wasn't enough to make her return to her former life.

And the friends she'd made had given her purpose. At least a purpose she actually enjoyed.

Jez gazed around the otherwise empty bakery and closed her eyes for a second. She breathed in deeply to calm her nerves, then mentally blocked the scent magic and persistent thoughts overwhelming her mind.

Thankfully, the buzzing at the rear of her sinuses settled after the third out-breath.

Taenya, wiping her hands on a white cotton towel, pushed through the swinging door leading out of the kitchen. Her butter-yellow apron with strawberries embroidered at the top was speckled with flour. Jez suspected the needlework was Doli's.

The elf, whose nature magic gave her an incredible talent for baking and decorating cakes, had won the Baking

Battle for the third time in a row. She, too, had moved to Adenashire after the competition to start over.

Funny how that competition had brought the group of unlikely friends together. As if the stars had aligned.

"Oh," the woodland elf said, her green eyes brightening. "Jez. I thought I heard someone come in." A grin quirked up the corners of her bow-shaped lips, and she dragged her hand over her bobbed auburn hair, which had been pulled into two short bunches on each side of her head and tied off with cotton twine. The arrangement looked a little like she had wings sprouting beneath her pointed ears, but Jez didn't mind the style. She wasn't one who cared much about fashion. That was Doli's thing.

The action, however, left flour from her pale fingertips in her hair, making a powdery mess.

"Uh, hi," Jez said, her brown eyes trained on the flour specks. She lifted her clawed hand and pointed. "You got a little something…"

Taenya reached up reflexively as if to pat her hair again but caught herself just in time, instead holding her hand out to examine the mess the towel had failed to remove. "Oh, stars!" she exclaimed, her eyes widening nearly as big as the swirly cinnamon buns that lay piled on display. "I'm a mess."

The fennex shrugged, her dark sand-colored tail flicking behind her. "Yeah. You are."

Taenya rolled her eyes at Jez before tossing the dishcloth on the counter and grabbing a fresh one from underneath. "You could *try* being a little less blunt sometimes."

Jez bit her lip, one fang pinching at the skin. She turned

toward the nearest table and dropped into a wooden chair but kept her body angled to make room for her pack.

"Arleta's not here?" The fennex knew she wasn't since her scent of "human" (they had a particular *non*-magical smell she'd grown used to since moving to Adenashire) peppered with a rotation of herbs from her constant baking experiments was too faint. Arleta Starstone, whom Jez had also met at the Baking Battle, was the other part owner of the bake shop.

Taenya pinched her lips together and shook her head. "She's practicing sledding with Theo for the Yule Games next week."

Jez scoffed and rolled her eyes. "Yule Games," she said with a heaping of disgust. She released her pack from her shoulders, lowered it to the floor, then unclipped the bag of fish. It landed with a dull thump. "You won't find me getting involved with that nonsense. Other than fishing, I'll be inside for the season with something warm to drink."

Thankfully for Jez, Adenashire was mostly a sleepy village, fueled by gossip she tried to stay out of.

"It's going to take over the whole town. I'm not sure you can avoid it." Taenya eyed the cotton bag and crossed her arms over her chest. "You understand that fish smell doesn't really go with…bakery."

"Why not?" Jez said. "Fish is delicious. Patrons will come in, think of lunch, then the dessert they might have when they're done." She threw her hands in the air as if in celebration. "More sales."

The elf gave a low chuckle and made her way to Jez's

table. She pulled out the second wooden chair, its legs scraping the floor, and sat. Then she planted her elbows on the tabletop and rested her slightly pointed chin on her hands, leaning closer to the fennex. "It doesn't work that way, Jez."

Jez blinked three times, then said in a dry tone without moving, "Do you want me to leave?"

Taenya leaned back in her chair. "What pastries would you like today?"

For a moment, Taenya's icing-sugar fragrance intensified. But Jez quickly clamped it down and looked at the counter, where frosting-slathered cinnamon buns sat next to a pile of brown butter chocolate chip cookies, one of Jez's favorites. She twitched her nose as the caramelly notes of the cookies broke through her barrier and made her mouth water.

"I've already got those ready for you," Taenya said. "In the back. I bagged them before I arranged the rest for sale."

"You knew I'd be in?" Jez flicked her attention to her friend, who sat with a slightly smug look on her face.

"You always come in after fishing. And you always fish midweek."

Jez tipped her head in interest and brushed her mop of white hair off her forehead. "Really?"

"Really." The elf's normally pale cheeks for some reason turned a light shade of pink, and she pushed her chair back from the table and stood. "Now, what else can I get you?"

Jez sat for a moment in thought before she said, "How about those bergamot cherry scones?"

Taenya turned to eye the array of goodies on the counter. "They're not even out yet. How'd you know?"

"I smelled them when I came in." Jez fiddled with the twine on her fishing pole. "It's okay if you haven't frosted them. I enjoy them both ways."

The corners of Taenya's mouth pushed upward. "Me too."

Voices wafted in through the shop window, and Jez looked toward the sound. It was Arleta, warmly bundled in a heavy wool coat trimmed with sheepskin, and her Fated Theodmon Brylar, a woodland elf like Taenya. His towhead was mostly hidden under a multicolored knitted cap, and he wore a coat similar to Arleta's. The pair had also met due to the Baking Battle and were disgustingly inseparable, except when Arleta worked in the bakery. Jez still didn't know exactly what Theo did with his time other than clean the home they shared, make dinner, and act as a servant to their forest lynx "house cat," Faylin. Jez couldn't fathom being around another person so much without considerable breaks, Fated or not.

Theo pulled a red sled behind him with one hand and held Arleta's gloved one with the other. As they reached the bakery door, he parked the sled and gave Arleta a twirl, making her loose, chestnut hair take flight from the spin.

"Are they coming in or not?" Jez asked, watching the display with raised brows.

The human giggled and nearly tumbled into his chest. He pulled her close and began kissing her with abandon.

Taenya chuckled. "Guess not."

Jez averted her gaze, suddenly feeling flushed.

"They're so cute," Taenya said with a sigh.

After what seemed like an age, Jez glanced up to her

friend, who must have gone to the kitchen to retrieve the scones and cookies *and* come back, as she held the bag out to Jez without looking at her. The elf's stare was trained on the couple making out on the bakery's stoop, a goofy grin on her lips.

"Shit," Jez said, her eyes briefly landing on Arleta and Theo again before she quickly averted them but not before noticing the green and gold magic radiating off the elf's pale skin. That tended to happen around Arleta…a lot. "I'd think *that* behavior would scare off customers considerably more than a few fish."

Taenya chuckled and returned her attention to Jez. "Could be. But don't you agree their story is romantic?" Taenya gently placed the bag on the table, sliding it over in front of the fennex.

The scent of chocolate and browned butter nearly made Jez forget about her friends' absurd behavior outside the window. "You'd think they didn't care if anyone was watching." She reached inside her coat and into a small pocket sewed into the lining. Jez tended to keep important things in that pocket. And one of those things was a silver flask.

The elf seemed to pay no attention to Jez's grumblings. "I mean, he'd seen her in his dreams hundreds of times, but he didn't know who she was when he showed up on her doorstep with a Langheim Baking Battle invitation. Can you imagine?" Her voice was lost in a daydream.

Jez took a swig from the flask and allowed the rum to pour into her throat. "No. I could *not* imagine," she said dryly as she returned the flask and opened the sack. She plucked out a cookie and took a bite. The sweet, buttery flavor with a slight bitterness from the chocolate made her melt a little bit. "But I *could* spend a lifetime with this." Jez held out and admired the large, golden, bumpy treat. "We might even be Fated."

Taenya smacked the fennex on the shoulder. "Are you truly that cynical, fox?" The elf's brows furrowed, and her lips pinched. "Theo and Arleta developed a close friendship before it"—she looked through the window at the still-kissing couple—"developed."

Jez took another bite of her cookie and spoke with her mouth full. "Now why would I spoil a perfectly good friendship for something as ridiculous as romance?"

"Because friendship is the greatest basis for romance," Taenya insisted, twisting to Jez. "Sometimes, when life gets difficult, you want reassurance that you actually like the person you love the most."

Jez dropped the half-eaten cookie back in the crinkly bag and looked up at her friend. "And I don't need romance for any of that. I like *and* love all my friends here. I'll do most anything for the lot of you. But romance messes things up—"

"It doesn't have to. Not for Arleta…or Doli and her gargoyle, Sarson." Taenya crossed her arms over her chest, then gestured out the window where Theo and Arleta were no longer visible.

Jez raised one brow. "I think they left. Probably to…you know."

"Or possibly to practice sledding some more," Taenya scoffed, obviously flustered.

"Is *that* what they're calling it these days?" Jez stood and reached for her fishing gear.

The elf didn't answer.

While arranging her pack on her shoulders, Jez said, "Look, friendship is easier. Romance always complicates life." She quickly re-clipped her bag of fish to her belt, grabbed her pastries, and then rested a hand on Taenya's shoulder. "And my life has been complicated enough. Having lots of friends but staying single is best for me. If *you* need something more, then go out and find someone. I'm perfectly fine watching from the side."

Taenya patted her friend's clawed hand. "It is a risk. I'll give you that."

"A risk I'm not willing to take," Jez said as she headed out into the snow toward the apartment she shared with Doli to prepare her fish.

About the Author

Baking magic into every page, J. Penner crafts cozy fantasy from her sun-kissed San Diego home. With a cat on her lap and a pen in her hand, she invites you into worlds as warm and comforting as a cup of tea.

Website: jpennerauthor.com
Facebook: jpennerauthor
Instagram: @jpennerauthor
TikTok: @jpennerauthor
Bluesky: @jpennerauthor.bsky.social